Jade's
COURTING DANGER

MARGO HANSEN

Jade's COURTING DANGER

◆ A NEWLY WEDS SERIES ◆

TATE PUBLISHING
AND ENTERPRISES, LLC

Published by Tate Publishing & Enterprises, LLC
127 E. Trade Center Terrace | Mustang, Oklahoma 73064 USA
1.888.361.9473 | www.tatepublishing.com

Tate Publishing is committed to excellence in the publishing industry. The company reflects the philosophy established by the founders, based on Psalm 68:11,
"The Lord gave the word and great was the company of those who published it."

Book design copyright © 2011 by Tate Publishing, LLC. All rights reserved.
Cover design by Kenna Davis
Interior design by Lindsay B. Behrens

Published in the United States of America

ISBN: 978-1-61346-818-0
Fiction / Christian / Romance
11.10.21

To Harlan and Marilyn Nygaard
Dad and Mom, thank you for raising me to
know the Lord and to desire to serve Him.

In memory of
Leo Hansen
and
To Patricia Hansen
You are more than a mother-in-law; you are my friend.
Thank you for your wonderful son.

To Bruce
Because I love you.

Acknowledgments

Writing is, to me, such a personal thing that to share my work with others has taken a bit of courage and some gentle prodding. For that reason I acknowledge the following:

To the *Lord Jesus Christ*: I give praise and thanks. He planted within me a desire to put thoughts into words and words into stories.

To *Bruce*: You have made it possible for me to fulfill my dream because you encourage me every step of the way. I know your prayer is that the Lord will use these words to help others. I love you.

To *Luke* and to *Travis*, my sons-in-law: I want to acknowledge you for taking such good care of my daughters and of your families. I am so proud of you for leading your homes to serve God.

To *Megan* and *Brooke*: I couldn't do this without your input. Thank you for not only caring for your families and your busy lives but also for taking time to lend an ear and give words of encouragement.

To *Casey*: for reminding me that dreaming is part of living.

To *my grandchildren: Alexis, Rylee, Traven, Zean, Jazlyn, and Nyah*: You know I don't sew quilts or knit or crotchet, but I ride snowmobiles with you and slide down hills. I ride four-wheelers with you and take you for walks. And I write books for you to read someday. You have been a huge motivation for me to write.

To *Tate Publishing:* for graciously leading me through the publishing process step by step to completion.

And a special thanks to all who said, "I can't wait for the next book!"

Sand Creek

Russ and Sky Newly
TYLER
LUCY
DORCAS
EMMA
REX
ABEL

Evan and Ella Trent
MICHAEL
GABRIEL
ESTHER
MARTHA
JOHN

Hank and Randi Riley
BUCK
DUGAN
MALLORY
JETHRO
PARKER
RODNEY
ROSS

Duke and Angelina Tunelle
REBECCA
ROBIN
RALPH
RAY
ROBERT

Jonas and Bridget Nolan
ROONEY
BERNADETTE

Harry and Gretchen Nolan
ANNIE
CAVAN

Jasper and Martha Riggs
PERCY SCOTT
PETER SCOTT
DEXTER
BERNARD
CLAYTON
RHODA
PENNY

Taylor and Violet Gray
PHILIPPA

Bert and Gertie Davies
MONTY

George and Janet Spencer
MALACHI

Clyde and Belle Moore

Gerald and Bertha Nessel

Roy and Nola Hill

The Brides	*The Grooms*
MELODY WELLS	MICHAEL TRENT
CORA MACARDLE	GABRIEL TRENT
LEIGH SHELDON	DUGAN RILEY
PEARL MADDOX	RALPH TUNELLE
GWYNETH KENT	RAY TUNELLE
HERMINE WETHERBY	BERNARD RIGGS
SALLY SMITH	

Chapter 1

Sand Creek

"Oh, Ty, it's good to see you!"

"Great to be home, Mom," the tall, sandy-haired man answered, lifting his mother off her feet and swinging her about the room.

"Tyler Newly, stop that this instant!"

He set her down gently and smiled into her sky-blue eyes. "I can hardly wait for Dad to get home. There's so much I have to tell you both."

Sky Newly looked lovingly at her handsome son while she straightened her apron and smoothed back her blonde hair. "He'll be back from town soon. I expect he's picked up the younger kids at school on his way and has been delayed. Lucy and Dorcas are out riding with Mallory right now."

Tyler chuckled as he pulled out a chair and sat down at the kitchen table. "Mallory Riley isn't happy unless she's on a horse or traipsing through the woods, is she? How do

Lucy and Dorcas keep up with her? Even her brothers say she's a better woodsman than they are."

"She gets it from her mother." Sky smiled as she reminisced. "Randi is happier in the woods than any place else too."

Then her brow knitted, and she said in a more serious tone. "Hank and Randi have been talking about sending Mallory back east to Hank's family to see if she can get some schooling at one of those ladies' schools."

"Why?" asked Tyler in surprise. "Mallory wouldn't be happy there. This is the life she enjoys. Why not let her be the way she is?"

Sky hesitated a moment. "I could ask you the same question, Son." She watched Tyler's face closely. He turned his head away from his mother as she spoke again. "You are the way God made you. Why do you want to try to be something you're not?"

"If you mean, why do I want to better myself, I see nothing wrong with that. All I want is to earn enough money to live a better lifestyle."

"If that were all, I wouldn't mind." Sky sighed. She didn't mean to bring up the old argument between them, but somehow she had to make him understand. "Tyler, I've had all that, and maybe my telling you about my life in England has led you to want it for yourself. But, Son, remember also that I said that living a wealthy lifestyle didn't bring me happiness. My happiness came when I accepted the Lord as my Savior and when I married your father."

"I know, Mom. I'm happy in the Lord too. I just want to—"

The sound of horses' hooves pounding into the yard made them both go to the window. Three girls with flying hair and laughing faces rode up and dismounted. One of them spotted Tyler's horse and quickly ran to the house.

"Tyler! Ty, are you in here?"

"I'm here, Lucy!" He held out his arms, and the blonde girl raced into them. "How's my little sister?" he asked as he gave her a big bear hug.

"Oooh!" she squealed. "It's been lonely around here without you."

Another girl flew through the doorway and screamed, "Tyler!" as she threw her arms around her brother.

"Dorcas! You're half a foot taller than you were three months ago. What have you been feeding these kids, Ma?"

Mallory Riley stood in the doorway watching the scene with pleasure. She knew only Tyler's horse was in the yard, but she looked past the kitchen into the parlor, hoping someone else might be with him. She sighed. No, he was alone.

"Mal! Come here and give me a hug!" Tyler noticed the quiet girl.

Mallory threw her gold braid over her shoulder and stepped in to give Tyler a good squeeze.

"Ow! Not so hard, girl! Save some of that muscle for chopping wood." He grinned mischievously at the tanned face of the young girl.

Mallory laughed. "Haven't you toughened up yet, Ty? I would think working in the woods would have made a man out of you by now."

He laughed as he ruffled her hair. "Maybe you should come and help us. We'd probably have the whole area cleared already."

The girls all laughed. Mallory was used to teasing from Tyler. Her own brothers were the same way. Everyone teased her about being a tomboy, but she didn't mind.

"Did you come alone, Ty?" asked Lucy. She had noticed Mallory looking around.

"Yep, just me this trip, but I've got messages from everybody and even a few letters. Here's some from Buck and Dugan for you and your folks, Mal, and would you mind stopping at the Trents'? Michael and Gabe wrote to Uncle Evan and Aunt Ella too."

"Sure, Ty. The horses need a rest first, so I'll go out and take care of them now."

"I'll come with you." Lucy started to follow her friend, but her mother's voice stopped her.

"Stay for supper, Mallory. I'm sure you'd like to hear all of Tyler's news to pass on to your folks."

"Thanks, Sky. I'd like that."

The two girls led the horses, including Tyler's, to the barn. Lucy watched her friend out of the corner of her eye.

"Wish Dugan would have come with Ty," she eventually said.

Mallory looked at Lucy and smiled. "I don't know what you see in him, Lucy. He's pesky and bothersome and bossy and—"

"And he's your brother, so you're bound to think so. But he's not like that to me. To me he's handsome and interesting and exciting." Lucy's eyes glowed, and her face turned pink. "Why can't he ever see me? I mean, really see me as a grown-up woman not just his little sister's friend?"

"Same reason your cousin Michael Trent can't see that I'm anything more than a tomboy, I guess," Mallory spoke quietly as she brushed her horse. She glanced at her friend, wishing once again that she had Lucy's thick blonde hair instead of her own plain brown braid. Lucy and her sisters all got a good portion of their mother's beauty, but Mallory knew that instead of being pretty like her own ma, she had more of her pa's features. While dressed in her buckskin clothing she had often been mistaken for a boy or for one of her brothers, usually Buck or Dugan, but sometimes even her younger brothers, Jethro or Parker. "Buck's different, though. He notices things. I think he has us figured out."

"It's not fair!" Lucy kicked the water bucket in frustration. "They go off and start a lumber business and start clearing land and planning homes. They don't even think about us. They don't even know we're going crazy thinking about them."

Mallory looked at Lucy's scowling face and started laughing. Lucy tried to keep scowling, but she couldn't help it, and she laughed with her friend.

"Men are so blind," she finally said.

They sat down on some hay, and Mallory stared out the door for a while before speaking.

"I used to follow Michael everywhere he went. He just got used to the idea that if he was going to do anything with Buck or Dugan, I was going to be there too. He never complained to me, but I heard him tell Buck once to try to sneak out so I wouldn't tail them.

"Once I followed him in the woods when he went hunting. He almost shot me because he thought I was a deer. Boy, was he mad! He yelled at me to quit acting like a boy. He said if I tried acting like a girl should once in awhile, someone might pay closer attention to me."

"What did you say?" Lucy asked in surprise.

"I told him if I had to act like that stupid Philippa Gray to make him like me, then he wasn't worth having."

"You didn't! Mallory, when are you going to learn to control your temper? Pretty soon you'll be as bad as Emma, and everyone will be saying, 'There's that look!' just like we all do when Emma's temper gets the best of her."

"Well, I was mad, but don't worry. I don't think I'm as bad as your sister yet! Do you remember that time back in school when Philippa got Michael to carry her books for her? She just flitted her eyelashes like this." Mallory imitated the action. "Then she puckered her lips out and said, 'Michael, dear, my books are so heavy, and you're so strong. Why don't you be a gentleman and help me out?'"

Lucy rolled over in the pile of hay, laughing at her friend's expression.

"The big dope did too. It almost made me give up on him, but then Philippa set her sights on your brother Ty, and Michael started being himself again."

Lucy scowled. "I think Ty likes her too. Don't ask me why! He must like the way she puts on airs and acts so important. You know Tyler has a dream to own a big mansion some day and have lots of money and servants and things. Mom and Dad have tried to make him see that those things don't bring happiness, but he hasn't given up yet."

"I'm glad Michael doesn't think like that."

"Or Dugan."

"Lucy, do you think we're crazy hoping that someday those two will wake up and realize we're in love with them?"

Lucy looked uneasily at Mallory. "Well, my mom talked to me about it one day. She said instead of 'mooning' over Dugan, I should ask the Lord to show me who I should marry. And if it's not him, I'll be glad as long as I trust the Lord."

She broke off some hay and cracked it into pieces. "She said Proverbs 3:5–6 are her favorite verses and that they led her to finding Uncle Evan, her twin, and they led her and Dad together. She said God would direct *my* path too."

Mallory sighed. "She's right. My mom and dad tell us the same thing." Mallory paused and then spoke hesitatingly, "Do you remember when I told you that my folks wanted to send me back east?"

Lucy nodded.

"I think I might go."

Lucy's head shot up in surprise, so Mallory hastened to continue. "At first I didn't want to at all because I didn't want to leave Michael, and of course, I wasn't too interested in becoming a 'lady.' But now…well, Michael's not even here, and maybe…well, maybe I should try to be more ladylike. Maybe that's the path the Lord wants me on, you know?"

"Oh, Mal, if you go, I'll miss you so much!"

"I know, me too. Pray about it for me, will you, Lucy?"

Just then, the girls heard the clattering of a wagon, so they walked out of the barn to witness the reunion between Tyler and the rest of the family.

Chapter 2

Sand Creek

Supper was a happy affair. Emma, Rex, and Abel talked nonstop about school events and kept their older brother busy with questions about the lumber business he was in. Mallory excused herself soon after and left with the letters in her hand.

After the younger children had been put to bed, Tyler sat with his parents for a quiet talk.

Tyler looked at his mom and dad with pleasure and satisfaction. They were his ideal of a happily married couple. Their love for each other was obvious, something they didn't try to hide, especially from their children.

"So let's hear how things are really going, Ty," Russ asked his son.

Tyler leaned forward on his elbows, anxious to share news with his folks. "Palmer Granville has been just great to work with. Remember how despondent he was when he first came to Sand Creek?"

"He was still grieving over his wife, even after two years," said Sky sympathetically. "I'm so glad we got to talk with him."

"You led him to the Lord, Mom. He said it was your testimony of how you got saved that made him see that he wasn't ready to meet the Lord. When he realized that heaven was a gift to be received and not a goal to be achieved, he finally stopped trying to work his way there and accepted God's way through Jesus Christ."

"That was so wonderful!"

"And he's growing every day. He reads the Bible, and we all get together for a study once a week. Michael led it last time, but we all take turns."

"Let's see," said Russ, "there are nine of you there now, right?"

Tyler nodded.

"Do all the men join in?"

Again Tyler nodded and grinned. "Yep! I guess our folks here in Sand Creek must've raised us right." He counted off on his fingers. "There's Palmer Granville— he's kind of the 'father' of all of us now. Then there's Mike and Gabe Trent, Buck and Dugan Riley, Ralph and Ray Tunelle, Bernie Riggs, and me."

"Sounds like a fine group to work with," said Sky. "Do you get along all right? Who does the cooking?"

"We get along okay. Sometimes we have arguments, like the time Gabe made pancakes for all of us. The things stuck to our plates like glue! We threw him in the river and made him start over, but the second batch wasn't much better. I guess none of us are very good cooks, but we take turns."

"What you need are some wives out there taking care of you," teased his father.

Tyler looked thoughtfully at his dad and just said, "Yeah, I guess." He thought about Philippa Gray. She was very pretty, and she knew how to act and look refined as if she had been born to wealth and lived with servants waiting on her, even though she had been raised here in Sand Creek just like the rest of them.

She had told him all about a book she had read about proper etiquette and how one would never acknowledge a servant's presence except to give an order. She explained how rich people ate at a table with all kinds of silverware for every course and how their homes had separate dining rooms from the kitchens and not only parlors but a library room and a den and a sewing room, and the bedrooms had little living rooms and dressing rooms attached to them. She had fed fuel to his dream of owning all those things, and he was beginning to think she was the woman to share it with him. No other girl in Sand Creek knew all those things or even cared to know them.

Tyler glanced at his mother as she put the dessert dishes away. She didn't care for Philippa much. He thought it was more that Philippa's mom and his mom didn't get along. Over twenty years ago, Sky and Violet, Philippa's mother, had traveled together by wagon train along with Mallory's mom, Randi, and several other women to become brides of the men who were homesteading in Sand Creek.

Tyler's folks had told their kids many stories of the adventures they had and how the Lord led them to each other. His mom was supposed to marry Evan Trent, but they found out that they were twins, brother and sister, who had been separated at birth. The story, along with his mom's testimony of God's leading, had always fascinated the children.

But Sky and Violet had not gotten along well on the journey. And Violet still treated Sky and Russ with polite disdain. Tyler admired Philippa even more for overcoming that barrier to befriend him.

Russ yawned, rubbed his chin, and said, "I've got to get to bed. Hank and I are buying some horses tomorrow, so we'll be gone most of the day.

"Oh, by the way, Ty, you'll be glad to know that those bank robbers are now in prison. The boss said to tell you you did a good job of undercover work for him. It must run in the blood."

Tyler smiled. "You like keeping your hand in detective work, don't you? I was glad to help. I learned a lot. You'll have to take Emma on your next job."

The men laughed. Tyler's younger sister had peppered him with questions about being a detective when he got back. She even started "spying" on other members of the family for practice.

Russ stood and held out his hand to Tyler. "Good night, Son. Glad to have you home even if it is only for a few days."

Tyler stood and clasped his father's hand then threw his arm around him and slapped his back. "Night, Dad. Sleep well."

"Good night, dear." Sky kissed her husband. "I'll be along shortly." They shared a smile, and Tyler watched with a grin on his face.

When his mother sat down at the table again, he said, "You and Dad have something pretty special, don't you?"

"I guess no couple on earth is as happy together as we are."

Tyler laughed. "I'm sure a lot of people say that about their marriages."

"They should," Sky replied. "If you aren't sure about the person you're going to marry, then you better not marry her. Marriage is for life, Ty. You can't afford to make a mistake."

"I know, Mom. You and Dad always tell us that." He fingered the tablecloth while they talked. "But something has always bothered me. When you came on that wagon train with all those women to marry the men here, you didn't even know them. How can you say, or any of them say, that that was exactly what the Lord wanted for them?"

His mother sighed and smiled a little. "I felt the Lord was leading me every step of the way. I got saved on that trip! The Lord led me to find Evan, and then he brought your father back here to me. I don't know how the other women felt. I think most of them truly wanted to do whatever the Lord wanted too, but they each made their own decisions. Now, you aren't in a situation like we were. You can choose a wife in your own good time. The best thing for you to do is pray about it now."

"I'm not in any hurry. Before I even think of getting married, I want to build the biggest, fanciest house Minnesota's ever seen. I want to make enough money and have everything ready so my wife won't have to work as hard as you have. I want servants to wait on us, and I—"

"Whoa, Tyler!" Sky shook her head then rubbed her forehead wearily. "I know you have a dream of owning a business and being an important person. There's nothing wrong with that, but don't sell your future wife short. If she's worth having, she'll want to share in the building of that dream. She'll want to be a part of it, working with you side by side. It will mean more to both of you if you both earn it."

Tyler pondered his mother's words. He couldn't imagine Philippa working alongside him to build anything. She was the kind of girl who would rather wait for everything to be done for her.

"I've got to get to bed too," Sky said after the long silence. "The kids have school tomorrow, and Lucy is working at Nolan's store in the morning. You know, I think Rooney Nolan is interested in her." She smiled at Tyler's expression. "She's eighteen, you know. Some young man's bound to snatch her away from us anytime now."

"But—Rooney Nolan? He's…he's just a clerk in a store!"

"If he is the man the Lord has for her, he's the right man no matter what he does. Think about that in regard to your future mate. Good night, Son. Sleep well."

Tyler lay in his old bed deep in his thoughts. Lately the men at the lumber camp had been talking about building a town right there. Palmer said it was an ideal location and they could all become business owners, and as the place expanded and grew, so would their profits. But he also said they needed to establish the place as a future community for settlers by having their own homes and families. People wouldn't move to an area of just a handful of bachelors. Those young men needed wives and families.

Chapter 3

Sand Creek

The visit with his family passed quickly. Tyler made the rounds to the families of his friends and got letters and packages that they wished returned with him. He borrowed one of his father's wagons and loaded it with supplies from the town.

The day before he left, he and Lucy went to see Mallory off. She was taking the stage out of Sand Creek and then the railroad back east. Lucy's eyes flooded with tears as she said good-bye to her best friend.

"Write to me, Mal. Let me know about everything." Lucy hugged her tightly and whispered, "Don't let them change you. Stay just the way you are."

"I think the whole purpose of this trip is to try to change me," Mallory said dryly. She was uncomfortable with Lucy's tears and with saying good-bye. It had been bad enough at home, and she had insisted that her family not accompany her to town. She tugged at the traveling suit her mother had made her wear. Mallory hated wearing "dress-up" clothes. She had even tucked her buckskins into one of her bags just in case this lady's school got to be too much for her and she decided to hightail it for home.

Tyler held out his arms. "Bye, Mal. Have a great time out there."

Mallory stepped into his embrace; then with her arms on his, she looked up at him and said, "Say good-bye to Michael for me, will you?" She turned suddenly and got into the waiting stage.

"Mike?" Tyler looked puzzled. He looked at his crying sister. "Why did she mention Michael?" he wondered.

Lucy waved her handkerchief at the departing stagecoach then looked at her brother with red-rimmed eyes. "Why do you think?"

Tyler's eyebrows rose as he realized her meaning. "But Mallory's just a kid. Michael's not interested in her. Why, he thinks of her as a pesky little sister like I think of you!"

Lucy groaned and slugged her brother on the arm. "You big dopes! Just because you all grew up with us, you think of us as 'little sisters.' Well, we're not! We're young women who are at marriageable ages!"

Tyler's eyebrows again shot up as he looked in surprise at his sister. "You're not—"

"I'm not what? Not old enough? Annie Nolan is younger than me. In fact, she's Mallory's age, and she and Monty Davies are getting married next month!"

Tyler studied Lucy for a few moments. "You mean you—"

"I mean I'm old enough to be married, but you and your 'lumberjack' friends don't even recognize that."

He shifted feet and tried again to understand her. "So you're saying—"

"I'm saying that men are blind as bats and haven't the sense to see what's in front of their faces!" She stormed off down the boardwalk in a swirl of skirts.

Tyler scratched his head as he looked after her. Mallory's leaving had sure upset her! She wasn't making any sense at all!

He headed down the boardwalk in the opposite direction. There were still a few things he had to pick up before he left for the camp in the morning. It would be a two-day journey back with the load he had now. It had only taken him one and a half days on horseback to get home, but now he'd have to slow down and take it easy.

"Tyler! Tyler Newly, is that you?"

Tyler halted his steps and turned to see Philippa Gray and her mother coming toward him. He swept his Stetson off his head and admired the picture she made in her fancy clothes and hat. She was even carrying a fancy umbrella, though it wasn't raining and didn't look like it was about to. He squinted up at the clouds then back at Philippa.

Philippa saw the appreciation in Tyler's eyes at her appearance. She twirled her new parasol and swung her skirts as she stopped in front of him. Violet stood behind Philippa and watched her daughter and Tyler closely.

"Tyler, how long have you been home and you haven't even been to see me yet? Haven't you missed me?" She pouted prettily at him, and he appeared dazzled by her attention.

"Philippa! It is good to see you!" He looked past her to Violet and said, "Good day, Mrs. Gray. How are you?"

Violet nodded and murmured a few words; then she put a hand on Philippa's arm and said, "Philippa, we have many errands to do. We must keep on our way."

"Oh, Mother, you go on ahead, and I'll catch up to you." Philippa slipped her hand through Tyler's arm and said, "Tyler and I must sit for a while and visit."

Again Tyler admired Philippa's willingness to be friendly even with her mother's disapproval.

Violet hesitated a moment longer even though the look Philippa gave her plainly insisted that she leave. Finally she nodded to the two of them and moved on. She always gave in to Philippa. She had spoiled her as a child, and now it was too late to change. But, oh! How she hated to see her precious daughter get involved with Sky's son! She still held a grudge against both Sky Newly and Randi Riley that stemmed way back nearly twenty-two years ago. She had to find a way to keep Philippa from Tyler; that's all there was to it!

"Tyler," Philippa crooned. She sat close to Tyler's side on the bench in front of Nolan's store. Tyler looked uneasily about him, hoping no one noticed. Her provocative move made him a little uncomfortable.

"Tell me about your house. Have you started building it yet? You know you should really hire some men to do it for you. A *gentleman* such as you really shouldn't be doing manual labor."

Tyler laughed as he slid slightly away on the bench, not too much but enough to put some space between them. He didn't notice the quirk of Philippa's eyebrow.

Although it made him feel good inside to know that she thought of him as a gentleman, he shook his head as he explained to her, "Philippa, I'll have to do the work myself. Right now I can't afford to hire anyone. After my business gets underway, I hope to be able to hire extra help to complete it, but that's a long way off yet."

Philippa studied Tyler's face. She assumed an innocent expression as she delicately asked her next question. "I suppose you could use some of your inheritance money on it, but maybe you're saving that for furnishing it when it's done?"

Tyler stared in front of him for a long moment while his mind raced. How did Philippa know about his inheritance? Actually, it was his mother's inheritance that she received from a relative in England before she was even married. Sky had insisted on sharing it with her twin brother, Evan, and the money must have come in handy for both brother and sister as they established their homes in Sand Creek. Tyler's folks had set aside a portion of it in the bank for each of their children, but he didn't even know what that amounted to. With six children in the family, he didn't expect it to be much.

He realized that Philippa was watching him out of the corner of her eye as she pretended to adjust her parasol. He asked himself again how she could know and why she had asked about it.

"I guess I prefer to earn my own money," he answered carefully. "I don't like to depend on other sources of income. One thing my folks taught me was that I won't appreciate something unless I earn it. I guess that applies to about everything except getting saved. Heaven's not something we can earn. It's something we can only accept as a gift."

Philippa's lips tightened. "Of course, Tyler, I understand. I just know how anxious you are to get your home made and be a proper gentleman and all, not that you aren't already in my eyes." She fluttered those eyes at him coyly.

"You know, I was reading about how rich gentlemen have their own servant called a 'gentleman's gentleman.' That's what you should have, Tyler. And I saw a picture of the most beautiful house! It had two side tower-like things and balconies on each of them. It was almost like a castle! I could draw it for you if you want to come over tonight." She looked prettily at him.

Tyler smiled at her again, but this time he wasn't so bedazzled. Her question about his money bothered him, and her interest in seeing him become a gentleman was equally bothersome. He had never realized before how she always encouraged him in his dream almost to the point of pushing him to achieve it. Which, now that he thought about it, was almost the opposite of what his parents did. He was about to speak when he felt someone standing directly behind him.

"I'm ready to go, Ty. How about you?" Lucy's voice sounded stiff, and Tyler glanced up at her and saw her looking at Philippa with anything but warmth.

"Uh, yes, Lucy. I'm almost ready."

He and Philippa stood, and Philippa took his hand in her free one and said, "Tonight then, Tyler?" She ignored Lucy.

"Uh—no, I'm sorry, Philippa, but I'm leaving early, and I still have a few things to finish at home. Thank you, though." He watched her carefully as her eyes hardened. He knew she was about to protest, so he quickly said, "Maybe another time. Now, if you'll excuse me, it was very nice seeing you again."

With a swirl of skirts, she spun around, nearly hitting Tyler on the head with her parasol, and angrily marched away from them.

Philippa groaned inwardly as she thought over their conversation. Religion again! She hated when he talked religious. She just didn't understand some of the people in this town like the Newlys, Rileys, Trents, Tunelles, and Riggs. Although they all attended the same church, those people practically gave you a sermon whenever you stopped to visit with them. They were always "praising God" for something! She just didn't see what was so special about it all.

Furious now, Philippa stormed off to find her mother. If only there was somebody else in this town with the prospects of being rich someday, she'd drop Tyler Newly in an instant. Ever since her mother had told her about Sky Newly having an inheritance, she had set her sights on getting it. First she'd tried Michael Trent, Tyler's cousin, but he saw through her schemes. She was coming along nicely with Tyler until today.

She stopped, nearly out of breath from walking so fast. She would try again. She wasn't going to give up the chance to be a rich woman, and Tyler looked to be her only hope at the moment. At least he shared the same dream she did. She'd have to think of a new way to entice him into becoming interested in her.

Lucy waited while Tyler finished his shopping. He led her to the buggy they had left waiting in front of Nolan's store and was helping her in when Rooney Nolan ran out of the store and called her name.

Lucy turned, and Tyler noticed an uneasy look come into her eye. He watched with interest as she spoke to the redheaded young man.

"What is it, Rooney?" she questioned him.

"I'm glad I caught you before you left. Hi, Tyler." He shook hands with Tyler and then turned back to Lucy. "Pa wants to know if you can work the next two mornings, Lucy."

Lucy sighed quietly. "Yes, Rooney, thank you. I've already spoken to your father about it. Well, good-bye now." She turned quickly and started climbing into the buggy again, anxious to be away from the persistent man.

Rooney took her hand to help her in, and once she was settled, he still held it. Lucy looked at his hand pointedly until he finally released hers.

As Tyler, hiding a smile, climbed in on the other side, Rooney asked, "Would you like me to pick you up for church next Sunday, Lucy? It would be no bother."

Lucy was startled, but, collecting herself, she said quite calmly, "I would think it would be a great deal of bother seeing how you live right next to the church and I live several miles from town. Thank you, but I'll be riding with my family. We must be going now."

Under cover of her full skirts, she kicked Tyler sharply, and he yelped, "Ow!"

"Good-bye, Rooney." Lucy kicked Tyler again, and he finally slapped the reins on the horse while he rubbed at his leg.

"Are you sure, Lucy?" Rooney called after them. "Really, it would be no bother!"

The buggy disappeared around the corner.

Tyler tried to hide his amusement while Lucy sat stiff-backed on the ride home. When he heard her mutter, "No bother!" in a scornful tone, he couldn't help himself, and he burst out laughing.

"Sure, you think it's funny! You don't have someone making a nuisance of themselves over you, or do you? Philippa wasn't too happy when you wouldn't agree to go see her tonight." Lucy hoped her brother was finally over his infatuation with the proud young woman.

"How long has he been interested in you?" He ignored her other comments, and laughter still danced in his eyes.

"Years!" Lucy moaned hopelessly. "He was making calf eyes at me way back in grade school. But it's only been these last few months that he's tried to actually approach me. I try to be nice, but somehow he has to realize that I'm just not interested in him."

"Well, I can see why. He's never going to be much. He'll probably just work in his father's store all his life and then take over after his father is too old. He has no head for business."

Tyler stopped speaking as he became aware of the way Lucy was staring at him. "What?" he asked her. "What's wrong?"

"Tyler Russell Newly!" Lucy exclaimed. "Do you think that would matter to me?"

"What?" he asked again, clearly puzzled.

"Do you think my interest in a man depends on what he does for a living?"

"Well, I—"

"You're crazy! I can't believe you're my brother, raised by the same people who raised me."

"Lucy, look—"

"Is that how *you* feel, Ty? Are you only going to look for a woman who has wealth and sophistication enough to suit you? What if you were to fall in love with some poor servant's daughter?"

Tyler sighed. Talking to Lucy was like trying to pitch hay with a one-prong fork. She never let him say his fill.

"That would never—"

"Never happen, Ty? How do you know? How do you know who the Lord wants you to marry?"

"Look, Lucy!" He raised his voice. "How do you know Rooney Nolan isn't who the Lord wants *you* to marry?"

He was surprised she actually let him finish his question, and then as the silence lengthened, he glanced over at her and found her deep in thought.

In a quieter tone, Lucy answered him, "It's kind of hard to explain, but deep in my heart, I just know he's not the one. I even prayed about it and asked the Lord to change my feelings for him if he wanted to, but one thing you have to understand is this: it's not because he's *just* a clerk in a store. It won't matter what my husband does—as long as he's not a criminal." Lucy smiled. "If he's someone the Lord would be happy for me to spend the rest of my life with, we'll be happy together whether we're pig farmers or millionaires."

She adjusted her position in the rocking buggy. "Rooney is a nice young man, but he's not the one for me. I'm sure of that."

Tyler stared ahead for a while; then he asked, "Have you any idea who that 'right one' for you is?"

Lucy reddened a little, but she gamely answered, "Possibly."

"Back in town you said something about my 'lumberjack' friends. Have you set your cap for one of them?"

Lucy's blush deepened. "That, big brother, is none of your business!"

"Okay, Lucy, but let me remind you of something else our folks taught us: 'Don't try to turn your will into God's will.' Better spend some time praying about it. You know, it could turn out differently than you expect."

Lucy nodded, and a comfortable silence settled between them.

Tyler realized as he guided the buggy toward home that the young girl beside him, who used to just be a pesky little sister to him, was now a young woman with whom he could actually discuss personal matters. She certainly had grown up!

Lucy's next question caught him off guard. "So what about you and that snob Philippa Gray?"

No, she was still a pest.

Chapter 4

The Settlement

What about you and that snob Philippa Gray? Lucy's words ran over and over in his mind. Tyler was almost to the camp, just a few miles to go. His thoughts the last couple of days had been on his visit and mainly on Lucy's conversation with him. He just didn't know himself. One minute he thought Philippa was the perfect partner for him, and the next he could see her calculating eyes as she asked about his inheritance. He would have to be careful not to encourage their relationship unless he was very sure of himself.

When he arrived at the camp, the men greeted him as though he had been gone months instead of days. Tyler hadn't thought of it before, but he could see what a lonely life they had at their camp.

"Are those boxes for me?" Ralph shouted.

"Oh! Please, please, tell me that my ma sent me some of her baking!" Gabe pleaded.

"Remember to share it with me, little brother, if she did." Michael laughed. "Good to have you home, Ty. We missed your bossing."

"We didn't miss his snoring!" teased Bernie Riggs. The group all laughed, and Tyler joined them.

"You know, this does feel like home." He looked with satisfaction at the logs piled high and the large tent that served as their dining hall. He scanned the surrounding Minnesota forest and the sparkling river; then he noticed something new.

"What's that supposed to be?" He pointed to a cleared area behind the camp.

"That's 'Main Street' of our new town," answered Palmer Granville proudly. "What do you think, Tyler?"

Tyler hopped down from the wagon and walked with the others to the large, cleared area. The faces around him were all beaming with pleasure.

"You did a lot while I was gone," he said in amazement.

Bernie grabbed Tyler's arm and began the tour by pointing at various stakes they had used to mark off locations of building sites. "My blacksmith shop is going over there at the end of town. Boy! Am I glad Mr. Moore hired me for the last three years to work for him! He not only taught me everything I know about being a smithy, but he also gave me all the stuff to get started on my own. My brother Clay is working for him now."

Tyler grinned at the man's enthusiasm. Bernie's face glowed with pride as he surveyed the area where the town would be. A muscular man from working with bellows and hammers, Bernie was shorter than most of the men in the new settlement but was without a doubt the most powerful physically.

Ralph Tunelle shoved Bernie playfully aside and said, "Enough about you. My turn."

Tyler laughed and followed Ralph and his brother Ray to the center of the area. In contrast to the stoutness of the blacksmith, the Tunelle brothers were almost thin in appearance, but they were strong and hardy and up to the challenges before them.

"We had hoped either Rooney Nolan or his cousin Cavan would want to set up a general store here, but they both want to stay in Sand Creek."

Tyler watched as his friend's face became animated. "So Ray and me figured that since we both worked at Nolan's store since we were kids that we know enough about running one to try starting our own. So here's where the 'Tunelle Brothers General Store' will stand." He spread his arms to indicate the area.

Tyler slapped Ralph on the back and shook his hand first, then Ray's. "Now, what's this supposed to be?" He pointed to the next area.

The men looked at Palmer Granville with expectation, and Tyler waited for the older man to speak.

"This will be the bank," said Palmer with a grin on his face. "And the reason these jokers are all smiling is because I've already authorized loans for their businesses from my own bank back in Chicago."

The men gave a cheer while Tyler looked at Palmer as though thunderstruck.

"Aren't you taking an awful risk on us, Palmer? What if this town doesn't succeed?"

"Ty, the logs you men have ready to transport down the river will bring you each a small fortune, and once you get established, your businesses will flourish. I'm a businessman, and I've seen how successes and failures come about. This will be a profitable venture, and I'm happy to help with it."

Tyler still looked at him in amazement. "You really are, aren't you?"

"Nothing in my life has brought me greater satisfaction. I mean it! I'm sure the fact that I finally accepted Christ as my Savior accounts for much of the peace I feel right now, but I feel good about this place, this town we're starting. My brother Amos would probably think I've lost my sense. He's a self-made millionaire back in Chicago. But with all his wealth, I don't think he's ever been as happy as I am right now."

Tyler reached for Palmer's hand and shook it heartily. "Well, I don't see how we could do this without your help. Thank you."

Palmer threw an arm over Tyler's shoulder and pointed to a distant corner of the clearing. "There's where the church will be. If it's all right with the rest of you, I'd like to finance the materials, but we can all put it up together. What do you say?"

"I say, let's get started!" shouted Dugan Riley. "Well, come to think of it, we'll have to all pitch in on all the buildings. Which should be first?"

"Hold on, Dugan. What are you planning in this new community?" asked Tyler as he laughed at the man's exuberance.

Dugan's handsome face beamed with pride. He pulled off his hat and wiped his forehead with his shirtsleeve then smashed the hat back on his wavy dark hair again. "This might surprise you, but Gabe and I want to set up a stagecoach line between here and Sand Creek and eventually from here to the next town down the line, which would be Norris. I want to build on a spot halfway between here and Sand Creek for a way station, and Gabe will do the same on the other side of town. What do you think?"

"I guess that would be a perfect way to get people coming through this area. What do you think, Buck?" Tyler asked the older Riley brother. He watched Buck with interest, noting that the tall, slim man wore the buckskins that were typical of all the Riley children, including their sister, Mallory.

"I'm in on the deal, even though Dugan neglected to include me." He laughed. "I'm going to start the hotel here in town for the travelers they bring through, and I'll have a barn and stable for the horses for the stage line." Buck grabbed both Dugan and Gabriel by the necks and said, "I'll keep these two busy!"

"I suppose that just leaves you and me," Tyler said to Michael.

Michael pointed to the area by the river. "I took the liberty of plotting out our lumber company where we talked about putting it. What do you think, partner?"

Tyler looked over the area his cousin showed him and nodded his approval.

"I know you're interested in the land on this side of the river," Michael continued, "so I decided to file for the land on the other side. The lumber company will be about halfway between us. Okay with you?"

Tyler couldn't have chosen better locations. And the land was exactly where he wanted to put up the house he had been dreaming of. He looked in amazement at the grinning faces around him. "I don't know what to say," he told them.

"I do," said Gabe. "It's your turn to cook!"

Chapter 5

The Settlement

"Let's take a break." Michael panted as he wiped the sweat from his forehead with his sleeve. His blond hair was damp as well.

Tyler agreed and went for the water jug and took a long drink then handed it to his cousin. The two men rested under a nearby tree, and soon the others joined them.

Palmer sank to the ground beside Tyler and groaned in mock agony. "I'm too old to work this hard!" His dark hair, streaked with silver and gray, used to have a trimmed appearance; but now, after being away from civilization for a time, it was brushing his shirt collar. He pulled off a glove and ran his hand through it, flattening it down.

Tyler laughed with him, but he secretly admired the man. Palmer had come from a life of wealth and leisure, but he worked alongside the rest of them as one of them. The reason why he chose to do so often crossed Tyler's mind.

The men were working together at the sawmill to make sawed lumber from some of the logs they had cut. Tyler and Michael had a saw rig already set up by the river's falls and had agreed to make the lumber in return for the help in getting the logs. It was a joint effort on all their parts. A good deal of trust and cooperation was necessary by all in order to make it work. And so far it did.

A week had passed in which the men had put all their efforts into making enough lumber to start drying while they used some lumber they brought with them to start on their buildings. They had been working from morning to night, only stopping to eat.

Tyler looked at the group sprawled out on the grass. Some of them had pulled the letters he brought them out of their pockets to reread again. They shared their news over and over until it was pretty much memorized by all of them.

Palmer folded his letter slowly, and Tyler noticed him stare into space with a frown creasing his forehead.

"Bad news, Palmer?"

Palmer focused his look on Tyler with a half smile. "Amos just wrote something that disturbed me. He said that an old friend of mine, Edmund Crandall, passed away several months ago."

"Oh, I'm sorry."

The other men expressed sympathy as well.

"I hadn't seen him for years, but I knew he was married and had a couple of children. We went to school together." Palmer smiled sadly as he thought of the past. "Edmund inherited a great deal of money, but apparently he never learned how to manage it. He died leaving his family in a sorry state. Amos says they had to sell their mansion, and though he's offered to help them, for he's become well acquainted with them, especially the children, they insist on working to earn their way now."

"Well, it's hard, but that's the only sensible thing for them to do, right?" asked Michael.

Palmer nodded slowly. "Yes. What you men here don't understand, though, is that this dramatically changes their status in society."

The men seemed puzzled, so he explained.

"Here, if you work hard and accomplish something, you are respected for that. Back east, you are only respected for who you are or who your ancestors were. If you become a member of the 'working class,' you chance losing your position in society's hierarchy, regardless of your background."

Some of the listeners shook their heads in disbelief.

"Unfortunately, it's true," Palmer continued. "But it doesn't work in reverse. If a poor man, say a butcher, suddenly comes into a large fortune and buys a fancy home and dresses like a gentleman, it won't change how society looks at him. He'll still be one of the 'lower class' and probably treated as such."

Tyler said in an angry voice, "That's not right!"

"No, it isn't," agreed Palmer. "One thing I like about being out here is that I could be the king of England and it wouldn't matter to you. I've also learned that God doesn't look at us as anything but equals either. It doesn't matter to him how much money we have or what color we are. We all need him the same way." The men nodded with him. "I hope that class system never infiltrates out here."

The men agreed with him again and went back to their letters. Tyler had been thinking of the plans they were making, and he had a few questions.

"Dugan," he called. "When you get your way station set up, who's going to run it while you drive the coach?"

Dugan looked up and smiled, but he didn't say anything.

Tyler frowned at the man's silence, but he turned his attention to Gabe and asked, "Who will run yours? And you, Buck, how can you handle a hotel alone and take care of the stable and horses?"

The men started to chuckle, and Michael said, "It took you longer to think of that than I thought it would, Ty."

"Think of what?" asked Tyler, puzzled. "What's going on now?"

"Well, Ty, it's like Palmer suggested weeks ago," said Ralph. "We figure we're going to need some wives to help us get this here town going." He grinned at Tyler.

"Wives?"

"Wives," repeated Bernie. "Who else will we get to work with us?"

Ray laughed. "Well, we want wives for more than just working in our businesses." Tyler looked at him in surprise, and, red-faced, Ray hastened on. "I mean, like Palmer said, we have to get our town established. Who will bring a family here to settle in a town of just men?"

"And we want to set down roots here and begin families and see this new community grow," added Gabe.

Tyler brushed his sandy colored hair off his forehead as he looked at the faces watching him. "Well, yeah, I know none of us are married yet, but I just figured that would come about all in good time."

Dugan spoke up. "I think the time has come. We want to build this town and get it running. I think we're all agreed that this is where we want to make our homes. The problem is, we have to stay here and work and keep our homesteads, and that makes it difficult for finding wives. So—"

"Wait! Wait just a minute!" interrupted Tyler. "You're not thinking what I think you're thinking!" He looked around. The men were watching him in anticipation. "Are you?"

"Our dads did it," stated Bernie.

"No! No, that was over twenty years ago. People don't do that anymore!" Tyler shook his head.

The men continued to look at him without speaking.

"Besides, *my* dad didn't do it. He thought the whole idea of 'ordering' brides was dumb, and so do I!" Tyler shook his head again.

"Your mom was a mail-order bride. All of our moms were," said Ray.

"No! No, you guys are crazy! They came because this area was just getting settled, and—"

"Just like here," said Ralph.

"Well, yeah, but this is different. There weren't any women in that area for the men to marry, and—"

"Just like here," put in Gabe.

"No! It is not just like here! We have towns on both sides of us. This area has lots more people in it now. It will just be a matter of time, and we'll all find someone." Tyler got up and started to walk away from the group.

"Ty."

He turned back at Michael's voice.

"You aren't for this, are you, Mike?" he asked in disbelief.

Michael sighed. "I'd like to have a wife and raise a family here. I think it's a good idea."

"But—"

"Sand Creek has some girls in it, but most of them are already taken or else they're too young. And Norris is an even younger town. There are no marriageable girls there."

The term *marriageable* caught Tyler's attention, and he remembered something Lucy had said to him. She *was* interested in one of them.

He took a step toward the men again and asked them, "Don't any of you have an interest in a girl from Sand Creek?" He watched their faces closely.

Buck looked at his brother Dugan. He doubted Dugan was aware of the admiring looks Lucy Newly had cast his way, but he had seen them. Would Dugan think of Lucy as a possible wife?

Ralph stood and spoke directly to Tyler. "Look, Ty, we've talked about this a lot. You know that. Who's available in Sand Creek?" He started counting them off. "Philippa Gray." He looked at Tyler again. "She's set her cap for you."

The men snickered, but Tyler only scowled at them. "There's your sister Lucy, but we've heard that Rooney Nolan wants to start calling on her. My sisters, Becky and Robin, are already married to Bernie's half brothers, Percy and Peter Scott, and Annie Nolan is getting married to Monty Davies. The rest are still too young."

Bernie added, "My ma wrote that Dexter has started calling on your sister Esther." He looked at Michael and Gabriel Trent.

Michael's eyebrows rose in surprise. "She's only seventeen. Ma won't let her court yet."

Dugan chuckled. "Mal is only seventeen too, and she moons over you, Mike."

Michael looked at Dugan in irritation. "Mallory's only a kid. Besides, she's always riding a horse in those buckskins, so no one knows whether she's a girl or a boy."

Tyler felt defeated. "So you all want mail-order brides?" he asked.

Palmer, who had been listening in amusement, answered, "I'm not looking for a wife. After my wife died, I didn't think I could go on. Then I met you people, and you led me to know the Lord, and now I feel that my life is complete. Building this town is just the challenge I need. But, no, I don't think I need a wife now."

Dugan slapped Buck on the back and announced, "And Buck is too bashful to get married. He said he didn't want to 'order' one yet."

Buck looked embarrassed, but he spoke for himself. "I want to wait for a while. I'm not sure the Lord wants me to marry yet."

"That's it!" Tyler pounced on Buck's words. "Have you thought about what the Lord wants for you?"

All the men had risen, and they stood facing Tyler, but it was Gabe who answered, "Pa told Mike and me about how hard it was for him to decide to 'order' a bride. His best friend, Michael Calloway, really was the one who convinced him that he should pray for the Lord's will. And, of course, he wouldn't marry anyone who wasn't a believer, and he wouldn't marry someone he wasn't sure of. Look how well it turned out for the people of Sand Creek, Ty."

"You don't have to get a mail-order bride if you don't want to," added Ray.

"Well, I don't want to! I'll find my own wife my own way. But if that's the way you men want to do it, then go ahead, I guess."

"Good! I'm glad you finally agree with us," said Michael with a grin, "because we're sending *you* after them."

"*What?*" Tyler looked at the grinning faces around him. "No! No, I'm not going after a bunch of women and traipsing over the countryside with them just so you fools can get married. Do you think I'm as crazy as you are?"

Palmer laughed along with the others then spoke to Tyler. "You remember I told you about my brother Amos in Chicago?"

Tyler nodded warily.

"I want you to go and conduct some business for me in Chicago that will be very important to our venture here. While you're there, the men want you to interview the women and bring them back with you."

As Tyler started to protest again, Palmer continued, "We voted for you while you were gone. It was unanimous. Michael was sure you would refuse to take a wife in this manner for yourself, so that was another reason you were the best choice."

Tyler interrupted as he pointed at Buck. "Why not Buck? He's not getting a wife."

"And," Palmer calmly continued, "I feel you are the best suited to handle my business affairs." He waited for Tyler's reaction.

"Why not go yourself, Palmer? You could do all the business and bring the women back yourself," he pleaded.

"I don't want to go back yet, Ty. I've found peace here, and I'd like to keep it. You understand, don't you?"

Tyler's shoulders slumped. "Boy, you people make a lot of decisions when a fellow's gone." He looked at the grinning faces and reluctantly capitulated, "When do I leave?"

Chapter 6

The Settlement

Tyler fought the idea of mail-order brides all the days leading up to his departure. But the men were adamant.

Evening was settling in on his last night at the settlement, and Michael was dogging Tyler's steps while he packed.

"You sure you got the letters?" Michael asked him for the third time.

"I've got them! They're right here in my saddlebags ready to go on my horse in the morning."

"Hope you don't have any trouble on the trail."

"Hey, Ty!" Ralph and Ray knocked and entered the cabin Michael and Tyler were sharing. "You all set? Do you need any help getting ready?"

Tyler couldn't help laughing. All evening the men had been showing up at their doorstep offering him help. If he didn't know any better, he'd think they were looking forward to getting rid of him.

"I've got my gear all packed, and I'll be picking up the rest of my things in Sand Creek before I head for the train. Was there anything else, fellas?"

Ralph nudged Ray, and Ray reddened and looked down at his feet, but he held out a packet of papers to Tyler. "I was wondering if these would be of any help to you."

Tyler set the packet on the table and opened it while Michael looked over his shoulder. Inside were drawings Ray had made of all the men. There was Dugan with his rakish grin holding an ax in his hands; Ray had caught the humor in Gabe's eyes as he stood beside a horse; Bernie, in his smithy apron with his muscles bulging, was working the bellows; Ray had drawn Ralph reading a book, and his face revealed interest and intelligence; Michael made a dashing figure on horseback; and Ray had even done a self-portrait.

Tyler paused in studying the pictures to praise Ray. "These are great, Ray! You have real talent, but what do you want me to do with them?"

"We thought you might want to show the ladies, if you think you should. Ma told us about the pictures they had of the men and how much it helped them to know a little about the man they were coming to marry. Course, Pa looked pretty mean in the picture, and Ma wasn't sure what to think about him, but at least she had that much. What do you think?"

Tyler looked the drawings over again. The men all looked pretty good in them, so he thought it might be okay to have them along.

Michael picked up the rest of the packet and said, "Hey, look at this, Ty. He drew you too."

Tyler took the paper from Michael and studied the drawing Ray had done of him. Tyler was standing on the hill where he planned to build his house, and he had his hands on his hips, looking down into the valley. He had stood that way many times.

"When did you do this?" he asked Ray.

"He draws every night," answered Ralph. "He just remembers what he's seen and draws it later. Pretty good, huh!"

"Yeah, it's okay, but I don't need a picture of me along."

"Leave it with your folks, then. I did everyone in camp, so I put them all in there, even Buck and Palmer."

Michael found the other two drawings. Buck was shown with his eyes squinting as he stared off into the distance; he looked like the rugged frontiersman he was. Palmer looked happy and contented sitting beside the river with a fishing pole in his hands.

"Thanks, Ray. These will be great to show to my folks before I leave. I'll take them to Chicago too, and if nothing else they'll help me not get so lonesome for all of you."

The men laughed at his comments then shook his hand and implored, "Come back soon, Ty!"

Tyler turned back to Michael and sighed. "Everything will be different around here once you guys are all married."

"You can still look for a wife too."

"Nope. I'm the only one who hasn't started on a house. I can't bring a wife here," he joked.

The men had worked hard the last months. Where there had once been an empty lot, there was now the beginning of a town. The hotel was up as well as the general store, and the bank. Bernie had a small cabin next to his barn and corral, and Gabe and Dugan had been away working on a cabin large enough to use for their first way station.

Michael and Tyler were now sharing the cabin that would be Michael's home. When Tyler returned, he would use the back of his lumber building for a home until he got his house built. While he was gone, the men would continue to work on the insides of their homes in preparation for their brides.

Palmer had sent the notice to the Chicago newspapers and also to some other eastern papers announcing the need for brides for their town. The men had thought long and hard about how to word the notice.

They had agreed on several points. First, they wanted women who believed in God as they did. How they were going to guarantee they would find such women, they didn't know, but they told Tyler they had confidence he would be a good judge of that.

Secondly, they felt the notice should indicate the age they were looking for. They didn't want girls who were too young or women who were too old, so they settled for the phrase: "of marriageable age but not older than twenty-five."

The things that caused Tyler to nearly tell them to forget the whole idea were the men's individual preferences. Some wanted blondes, some brunettes, some tall, some short; the list went on. Finally Palmer put a stop to it.

"You men have to realize that you will not be there to choose. The women who show up are the choices you will have."

Tyler silently thanked him.

Buck brought up another point. Although he wasn't partaking in the enterprise, he mentioned something that had been on his mind. "Do you remember how our moms talked about how much they hated having a contract saying they had to get married?"

Heads nodded, so he continued.

"I can't see how you should make these women marry you just because you paid their way out here. They should be able to turn you down, and you should be free to turn them down if they aren't what you want."

"What do you mean? Send them back?" Dugan asked his brother.

"I don't know. I guess it could get kind of uncomfortable."

The men pondered the problem a while, not sure of themselves anymore, until Michael spoke up.

"Look. All we can do is hope and pray they will be the right ones and not sit here frettin' and stewin' about it. I'm willing to leave it up to the Lord. How about you?"

Glad to have the problem set aside in that manner, the others agreed. Their notice finally read:

Wanted: Women Willing to Begin a New Life in Small Minnesota Town as the Wives of Men Building a New Community. Require Bible-Believing Women of Marriageable Age—No Older Than 25.

Tyler was restless that night and unable to drift off to sleep.

"Mike?"

"Hmmm?" Michael was just dozing off.

"Did Uncle Evan give you and Gabe your inheritance money yet?"

Michael yawned and rolled over to look at Tyler across the room. "You want to talk about money at this time of the night?"

"Sorry. Go back to sleep."

"No." Michael sat up and rubbed his hands over his face. "Dad and Mom used some of your ma's inheritance money right away. Dad told me he hadn't wanted Aunt Sky to share it with him like she did, but she insisted." He yawned again as he ran a hand over his thick blond hair, causing the overgrown mass to stand on end.

"They got the farm going and then put the rest of it away for us kids. Even with five of us to share it, there's still plenty for each of us to get a good start too. I already got mine because we get it when we're twenty-one. Gabe gets his next month.

"Some of mine is going into our lumber business. Then I'm going to put the rest of it away for my kids too." He grinned sheepishly at Tyler. "Anyway, it sure has helped. Gabe will do the same with the stagecoach company. When did you get yours?"

Tyler stared thoughtfully at the moonlit floor. "Haven't. I'm past twenty-one too. I don't know what my folks have planned, because they don't talk about it much. I'm glad we made that cattle drive a couple years ago, and I've worked for my dad's old boss a few times doing detective work. At least I have that money to fall back on if our business here doesn't take off."

"What are you worried about? We've already got orders for lumber we're having trouble keeping up with. We'll do great! And your idea for a furniture shop is good too. With the stage line running, we can ship goods across the country even."

Michael watched Tyler wrestle with his thoughts for a while; then he decided to speak again.

"You know, I don't know what your ma and pa have planned either, but I do know that they haven't used much of that money themselves."

Puzzled, Tyler looked up at Michael.

"I heard my folks talking about it. Aunt Sky was so upset about all the trouble the money caused with that English guy following her here and all that she didn't want anything to do with it. She said her stepfather never liked her anyway, so the money didn't mean much to her. I guess they just used what they needed and put the rest in the bank."

Tyler's thoughts swirled in his mind after he said good night to Michael and lay down. After what Palmer had said about money and how people gave respect to those with it or not, he had been wondering if he was way out of line in his dreams for a fancy home. He knew enough to admit to himself that respect had to be earned, not inherited. He also knew God was no respecter of persons. Why, then, did he feel so drawn to wealth and position?

He sighed as he rolled over to get more comfortable. Maybe this trip to a city would help answer his questions.

Chapter 7

Chicago

The house was quiet as Jadyne Crandall, Jade to her friends, of whom there were very few these days, made her way to the kitchen with the breakfast tray. The ornate grandfather clock ticked loudly in the stillness while the pendulum swung with graceful dignity. She noted that it was just past 6:00 a.m. and hastened her steps, thereby disturbing the stillness with the rustle of her heavily starched apron. Mrs. Stanwood would be impatient to give her her orders for the day.

Mrs. Stanwood was always impatient, but to Jade it seemed she was particularly impatient with *her*.

Jade backed into the kitchen then turned and set the heavy tray down as gently as possible.

"I think I'm getting the knack of doing that without making the dishes clatter, Mrs. Todd," she said to the cook. She shook the soreness from her arms and quickly readjusted the white, frilly maid's cap on her head. Feeling a wayward curl, she tucked it into place. The maid wasn't supposed to let her hair show; every strand was to be kept under the hat while she was in service at the Granville mansion, according to Mrs. Stanwood.

"Mr. Granville said to tell you the hot cakes were superb, Mrs. Todd. He wants to know what's for lunch, and he said to remind you that he will be having a guest today." Jade smiled pleasantly as she relayed the messages to the petite woman.

Mrs. Todd looked up from the eggs she had been counting and shook her finger at Jade. "Now you've made me lose count, Jade." She teased. "Of course I remember there's to be a guest. Does he think my mind has gone?" She resumed her counting as she talked. "Lunch is to be roast chicken, naturally, and I'll be making a peach pie for dessert and—"

She was cut off by the entrance of Mrs. Stanwood, the housekeeper. The thin woman barely glanced at the cook but instead turned her attention to Jade. "Is that a strand of hair I see, *Miss Crandall?*"

Jade poked the erring copper curls back under her cap and smiled apologetically at the woman. "Sorry, Mrs. Stanwood. It just has a mind of its own sometimes." She tugged the cap down more firmly. "I'll try to keep it under control."

Mrs. Stanwood did not return the smile. Quickly she rattled off Jade's instructions for the day. "Start with the linens and then dust the library. After lunch, you must do the windows in the dining room." She turned and left.

Mrs. Todd looked after her with a frown. "She could have said 'please' at least. Never mind, Jade. You're doing just fine. Nothing to worry about." She paused and looked at the eggs in her bowl. "Now *she* made me lose count!" She reached for another egg as she continued, "You can tell Mr. Granville thank you for the compliment on the hotcakes. I'll bet he ate every one. Don't see how a man his age can eat so much and stay so trim." She looked up at Jade again. "I'll need you to serve at lunch with the guest here and all. Think you can fit it in?"

"I'm sure I can. Oh, Mrs. Todd, I almost forgot. Mother said to thank you for the cake you sent home with me last night. It was delicious!" She smiled again at the busy woman. "And ... will you have time to show me how to do the pie?" she added coaxingly.

The cook paused in her labors and glanced again at Jade. Her face softened. "You tell your mother she's welcome, dear. I'll bake an extra loaf of bread for you to take to her tonight. And if you hurry, we'll work on the pie together." The two women shared a special look; then Mrs. Todd exclaimed, "Jade, you made me lose count again! Get on your way now."

The door swung shut after the laughing young woman, and Mrs. Todd watched its swaying movements absently.

"Shame that girl has to work. It's a real shame!"

"And just who are you talking to this fine morning, my dear? No one seems to be about." A gray-haired man entered the spotless kitchen from the back door. He was dressed in a distinguished black suit and was adjusting his collar.

"I was talking to the only person who has sense enough to listen to me, Mr. Todd. Myself!" answered Mrs. Todd pertly. From her petite but rounded frame, she looked up at her husband then continued in a quieter tone. "I was just thinking that it is such a shame that Miss Crandall—I mean, Jade, has to work."

"I know, dear, but give the girl credit. Since her father passed away and left her and her mother and brother penniless, she's not once complained about her change in Chicago's society. She just took charge of affairs by moving the family to the gardener's cottage here and getting this job from Mr. Granville to keep them going."

He tugged white gloves on over his hands as he continued. "The thing that I think is such a shame is the way her old friends treat her. Why, I remember her coming to this very house for parties, and all her friends were falling all over themselves to be near her. She was so popular. Now I hear they don't even speak to her when they pass on the streets." He scowled.

"Well, I can tell you, it was the hardest thing I ever had to do when I had to start giving her orders. At first I just couldn't. But she sat me down and told me I must. She said if she didn't do well at this job, she didn't know what to try next. The poor girl! But she does everything so well, I told her there was no danger of that. I wish Stanwood wouldn't be so stern with her. I never have gotten along with that woman."

The cook picked up a new bowl and started breaking eggs into it as she talked. "At least Stanwood knows better than to try to boss me around. The kitchen is my territory, and she had better stay out of it."

"Yes, dear," her husband dutifully answered.

"Jade is doing very well under the circumstances. She's so cheerful about everything. I never would have thought she would be. You know what she told me once, Roland?"

The gentleman quirked an eyebrow at his wife.

"She said the Bible has verses that help her. Have you ever heard any of those other society girls talk like that? No, our Jade is someone special, someone very special."

She heard the clock chime and looked up at her husband. "Roland, you'd better get going. Mr. Granville has already eaten, and he'll be expecting you."

The butler stooped and gave his wife a quick kiss on the cheek. "See you later, Hettie."

The cook smiled up at her husband and then, glancing down at her bowl again, exclaimed, "Now *you've* made me lose count! Off with you!"

Jade hurried from the laundry room to the servants' quarters with her arms full of fresh linens. She stopped at the closet between two of the rooms and set down her load; then she began to sort the slightly worn linens from the freshly laundered newer ones. The older things would go here. She looked around her for the hundredth time. Her home had been similar to the Granville mansion, maybe not quite as elaborate, and they had had servants' quarters too, but she had never ventured into it. Her mother always said the servants deserved their own privacy in the home.

She couldn't get over the difference between this part of the house and the rest of the mansion. Oh, it was nice, and everything was clean and neat, but there were no carpets, no fancy furniture, no pictures on the walls. Everything was painted a stark white.

As she stooped to sort the linens, she glanced over at the door that separated the servants' quarters from the rest of the mansion. She knew what lay beyond that door. There were thick carpets, ornate woodwork, priceless paintings, fine furnishings, even gold trim on the doors and chandeliers. She shook her head. A doorway was all that stood between one style of living and another, and she had crossed over the threshold of that doorway.

Her hands stilled, and her gaze looked through the linens into the past. Her home had been beautiful too. She had loved it dearly. When she and her mother learned the awful truth about their finances, Jade had been angry. She had been angry at her father for dying and leaving them in that state; she had been angry at the creditors who came and took their possessions away from them; she had been angry at the bankers who told them they must sell their home to pay the rest of what her father owed; she had been angry at God for letting it all happen.

In time the anger passed. God wasn't to blame; God was still in control of their lives. Her mother handled each new catastrophe with a prayerful heart and led her children to do the same.

Jade sighed. Working for Mr. Granville wasn't so bad. It was better than the governess position she had tried. Blinking, Jade realized she was daydreaming instead of doing her duties. She stood up swiftly and gathered the pile of linens in her arms; then she turned and found herself face-to-face with Wilbert Tait, the stable hand. His arms went around her waist, and he pulled her to him with the pile of linens crushed between them.

"Wil, let me go this instant!" Jade insisted. Her green eyes sparked with anger.

"What's the matter, Jade? You think you're too good for me? Remember you're just one of the hired help now, not the Miss Crandall who would tell me to stable her horse when she used to come to visit the old man."

Jade squirmed, and her face flushed with the exertion.

"You would never have dared treat me like this then, would you? Just because I work here now, that doesn't mean you have the right—"

"Wilbert!"

Wilbert snatched his arms away from Jade and spun around to face the butler's stern expression. Jade stumbled back and clutched at the linens that were threatening to fall to the floor.

"Your duties do not extend to the house, only to the stables, Mr. Tait."

"Yes, sir."

Mr. Todd approached the groom. His tall form and bearing radiated authority with each advancing step, and Wilbert stood at attention with his eyes staring straight ahead. A tic began in one eye.

"You will apologize to Miss Crandall for your rude behavior, Mr. Tait."

"Yes, sir. I beg your pardon, Jade."

"Ahem!"

"Uh—I mean—I beg your pardon, Miss Crandall."

Jade nodded then looked to Mr. Todd.

"You may go now, Jade," he said smoothly.

She hastily gathered her linens and passed through the doorway to the other part of the mansion.

Mr. Todd studied Wilbert Tait's face with his own only inches from it. "You are never to treat that young lady with disrespect again," he said quietly. "Is that perfectly clear, Mr. Tait?"

"Yes, sir." Wilbert's eye was jumping erratically now.

"Because if you do, you will leave this position with no reference and no recommendation and quite possibly a few broken bones. Is *that* clear, Mr. Tait?"

"Yes, sir." A bead of sweat rolled down the side of the young man's face.

The butler continued to stare at the groom until apparently satisfied that his meaning was understood. He dismissed him with a curt nod of his head.

Wilbert quickly left the house and headed back to the stables. The farther he got from the house, the less was his fear of the older man. As soon as he was out of sight, he said with a sneer, "Oh, I'll treat her with respect all right."

He entered the large barn and immediately noticed a strange horse in the first stall. He walked over to it, and a man stepped from the shadows.

"Wilbert Tait?"

"Yeah, who wants to know?"

"I'd like to have a word with you, if I may."

Chapter 8

Chicago

Jade hurried down the luxurious hallway to put her linens in the proper cupboard. Her hands were a little shaky as she piled them in neat, orderly stacks.

That stupid Wilbert! Was he going to cause trouble for her now? She had left the governess position because of a similar circumstance. Only the problem there had been the man of the house. He had never outwardly approached Jade as Wilbert had just done, but he had made a point of always being around her and of watching her until even the mistress of the house noticed and decided to let Jade go.

"I'm sorry, Miss Crandall," she had told Jade. "It's not your fault, but I just can't afford to have such a distraction in my own household."

And that had been that. Jade didn't know where to turn next when Mr. Granville, an old family friend, had offered her family a home with him. He was in his seventies and a widower. He told them he had plenty of room and would enjoy the company. Of course, her mother had politely but firmly turned him down, saying that they would earn their way as God intended.

That's when Jade had gotten the idea to work for the old gentleman. When she made the suggestion, he had almost laughed at her. Then, seeing her sincerity in wanting the job, he had hired her; and because he didn't want her to totally lose her status in society, he had requested that Jade become his secretary, a position that a lady of limited resources was quite respected for doing.

Jade went to work that first day full of ambition and eagerness to do a good job, but it soon became apparent that Mr. Granville had no need of a secretary. He already had men taking care of his businesses and his accounts, and though he tried to find something for Jade to do, it was obvious to both of them that there wasn't enough work to justify her being there. Jade would not accept payment for her idleness, so Mr. Granville asked that she spend her afternoons reading to him.

Amos Granville was a man who read every day, and he had an extensive library. The first day or two went well; then Jade noticed that her employer kept dropping off to sleep while she read. Sitting quietly through one of his "naps," she made up her mind that she was going to have to take matters into her own hands. When he awoke, she laid out her plan to become the maid. He argued that it wasn't fitting for her to do so; she argued that she needed to feel useful and she didn't give a wit for society anyway. Seeing her determination, he capitulated. Now Jade was doing all in her power to make the switch from one way of life to the other.

The change hadn't been as hard as she thought it would be. Jade gathered her dusting materials and began work on the masculine library. She didn't mind being a maid. In fact, she didn't really feel any different than she had before except that she didn't dress in her fancy dresses now. She mostly wore the uniform of a maid along with the ridiculous cap.

She grimaced as she tucked a curl back under the frilly cap; then she laughed as she saw her reflection in the large, round mirror on the wall. She looked just like her twelve-year-old brother, Sidney, with all her hair tucked up in the silly cap! He always wore a cap pulled down over his ears too. With their green eyes and reddish-brown hair, they could almost pass for twins, although Jade was six years his elder.

A noise made her turn, and she smiled as Mr. Granville came into the room.

"Oh, hello, Jade. Hard at work, I see." The elderly man used his cane to reach a chair, and Jade hastened to bring him a pillow and footstool. "Sit down and visit with me for a while. That dusting can wait."

Jade hesitated; then knowing it would please him, she sat down in the chair opposite him. She used to come and visit and play chess with him in the "old days." He scoffed at her insistence on being only the maid now and treated her in their old manner as if nothing had changed.

"Do you remember my brother Palmer, Jade? He was a friend of your father's years ago."

She thought for a moment. "He's your half brother, right?"

"Yes, that's right." Mr. Granville chuckled. "He's quite a bit younger than me. I think he's only in his late forties now."

"Isn't he a widower too?"

"His wife's been gone two years. I think that's why he's decided to get adventurous in his old age, or else he's lonely and looking for something to do with himself."

Jade looked puzzled, so the old gentleman explained.

"He's starting a settlement with some young partners out in the Minnesota wilderness. The guest I'm expecting today is one of the partners in the venture. He's here on some business for their group, and Palmer sent him to see me. It will be good to get some news about my wayward brother. He isn't much for writing."

"You must miss him."

"Oh, yes. I haven't seen him now for ten years. I wish he would have come himself."

"You have another brother too, don't you?"

"Had, dear, had. Melvin died last year. He was between Palmer and me in age, and he was a widower also, but he had two children. Neither Palmer nor I had any."

Jade sank back in her chair and dangled the feather duster over the side. She listened, not just out of politeness, but with genuine interest in what Amos Granville was saying. "What did he die from?"

Mr. Granville sighed and rubbed a hand over his chin. "They tell me it was a carriage accident in Philadelphia. His children must be about your age, dear. I saw them once when they were youngsters. Little terrors they were. Tore up and down in the hallways scaring the help half to death." He chuckled, and Jade joined in his laughter.

Out of the corner of her eye, Jade caught sight of Mrs. Stanwood. She was standing outside the door and was directing an icy glare in Jade's direction. Jade dropped the duster as she jumped to her feet and stammered, "I really must get back to my work now, Mr. Granville."

"Oh, forget the work, Jade. I haven't seen any dust in this house for years."

"That's because we keep it so nice for you, sir," said Jade with a comical curtsy.

The elderly man laughed then spoke seriously to her. "You really don't have to work here, my dear. You and your mother and Sidney are welcome as my guests, as my 'family,' even."

"Please, Mr. Granville!" Jade dropped on her knees beside his chair. "We've been over this enough. Mother won't hear of it, and neither will I. You've already helped us out so much by renting us the cottage so cheaply, and I insist on earning our money." She smoothly changed her tone. "What's the matter? Don't you think I make a good maid?" she asked teasingly.

He smiled. "I do enjoy seeing you here, but it bothers me to have you working. You should be out to parties with the other young people, enjoying life. What ever was your father thinking of to let—I'm sorry, dear, that's none of my business."

Jade rose to her feet again and picked up the duster. "I don't know either. Most of our money came from my father's inheritance. I guess he just slowly used it up without bothering to invest or replace it." She tugged at her cap. "If nothing else, I've learned one lesson from all this. You can only count on the money you work for yourself." She gave an emphatic nod of her head and with a determined look in her eye went back to her work.

Amos Granville watched her admiringly, and Jade felt she had won their debate once more, but as she glanced at him again, she had the suspicious feeling that he wasn't ready to admit defeat quite yet.

Jade finished her work quietly and tiptoed out of the room when she saw that her employer had fallen asleep. She had time now to learn how to make a peach pie from Mrs. Todd. Cooking was something new to her, and she was proud of her accomplishments in the kitchen so far. Mrs. Todd really was a dear! Jade was hurrying along the corridor to the kitchen when she heard Mrs. Stanwood hail her. With a sinking feeling, she turned and awaited the approach of the stern woman.

Mrs. Stanwood looked pointedly at Jade's cap until Jade realized something was amiss. Her hand quickly checked and tucked back the rebellious curls. She remained quiet, waiting for the woman to speak.

"Miss Crandall," the housekeeper's sarcastic voice mocked her. "I realize that you haven't worked here long, but I would think that a 'society girl' like yourself could remember her place by now. You are *not* to sit in Mr. Granville's furniture while you are in his employ. Maybe your mother allowed familiarity with the servants, but I assure you, it is not proper and will not be allowed to continue here."

Jade's face hardened at the slur to her mother, but she kept her silence.

"Furthermore, if you haven't enough duties to keep you busy, I can certainly find more to keep you from the temptation to bother Mr. Granville again." She lifted her chin and walked away.

Jade fumed inwardly as her green eyes sparked her fury. The woman was hateful! She did everything she could to make the job difficult for Jade, but the adversities only seemed to make Jade more determined to succeed. She drew a deep breath, breathing a prayer for divine help, and continued on her way to the kitchen.

The pie turned out beautifully, and Jade breathed in its fragrance and admired its golden beauty with pride. Mrs. Todd nodded her approval.

"You've got the knack for it, Miss Jade. You're a natural at cooking and baking."

Jade beamed. "Thank you, Mrs. Todd, but remember, just Jade now, no Miss."

The cook looked thoughtfully at the younger woman. "It really doesn't bother you, does it?"

At Jade's questioning look, she continued, "Working here, I mean. It doesn't bother you to be serving the lunch instead of sitting down and being waited on." She studied Jade's face.

"No … well, sometimes. I guess I feel that I'm the same person I always was, Mrs. Todd. I'm still Jadyne Kathleen Crandall no matter what clothes I wear or what tasks I perform. And I've never done anything so enjoyable as this." She pointed to the pie as she dusted her hands off and smiled at the woman. "Galatians 3:28 says, 'There is neither Jew nor Greek, there is neither bond nor free, there is neither male nor female: for ye are all one in Christ Jesus.' If it doesn't matter to God who I am, why should it matter to me?"

Mrs. Stanwood's dry voice came from behind Jade. "If you are quite through giving sermons, Miss Crandall, maybe you could begin serving lunch. Mr. Granville and his guest are entering the dining room now."

Jade and Mrs. Todd exchanged a private look then both scurried into action. Jade washed and put on a fresh apron then adjusted her cap. Mrs. Todd had the first tray ready, and Jade carefully picked it up and backed through the swinging door into the dining room.

Mr. Granville was taking his seat and motioning his guest into the chair at his right when Jade turned from the door. She glanced at them briefly before setting her tray on the sideboard. The gentleman was young, probably not much older than herself, and he looked genuinely interested in what Mr. Granville was saying. Jade was glad the old man had someone to visit with today; he was sometimes lonely.

As she served the creamy soup, Jade saw Mr. Granville give her a smile, and she cautiously returned it, hoping Mrs. Stanwood's eagle eye hadn't detected the exchange.

Once at a dinner party the old gentleman had turned to Jade and asked her opinion of something the guests had been discussing. She had answered without a thought;

then they both realized there was shock on the faces of the people at the table. Mrs. Stanwood had sternly lectured her. After that, she had begged Mr. Granville to remember that she was only one of the hired help. It would be more comfortable for all concerned if he treated her as such. Jade glanced again at the young man, but he didn't seem to notice anything wrong. In fact, he hadn't even looked at her since she entered the room. Jade returned to the kitchen for the next course.

After setting the tray with the covered dishes of the main course on the sideboard, she stood quietly beside it, waiting for the two men to finish their soup. Apparently they had so much talking to do that they hadn't attended to the business of eating and weren't done as she had anticipated. She had a new appreciation for the servants who had kept her own home running smoothly and without any noticeable effort. There was a trick to this.

"Your brother is in excellent health, sir," the young man was saying. "If only you could see him, you would understand what I mean. Palmer has been out in the woods with us surveying the area. We live a very rustic lifestyle at the settlement, but the combination of fresh air and hard work is good for both body and soul."

"So he's happy? He's not brooding anymore?" asked Mr. Granville. "He was deeply depressed after his wife died. I could tell that by the few letters I received."

"Mr. Granville, I can say with great assurance that he's a very happy man right now. Starting this new business venture, the work—I'm sure all that has helped, but he has also found happiness by accepting Jesus Christ as his personal Savior. My parents spoke with him and showed him that God loved him and sent his Son to pay for his sins. Palmer accepted him at our own kitchen table. I was there." The sandy-haired man smiled his enthusiasm at the older man.

"Yes, he did mention something about that in one of his letters recently. That's good. That's good. I'm glad he's found something to help him." Mr. Granville seemed uneasy. "Tell me about this lumber business, Mr. Newly."

He set his spoon down beside his empty bowl, and Jade, who had been caught up in the conversation and silently thanking the Lord for a new soul saved, came to herself with a start and remembered her duties. She had also been distracted as she watched the guest's face as he related the story of Palmer's conversion.

She was aware that he was a very good-looking man, and for the first time in a long time, she felt sorry that she was only the maid here and not a guest herself. As she cleared away the empty dishes, she again noticed that he seemed to ignore her presence. She was curious, for she was not unaware that men usually noticed her. Normally such attention bothered and even irritated her. Right now, she keenly felt its absence.

"Our camp is not very large. There's only about nine of us right now." The young man began with obvious pride. "But we don't need too many yet. We're about a two-day ride from Sand Creek where my family lives. It's wilderness and beauty, and we are starting a community there. The lumber is plentiful, and there are falls on the river that can be harnessed for a mill. It's a great location."

Amos Granville smiled at his guest's exuberance. "And my brother wants a part in building this community?"

"Yes, sir. In fact, it was his idea. He said if we settle the area and each start businesses where we can service the newcomers, we'll soon see profits."

The old gentleman chuckled. "Palmer always did know how to make a profit. You listen to him, Mr. Newly. You can learn a lot from my brother."

"Please, sir, call me Tyler. Palmer said we'd better get established first, build our homes, and make the place ours. People may not want to move to an area that is too primitive."

Jade finished her serving and stepped back into the kitchen. She really wanted to stay and listen, but she knew she couldn't. How interesting to start a town! She imagined for a minute what business she would choose to start if she were a part of it. A restaurant! She loved cooking. Mrs. Todd looked at her strangely, and Jade realized she was daydreaming again.

"Are they nearly ready for dessert?" she asked.

"Oh, goodness! I don't even know. I was listening instead of watching." Jade laughed in embarrassment. "Sometimes it's hard for me to remember which side of the fence I'm on, Mrs. Todd. I'm sorry. I'll go check."

"Well, you can't just run in there empty-handed. Here, take the coffee tray and set it on the sideboard. It'll stay hot enough. Then you can look things over without seeming to."

"Thanks, Mrs. Todd. What would I do without you?" Jade smiled and took the tray.

She backed through the door again and heard Mr. Todd announcing a visitor. She noted the progress the men had made with their dinners then looked up to see the butler lead a young woman into the room. The newcomer was dressed in a fashionable gray coat and had a matching hat with a feather tipped at a becoming angle on her raven-black hair. She was quite lovely.

"Miss Cecile Granville," announced Mr. Todd.

The two gentlemen rose from their chairs, and Amos said in a puzzled tone, "Cecile?"

"Oh, please do sit down, Uncle Amos," the woman said in a cultured voice. She walked leisurely to his side and pressed her cheek to his. "Surely you haven't forgotten your very own niece, Uncle Amos!" She began pulling off her gloves while she looked with interest at Tyler Newly.

Amos's expression cleared, and he said, "Of course! Cecile. Is Hunter with you too?" He looked past the woman at Mr. Todd, who shook his head.

"No, Uncle. Hunter is off somewhere doing I don't know what. I've come to stay with you for a while, if I may, but I see you already have a guest, so maybe I should check the hotels?"

"No, of course not, my dear. You are most welcome here. Mr. Newly is also welcome to stay. I have plenty of room. Oh, pardon my manners. Cecile, let me present a young friend of mine, Tyler Newly. Tyler, this is my niece, Miss Cecile Granville." Amos looked at Jade, including her in his introduction of his niece. She nodded in acknowledgment.

"How do you do, Miss Granville?" Tyler took the hand Cecile offered him and gently shook it. His eyes showed their appreciation for her beauty, and she gave him a coy look that said plainly she returned his interest.

Jade stood perfectly still while she witnessed the exchange. Never before had she felt the loss of her status in society as she did at this moment. She could easily visualize herself looking into Tyler Newly's blue eyes and seeing that admiration, and she felt a sharp pang of jealousy go through her.

"Would you join us, Cecile? Have you eaten?" Mr. Granville indicated the dinner table with his hand.

"No, thank you, dear Uncle. I would like to freshen up, though, and change and I'll join you later for a chat."

"Will you take Cecile to a room, please?" Mr. Granville smiled pleasantly at Jade. "We'll take our coffee in the library when you are through."

Jade nodded and stepped forward to show Cecile the way. Cecile gave the gentlemen at the table a smile and, with a lingering look at Tyler, turned and followed.

As soon as the dining room door closed, she turned to Mr. Todd. "I need my bags right away!"

"Yes, miss. I'll have to make two trips, though." The butler picked up the two largest of the five bags in the entry.

"No! I need all of them at once. You, girl!" She pointed to Jade and motioned to her luggage. "You carry those."

Mr. Todd looked horrified for a moment and then quickly said, "I'll get the groom to help with the rest, miss."

He set down the bags and headed for the door. Cecile's angry voice stopped him.

"Did you hear what I said? I want my luggage *now*, not at your convenience."

Jade stepped forward and lifted two bags. "It's okay, Mr. Todd. I can manage these." She avoided looking at Cecile, for she knew what message her green eyes would be flashing. She had seen other people treat servants in this condescending way, but she never had, and she didn't stay friends long with those who did.

The dining room door opened, and the two men stepped out and looked at the group in surprise.

"Is there a problem?" asked Amos.

Cecile laughed and picked up one of the large bags with an obvious struggle. "No, no, we're just trying to get my bags to my room."

Tyler immediately took the bag from her hands and said, "You shouldn't be carrying that. Allow me." He picked up a second one, completely ignoring the two that Jade held. Mr. Todd and Amos both looked skeptically at the young *gentleman*.

Mr. Todd picked up the remaining bag and took one from Jade. She thanked him with her eyes then led the way to Cecile's room.

Cecile thanked Tyler profusely and flirtingly. After he and Mr. Todd left, she turned to Jade and started her commands. "Unpack the three largest and see that everything, and I mean *everything*, is pressed. I will require a bath and someone to fix my hair before the evening meal. I will be resting now. See that I'm not disturbed." She disappeared into the bedchamber.

Jade grit her teeth at the woman's rudeness. How was she to do all this work when she still had work downstairs waiting for her? She opened the bags quickly and began hanging the dresses. At least some of the wrinkles might come out if they were out of the bags. Finally she was done, and she hurried back downstairs. Mrs. Stanwood was waiting for her.

"I suppose you and the new guest have been getting acquainted. I am sorry to disturb your social hour, Miss Crandall, but you are being negligent of your other duties."

"I apologize, Mrs. Stanwood. Miss Granville expects all her belongings to be ironed, and she wants a bath and her hair dressed before supper. Should I attend to her or work with Cook or both?"

The housekeeper's smile was malicious. "Oh, I think it would be best if you attend to our guest, don't you? But she won't be needing you for some time, so finish your duties here first. The dessert and coffee still need to be served and the dining room has to be cleared."

"Yes, ma'am." Jade headed back to the kitchen.

Mrs. Todd was waiting for her with a sympathetic look on her face. "Roland told me about Miss Granville. She hasn't changed from the little brat she was years ago. Only now I think she is sneakier. I'm sorry, dear. What's wrong?" she asked when she saw the look on Jade's face.

"Oh, Mrs. Todd," Jade looked dazed, "I'm supposed to serve the dessert and coffee now, then clean the dining room, iron all of Miss Granville's things, prepare her a bath, fix her hair, and still find time to help you with the supper." Jade looked past the cook as if deep in thought. Then spurred to motion, she said, "I can do this!"

The cook muttered, "And just what is Stanwood planning to do all this time? She just wants to run you ragged. Now look, Jade, you take this tray in. I heated the coffee again, so it's ready. I'll get the irons heating, and I'll help you with the dresses. We'll manage together."

Jade bent down and kissed the older woman on the cheek. "Bless you, Mrs. Todd. I'll be back as soon as I can."

The men were in deep conversation when Jade entered the library. She set the tray down and began to serve the peach pie and coffee.

"This is what I plan to have someday," Tyler Newly was saying. He indicated the surroundings including Jade as she handed him his dessert. "A beautiful home, servants to wait on me, prestige. This is the way to live."

Amos Granville studied the young man before him. He saw only too well that his young guest was hungry for money and power. He shook his head, knowing the futility of heading down that path. How did one convince youth of what he in his old age had learned? Money and power were no guarantee of happiness.

"Has Palmer encouraged you to try to obtain all this?" He lifted his arms to indicate his own wealth.

Tyler shifted uncomfortably. He didn't want to go through all that again, especially with this man. How could they understand? The Granvilles already had their wealth.

"Palmer is content to live as he is now without a home like yours," Tyler admitted. "But I've never had all this. I plan to get it. I plan to be somebody."

Jade saw the look of disappointment that crossed Amos's face. She looked carefully at Tyler and wondered why he wanted to be "somebody." He turned, and his eyes locked with hers for an instant before he turned away and again ignored her presence.

Jade felt in that instant that he knew exactly what she was thinking. She nervously finished serving and prepared to leave the room when a new thought struck her. He had been told to act like this to servants! She was sure of it! Someone must have told him that this was the proper way to act if you were "somebody" important. Somehow she knew it was an act. Now, with Cecile Granville, it was the real thing, but Tyler Newly didn't seem to be acting naturally at all. Yes, that was it!

She headed for the door and heard Amos's voice behind her say, "Would you excuse me a moment, Tyler?" The old gentleman made his way to the door after her.

She waited in the entryway.

"Jade, dear, I have a big favor to ask of you," he said after he had shut the door. "Mr. Newly will be staying with us, and so is Cecile. Now, tonight for supper I would like to invite a few more people. I'm on my way to see Mrs. Todd about it now, but what I wish to ask of you is, would you be one of my dinner guests tonight?"

Startled by his request, Jade shook her head emphatically. "No, sir, I can't do that. I'm your maid now. I can't suddenly appear as your guest!"

"Jade." Amos chuckled. "No one will recognize that you are the same person. Honestly, even I hardly recognize you in that outfit."

She again shook her head, but he spoke before she could.

"I thought that might be your answer, so you leave me with no choice. When I have overnight guests in my home, you know you are required to stay here and help out, even sleep here if necessary, right?"

She nodded cautiously.

"So you will be 'on duty' tonight, so to speak, and I *order* you to appear as my guest." He spoke with a stern voice and a twinkle in his eye.

"But … why?" she wondered.

Amos became serious. "You've seen Cecile, dear. I can tell already that that girl is up to no good. I don't want her troubling our young friend in there and confusing him anymore about how rich people ought to behave. His ideals are certainly mixed up."

Jade nodded in agreement and Amos said, "You noticed it too, didn't you? I thought you would. Somebody has given that poor man some misinformation. I don't understand how he can think like that and still talk like he did about Palmer accepting his religion. Anyway, that's where you come in."

"But what can I do?" Jade was still puzzled.

"Just be yourself, dear. You will do more than you realize by just being yourself. I'm an old man now, and I've seen a lot of different people act a lot of strange ways. You, on the other hand, never put on an act. No matter how you look on the outside, you are the same wonderful person on the inside. Trust me. Please do this for me."

Jade gave in uneasily. "What about my duties? Mrs. Todd will certainly need help tonight."

Amos chuckled again. "That's what I like about you. You're always concerned about others. I'll get more help in for tonight. Don't worry about a thing. Just be ready for a relaxing evening." He walked to the kitchen in a cheerful mood, and Jade looked after him, wondering what she had just gotten herself into.

Chapter 9

Chicago

Tyler paced the luxurious library not appreciating its obvious wealth and good taste any longer, for his mind was occupied with trying to figure out what was wrong. There *was* something wrong! He rubbed his hand over the mantle of the fireplace while he stared into the flames without seeing them.

Amos Granville did not act like Tyler thought a wealthy gentleman would act. Of course, Palmer was just as wealthy, but Tyler had gotten used to looking at Palmer as an ordinary person because he wasn't surrounded by the signs of his wealth back at the camp. Tyler scanned the library again. He was painfully aware of his own inadequacies. In his dream of a fancy home, he had never envisioned anything as grand as this. He didn't even know such beautiful things existed. Strangely enough, he found that it didn't appeal to him as much as he thought it would.

He turned back to the fire. But that wasn't his problem at the moment. He was acting oddly. He could tell by the expression on Amos's face. He was trying so carefully to follow the instructions Philippa had given him on the proper etiquette for a gentleman! He smiled ruefully. Philippa. He had been in the city for only a day, but he already knew that no one in Sand Creek, including Philippa, had any idea how different people in the city were compared to them. No one, perhaps, but … his mother. He rubbed his chin thoughtfully.

What was he doing wrong? He puzzled over his actions and behavior in the last couple of hours. He had seen Amos smile his thanks at the maid during lunch, but he had ignored it. After all, these were the man's servants; he would be friendly with them. Now Cecile treated them more like he imagined Philippa would. It had bothered him to let that girl carry those bags, but he supposed that was part of her job.

"Well, Tyler," Amos's voice startled him out of his musings. "I imagine you would like a chance to rest after your journey too. Would you like to be shown to your room and have your things put away?" Amos smiled at his guest.

"Thank you, sir, but I already took a room at a hotel, so I—"

"Nonsense! You're a friend of Palmer's, and I'd like to have you here to tell me more about him. You're welcome to stay as long as you are in the city." Amos beamed at the younger man.

Tyler hesitated.

"Please, son, I'd enjoy the company. I'm getting to be a lonely old man."

"What about your niece, sir?"

"Plenty of room in this place, Tyler. Now, tonight I've planned a small dinner party to acquaint you with some of my friends and with Palmer's associates with whom you'll be conducting business. Will that be satisfactory with you?"

"Uh, yes, sir. Thank you, sir." Tyler was impressed with the generosity of his host. "Would it be all right if I return to the hotel for my things and do some of my business yet this afternoon?"

"Fine, fine. I generally take a nap about now anyway. Please help yourself to the stables. Have Wil Tait, my groom, take you where you want to go or take a carriage yourself. My home is at your disposal, and I want you to feel completely welcome here."

"Whoa!"

"Look out there!"

"Keep moving! Get out of the way!"

Tyler kept a tight hold on the reins of the moving carriage. The crowds, the noise, the buildings were pressing in on him. He didn't know which way to turn when he reached the end of the street.

"Come on, Bub, right or left? I ain't got all day!" shouted a voice behind him.

Tyler chose right and found himself in another maze of streets and alleyways and houses. He was lost.

He had found the hotel and gotten his things; then he tried to locate Palmer's offices. He would get started conducting business affairs tomorrow, but he wanted to find the places now to save time. It was hopeless. He gave up. Next time he'd have a driver take him. All he wanted to do now was get back to the Granville mansion before the dinner party began. Fine impression he'd make coming in late!

He spotted a group of boys playing at the next corner, so he directed the horse toward them.

"Excuse me!"

The group turned as one to the sound of his voice. Several pairs of eyes, blue, brown, and green, looked with interest at the fancy carriage and fine horse. They narrowed with speculation as they perused Tyler and his western attire, including the Stetson hat. One lad reached up and took hold of the horse's bridle. The others gathered around the carriage on all sides until Tyler felt he was surrounded. It reminded him of the time he and Mike and Gabe had been attacked by Indians on all sides during their cattle drive. The Indians only wanted to keep them busy while they helped themselves to a few head of cattle, but the feeling of being surrounded was a terrifying one.

Tyler swallowed and smiled uneasily at the youthful faces around him. They didn't look too dangerous, but there were quite a few of them.

"Is he wearing gold spurs?"

"No, stupid! Cowboys only wear spurs when they ride a horse, not when they sit in a buggy."

"He's probably got a six-shooter under that coat."

"Maybe he's an outlaw!"

"Look at them boots!"

Tyler relaxed, and a grin slipped over his face as he realized he was the object of some admiration. He tipped his Stetson to the young audience and drawled, "Howdy."

"Howdy!"

"Howdy, mister!"

"No, it's, 'Howdy, pardner!'" The slim, freckled-face boy nudged his chubby companion.

"Yeah? How do you know so much about it? I guess I know as much as you do!"

Tyler quickly intervened before a scuffle could ensue. He leaned back in the seat and placed a booted foot up where the lads could get a better view.

"Wow! Look at them fancy boots! Are you wearin' ivory-handled pistols, mister?"

"No, son." Tyler opened his coat so they could see he was unarmed. "A cowboy only needs his guns on when he's working out on the range protecting his cattle from wolves, rattlers, and rustlers."

"How 'bout Injuns? Ya ever bin in an Injun fight?"

"Only once, but I never fired a shot. The Indians had me and my partners surrounded. They were a whoopin' and a hollerin' and shootin' off their rifles. It was enough to make your scalp prickle."

The eyes of the would-be cowboys widened in suspense as they hung on Tyler's words.

"Whad'ja do, mister?" the freckled-faced boy asked breathlessly.

"We waited." Tyler crouched forward and lowered his voice. "We waited until dawn, and then we slipped away and got our herd away from there as fast as we could go." He shook his head solemnly. "Never want to go through that again. No, sir."

"I would've shot my way outta there!" The chubby boy began blasting his make-believe gun, and the others joined in the impromptu Indian battle. War whoops and death cries filled the air with the imagined sounds of banging guns and whistling arrows.

Tyler nearly joined in the battle; he was having so much fun watching them. Then he recalled his dilemma, and when the battle was near an end, he called to one of the survivors, "Say, I could use some help finding my way around this city."

The war stopped in an instant, and the warriors gathered around the carriage once again.

"You lost, mister?"

"Well, I'll tell you." Tyler took off his hat and scratched his head. "If I were back out in the wilderness, I'd just get down and start back-tracking my trail to find my way out of the woods. But here, there's no trail. Horses and buggies have packed the ground hard as rock, and though I hate to admit it, fellas, I don't know up from down in this here city." Tyler gave the boys an ashamed look. "And me able to track a black bear on ice."

The young cowboys gasped, and sympathy for the great tracker lost in the city inspired them to show him their skills.

"You just tell us where you need to go, and we'll get you there, mister." The freckle-faced boy spoke with confidence.

Tyler chuckled to himself as he looked at the young-ster. The boy had on an old cap that was several sizes too large for him. All Tyler could see were a nose, mouth, and freckles peeking out. The boy's eyes were almost lost in the cap.

Tyler flicked the bill of the cap up and laughingly said, "You sure you can see where to go yourself under that thing?"

He was sorry a moment later when the boy's angry green eyes flashed at him.

"Keep your hands off my property, mister," he snarled. He pulled the cap firmly back in place.

The chubby boy spoke up. "Don't mind Sid, mister. Since his pa died, he's always worn his cap. He don't take it off for nobody."

"Oh, I see." Tyler berated himself for his action. "I'm awfully sorry, Sid. I'll never do it again."

Tyler noticed the lad's lip tremble, so he hastened to continue. "So you think you could help me find my way back to the Granville place? If I don't hurry, I'll be late for supper."

"I'll take you there, mister, if you let me ride with you," Sid swiped his sleeve across his nose and offered the deal.

"Sure, come on." Then Tyler hesitated. "But won't your mom mind?"

"I live near there anyway, so you'll be doing me a favor." Sid called to his pals as he climbed into the carriage, "See ya tomorrow, fellas."

They waved him off with a volley of make-believe bullets and arrows.

Once on their way, Sid gave Tyler directions and then remained silent for the journey. Tyler cast side-glances at his guide from time to time. The boy was about the same age as his brother Abel. Finally he spoke, "Say, I'm going to be here for about a week or more. Do you suppose you could take me around to the places I need to go?"

The freckled nose turned to Tyler, but no answer was given.

Tyler was perplexed, not sure if he had offended the boy again, but he ventured to add, "I'll gladly pay you."

"Got yerself a deal, mister," came the quick response. A gloved hand was thrust out at Tyler, and Tyler, chuckling, shook it with his free one.

Chapter 10

Chicago

"Jadyne, hold still!"

Jade scurried around the garden cottage, trying to complete her preparations for the dinner party. Her mother was attempting to finish pinning the coppery curls but was finding the task impossible.

"You must sit here if I am to finish your hair, dear. Why are you digging in that box now? You'll wrinkle your dress."

"I'm sorry, Mother. I'm being as careful as I can. Believe me, I'm thankful not to have had to press this one. Mrs. Todd and I ironed Cecile's things all afternoon!" Her head disappeared into the box again, and in a muffled voice she said, "I'm looking for the slippers that go with this gown. Oh, here they are!"

"You can't wear them on this wet ground," said her mother practically. "You'll have to carry them and wear something else."

"I'll wear the ones by the door and carry these. I just hope no one sees me arrive. I told Mrs. Todd I'd come in the back way, and Mr. Todd can announce me as if I just came in the front door. Oh, bother, why did Mr. Granville put me in this predicament?"

"Shhh! I'm sure Amos Granville has a very good reason. He's been so good to us already. The least we can do is comply with his wishes."

Jade smiled at her mother. "I wish you were coming too."

"I'm very glad that I am not. No, Sidney will regale me with his adventures of the day, and I'll enjoy a nice cup of tea after he's gone to bed. I'll wait up for you. Oh, and do thank Mrs. Todd for the bread. I hope you've learned that skill from her too." Her nimble fingers worked on fastening her daughter's hair in place.

Jade grimaced. "Well, I made cherry pie for the dessert tonight, but bread is a little difficult. The one time I had a chance to try, my loaf came out hard as a rock."

Hazel Crandall laughed with her daughter and the green eyes that her children inherited sparkled with mischief. "Is that what I saw Wil Tait burying behind the stables yesterday?"

"Mother!" Jade turned her head and was promptly tugged back. "Ow!"

"Who is the young gentleman that Amos is entertaining?" Hazel inquired innocently.

Jade looked suspiciously at her mother's reflection in the mirror. "He's a business associate of Mr. Granville's brother Palmer, Mother. Don't get any foolish notions."

"What do you mean, dear?" Hazel put on the finishing touches and remarked as Jade stood for her inspection, "I'll bet he's handsome, isn't he?" Before her daughter could reply, she exclaimed, "Goodness! No one will recognize you as 'Jade the maid,' will they?"

Jade giggled at her mother's comment and then looked at herself critically in the mirror. "I wager that if I stuck that silly maid's cap on right now, they'd know in an instant."

"Or else they'd think you were Sidney. Of course, the dress might give it away!"

The women laughed together. Jade had modeled her maid's outfit for her mother and Sidney, and they had all laughed together when she and Sidney had switched caps. Jade was of average height, but at twelve years of age, Sidney was already nose-to-nose with her, and it was fairly certain that he had inherited their father's lean and lanky frame.

Jade checked the time and exclaimed, "Mother, I must go! I don't want to be caught running between here and the mansion. Fortunately Mr. Granville hired someone to replace me who doesn't know me. I just hope Mrs. Stanwood is kept busy somewhere else." She paused for breath. "I...I don't think I can go through with this!"

"Jadyne Kathleen Crandall!" Hazel Crandall spoke firmly. "If the Lord could get us through all the troubles we faced after your father's death, don't you think he can help you through a little thing like a dinner party? 'Cast *all* your cares upon him.' Nothing is too trivial or unimportant to him."

Jade sighed deeply. "I know, Mother. It's just that sometimes I feel that I have to do all the planning and try to work every detail out ahead of time. I *will* quit worrying and just leave the evening in the Lord's hands." She kissed her mother's cheek. "Thank you."

"Good-bye, dear. Enjoy yourself."

As the door closed behind her daughter, Hazel turned to the Lord herself. *Help her understand how to trust you, Father, even when she can't see around the next corner. Help her see that she needs faith in your abilities to work out details, not in her own abilities. Help her follow where you lead.*

Jade hurried along the wet, dark path carrying her good slippers. She was very nervous about being recognized tonight by Tyler Newly. True, he appeared not to be aware of her while she was serving him, but their eyes had met once. Jade felt again the warmth that had spread through her. And her green eyes might give her away; they were very distinctive to her, Sidney, and her mother. Jade mused the problem over in her mind. Then, remembering her mother's admonition, she paused on the path and gave the worry over to the Lord.

Her burdens felt lighter after her moment's pause, and feeling more confident, she was about to go on when a noise on the path behind her made her spin around in sudden fright. The shadows of early evening made the trees appear large and sinister, and the swaying of the bare branches in the light wind seemed as figures darting in and out of hiding.

She laughed nervously while her racing heart slowed, and she turned back to go on. A few steps later she spun around again, and this time she saw more than imaginary figures in the branches. There *was* someone there!

"Who is that?" Her shaky voice did nothing to hide her fear. She stood trembling while her eyes scanned the area. Gathering courage, she called, "Wil Tait, that's a mean thing to do, trying to scare me!"

With false bravado, she turned back on her way and with increasing speed finally made it to the back door of the Granville mansion.

The warmth and light of the kitchen enveloped her, and she stood for a moment just breathing deeply after her flight. That Wilbert Tait! She was going to put a stop to his shenanigans as soon as she saw him again.

Mrs. Todd scurried into the kitchen from the pantry with her arms full of canning jars. At the sight of Jade, she jumped and gave out a little scream. Jade rushed forward and caught the jar that slipped from her fingers.

"Goodness, Jade! You startled me standing there like that!" She set down her supplies and looked at Jade again, this time in admiration. "You look lovely, Miss Jade, just lovely." Then she noticed the whiteness of the young woman's face, and she asked, concerned, "Are you all right?"

Jade smiled at the friendly cook. "I'm fine, Mrs. Todd." She didn't wish to worry the woman. "I guess I'm a bit nervous, though." She bent down to change her shoes.

"Well, there's absolutely no need for that, Miss Jade. We've got everything worked out. Roland will come get you when the coast is clear."

The butler appeared in the kitchen door at that moment. "Tait just drove up with Simonsons. I'll come for you, Miss Jade, after I announce them." He smiled briefly then hurried off to get the door.

Mrs. Todd looked pleased with herself. "See, dear, everything is going fine. Now, let me take your cape. I'll just put it and your shoes here in the pantry. How would that be? Miss Jade? Jade?"

Jade stared at the cook but wasn't seeing her. Wilbert Tait wasn't the figure in the woods! He couldn't be; he just chauffeured someone to the front door! Jade swallowed the nervous lump that had begun again in her throat and shook off the shiver that enveloped her.

"Why, you're still freezing, child! Stand over by the stove until Roland comes back for you." Mrs. Todd led the silent girl to the cook stove and took the cape from her shoulders. "Where is that girl Becky? I tell you, Miss Jade, she can't compare to you in the kitchen. I've had to teach her to do everything, and Stanwood keeps taking her away to wait on Miss Cecile upstairs. It's been busy here this last hour. Believe me!" The woman kept up a steady chattering until she saw some color return to the girl's lovely face. "Are you feeling better now, Jade?" She looked anxiously into Jade's face.

Jade smiled absently at the woman as she silently berated herself for letting her imagination run away with her. There was probably nothing there at all! She was just nervous about the evening ahead.

"I'm fine now, Mrs. Todd. Thank you for taking such good care of me. Who is the new girl tonight?"

The cook studied Jade closely, and worry puckered her forehead. "Her name's Becky."

"Well, I hope she has been a good help to you so far. I feel terrible about leaving so much for you to do. Cecile was very demanding before I could get away."

Perplexed at Jade's inattention, the woman was about to explain again when Mr. Todd hurried into the room.

"Are you ready, Miss Jade? I mean, Miss Crandall?"

Jade's heart doubled its beating. "Yes." She smoothed her skirt and looked to Mrs. Todd for approval. Receiving her answering nod, she turned to follow Mr. Todd into the entryway.

Jade stood a little behind the butler as he opened the front door and shut it again. He winked at her as he pretended to take her wrap and hang it up. Then with a smile as if he were enjoying the secrecy, he led her to the front parlor.

"Miss Jadyne Crandall."

With some trepidation, Jade stepped into the room.

Two older couples were in a conversation with their host on one side of the parlor. Across from them was Cecile Granville, holding court for two young gentlemen who seemed to be hanging on her every word. One of them was Tyler Newly. They all turned at Jade's entrance.

Jade stood with quiet grace as Amos made his way to her side. His welcoming smile and the twinkle in his eye put her at ease. She owed this man much, and she would not disappoint him.

Amos saw the lift of her chin and the determined gleam in her eye, and he gave her an approving nod. Together they made their way around the room.

"Jadyne, let me introduce you to Mr. and Mrs. Simonson." Jade smiled her thanks at Amos for using her formal name. "Lee is my lawyer, and he handles Palmer's affairs as well. Lee, Edna, let me introduce a dear friend of mine, Miss Jadyne Crandall."

At Jade's surname, the lawyer's eyebrows rose. Every lawyer in Chicago had heard about Edmund Crandall's death and loss of his fortune. The man had been a poor manager of his money.

Jade saw the look and steeled herself for the snub she had come to expect, but Mr. Simonson spoke with genuine sympathy. "Our condolences on the passing of your father, Miss Crandall."

Jade's green eyes lost their wariness, and she warmly thanked the couple.

"These are the Pullveys, my dear, Harold and Elizabeth. Harold is a business associate of Palmer's, and his son…" Jade quickly shook hands with the couple as Amos led her to the younger people. "His son Wade is a partner now too. Wade, meet Miss Jadyne Crandall."

The dark-haired man took Jade's hand and kissed it with great debonair.

"A pleasure, Miss Crandall." His eyes frankly admired her.

Jade smiled and nodded politely to the man. He was like a dozen other men she knew who thought themselves irresistible to the ladies. She gently pulled her hand away from his as Amos turned to Tyler.

With a touch of glee in his voice, Amos said, "Jadyne, please meet Mr. Tyler Newly, a business partner of Palmer's. He's recently come from Minnesota and is staying with me while he conducts his business affairs. Mr. Newly, my good friend Miss Crandall."

Jade willed herself to bring her eyes up to meet Tyler's. This would be the moment he would recognize her. She was sure. Her eyes traveled up the buttons on his coat, his shirt, up to his bow tie, his firm chin, his straight nose, and then into his eyes. There they stayed while the moments ticked past.

Amos hid a smile as he waited for one of them to speak. Wade Pullvey scowled, and Cecile fairly bristled as her eyes narrowed. Tyler Newly had never looked at *her* like that!

"How do you do, Miss Crandall?" Tyler finally reached for the hand Jade held in midair. His gentle pressure on her fingertips sent an invisible shiver through her, and her eyes reflected a momentary gleam.

As if suddenly realizing how long she had been standing there, Jade quickly withdrew her hand and murmured, "How do you do, Mr. Newly?" in a soft voice.

"And this is my niece, Cecile Granville, who has come to stay and visit her old uncle for a while." Amos turned Jade finally to Cecile with not a little apprehension.

Jade caught the slight worry in his tone and with as much delight as she could muster, said, "How nice to finally meet you, Miss Granville. Your uncle has told me about you. I hope you are enjoying your visit?"

Cecile looked at Jade closely. Her eyes roamed over her face and eyes and hair, and finally she said, "Oh, yes. Dear Uncle Amos and I are very close. We get along famously."

Amos led Jade back to the Simonsons, and they continued their conversations there. Cecile and Wade took up where they left off, and Cecile tried to coax Tyler into the little flirtations he had been enjoying only moments before, but now he was strangely quiet. Cecile's face hardened when she saw his attention was on the young woman across the room.

Tyler didn't hear the voices around him. He sat very still trying to analyze the emotion he was feeling. Ever since Jadyne Crandall had been announced, she had mesmerized him. She seemed almost frightened to be here, yet she was calm and regal. Her beauty astounded him, and he reddened slightly, remembering his reaction to her introduction. He had stared dumbfounded at her like a schoolboy with a crush! What she must think of him!

He watched her smile and converse with Amos Granville. Philippa hated talking to older people. She was barely civil to her own parents. He watched the light flicker on Jadyne's coppery curls and marveled at the green eyes he could see sparkle with intelligence and interest.

Green eyes! Where else had he seen eyes like that? He searched his mind uneasily, wondering if he had met her before. How embarrassing if he had! No, he knew! It was that freckle-faced kid he met today. Sid. He had green eyes too. Tyler sighed in relief.

"She's something, isn't she?" Wade Pullvey leaned over and spoke quietly to Tyler while Cecile answered a question the elder Pullvey had put to her.

Tyler felt his face flush a little, but he didn't say anything.

Wade looked speculatively at the man then said in a challenging voice, "I think I'll ask Miss Crandall if I may take her into dinner." He rose and walked to the group, who were enjoying a laugh together at something Amos just said.

Tyler could have kicked himself for not thinking of it first. He saw Wade speak into Jadyne's ear, but before she could give a reply, Amos announced, "I believe our meal is ready for us. Wade, would you and Mr. Newly kindly escort Cecile?" He held out an arm to Jade. "I'll take Miss Crandall and lead the way. Gentlemen, bring your wives to the dining room, please."

The group rose to follow, and Tyler felt Cecile slip her hand into his arm. Wade took her other hand, and she smiled and said, "What handsome escorts! What more could a girl ask for?"

Wade's eyes met Tyler's over her head. He looked up ahead to where Jadyne and Amos led the way and then back to Tyler again. With a slight mocking tone in his voice, he said, "And what an honor to escort such a lovely lady as yourself, Miss Granville. Isn't that right, Newly?"

"Indeed." Tyler met the challenge he saw in the other's eye.

Cecile reveled in the competition she saw between the two, missing completely the focus of their attention. She poured on the charm. "You must each sit on one side of me, gentlemen. There is so much I want to know about both of you."

Jade admired the loveliness of the table. She had a new appreciation for the efforts of those who prepared the elegance that others enjoyed. A plump young girl in the maid's uniform and frilly cap stood beside the kitchen doorway waiting for the signal to begin. Jade noticed the nervousness she was trying to hide, and catching the girl's eye, she gave her a warm smile. The girl timidly smiled back.

Tyler noticed the exchange and wondered. He was uncomfortably aware that he was out of his element in this new environment. More and more he was longing for the simple things back home. As he took in the table and all of its dishes and silverware, he knew he was in trouble. Lunch hadn't been bad with only Amos watching him, but tonight he was surrounded with people who no doubt would notice his ineptness.

Amos directed the seating arrangements, and Cecile got her wish of having the men on either side of her. Tyler could hardly believe his good fortune when Jadyne was placed on his other side, on Amos's right hand. The Simonsons and Pullveys lined up across from them. Before they were seated, Amos turned to Tyler and said, "Mr. Newly, would you ask the blessing, please?"

Surprised but pleased, Tyler nodded. In a clear voice, he prayed, "Heavenly Father, we thank thee for these blessings you've so graciously provided, for these friends gathered together, but mostly for your Son, Jesus Christ, for providing an eternal home in heaven for those who believe in him. May we live to serve you in his name. Amen."

The room was quiet, and Tyler heard the very soft "amen" of the woman beside him. On his other side, Cecile looked up at him curiously. As Amos asked them to be seated and motioned for the serving to begin, she asked Tyler in an incredulous voice, "You're not a minister, are you, Mr. Newly?"

Tyler laughed and said, "No, Miss Granville, but I was raised in a Christian home, and prayer was and is part of my daily life."

"Well," said Cecile with a knowing smile, "that should certainly get you into heaven."

Wade chuckled.

"No, Miss Granville. That's not what I believe at all. You see, heaven can't be worked for. It's given to us as a gift. Jesus Christ did all the work for us when he died on the cross for our sins."

"'Not by works of righteousness which we have done, but according to his mercy he saved us...'" quoted Jade. She stopped as the surprised faces turned toward her and then bravely continued. "All we do is place our faith in the Lord Jesus Christ's work instead of our own."

"That's right, Miss Crandall." Tyler smiled with pleasure at the lovely lady beside him.

Amos watched with interest as they smiled at each other. Then noticing the black look on Cecile's face, he changed the subject. "Harold, tell us about the business you and Wade are in now. I'm sure Palmer would appreciate having Tyler know some details to pass on to him."

The first course began as Mr. Pullvey went into a narrative of business, of which Tyler heard little. His mind was on the woman beside him, and more and more he wanted to talk alone with her and find out more about her.

The maid placed a plate in front of him and then one in front of Jadyne. He heard the young woman quietly thank her. Closely he watched and listened to the others. Amos smiled and said, "Thanks, Becky. You're doing fine." The Simonsons both smiled their thanks at the girl, but the Pullveys, Wade, and Cecile ignored her as he had done to the maid at lunch. He felt chagrined. Apparently Philippa's instructions had been right—if you wanted to act like *some* rich people. Tyler knew now that it was not right for him.

As the others began to eat, Tyler realized he was in another quandary. In the myriad of silver laid out before him, he had no idea which to pick up and start eating with. Unobtrusively, he looked around.

"The one farthest to your left," Jadyne whispered behind her napkin.

The words were unheard by the others, and Tyler silently thanked her with his eyes. Cecile then claimed his attention and kept him monopolized through most of the meal.

Tyler was rewarded with a slight smile from Jadyne each time he politely thanked Becky during the rest of the dinner. He continued to watch her closely for directions. Then as the housekeeper came in with the dessert, he heard Jadyne make a choking sound, which she quickly turned into a cough.

Tyler felt the change in his companion immediately. Jadyne was sitting very still and quiet, her eyes fastened on the woman who was about to serve the dessert. Tyler saw the woman give Jadyne a cold, hard look, and then she began to serve, beginning with Amos.

Tyler didn't understand what was wrong, but he stayed aware as the rest of the party visited with each other. Fortunately Cecile was occupied with Wade at the moment. The dessert finally came around to their side, and the woman served his, and he quietly thanked her. He saw her pick up the plate of cherry pie and start to place it in front of Jadyne. Then her wrist turned, and the pie began to slide toward Jadyne's lap. Without thinking, his hand darted out and caught the pie. He slid it back on the plate, and as the others turned curiously at the sudden movement, he laughed and said, "Sorry. Here, Miss Crandall, trade with me. My fingers are all over this piece."

Jade's white face turned to him, and he saw her tight, pained expression. "Thank you, Mr. Newly. You were very quick."

"Why, that would have ruined your lovely gown!" exclaimed Mrs. Pullvey.

"Nice work, Newly," said Wade.

"I'm awfully sorry, miss. Please, sir, allow me to bring you a fresh piece." The serving woman smoothly apologized.

"No, that's not necessary." Tyler took a bite, and the others relaxed and followed suit. Before the woman left the room, Tyler said, "Please tell the cook the pie is excellent."

The woman nodded and left.

Jadyne's smile lit up her face, causing Tyler to wonder if what he said or did had caused it.

When the meal finished, the gentlemen excused themselves to the library to discuss some of their business affairs. The women returned to the front parlor, and Becky brought their coffee and tea.

"Your hair is a beautiful color, Miss Crandall, and so stylish," remarked Mrs. Simonson. "Your maid must be very clever."

"My mother helped with my hair tonight. Thank you. I'll tell her what you said."

"Well, I had to resort to doing my own," complained Cecile. "The maids around here know nothing of the latest styles and nearly ruined my hair. I really must speak to Uncle Amos about it."

Jade looked at her hands and willed herself to keep quiet. She had done Cecile's hair before running home, and the style hadn't been changed when she came back.

"How ever did you manage it alone?" asked Mrs. Pullvey. "It looks quite difficult." The two older women exchanged a knowing look, and Jade hid a smile. Clearly Cecile wasn't fooling anyone.

The evening passed quickly, and Jade wondered about leaving. Mr. Todd said he would signal when the coast was clear. She enjoyed herself, she admitted, and mostly because of Tyler Newly. She wondered if she would ever see him again when he left here and was surprised at the lonely feeling that came over her.

The men rejoined the ladies, and Jade did her best to politely refuse Wade's offers of a ride home, a ride in the country, a concert—the man was persistent! She had no time to speak privately with Tyler, and the disappointment was evident on his face. Cecile again claimed his attention, and manners prevented him from leaving her side.

The Simonsons left and then the Pullveys. Jade was about to excuse herself when Mr. Todd announced that her carriage had arrived.

Both Amos and Jade looked at him in surprise. *Carriage?*

Tyler managed to escape Cecile for a moment and came to Jadyne's side. He took the cape from Mr. Todd and helped her into it and then said, "I would be happy to escort you home, Miss Crandall."

Four startled faces looked at him as though he had committed another social blunder. Surprisingly, Cecile came to Jade's rescue.

"You were going to escort me to my room, Tyler. Don't you remember?"

Tyler seemed irritated for a moment, and Jade doubted that he had made Cecile any such promise.

"Thank you for the offer, Mr. Newly," Jade said. "I'm sorry, but I've made other arrangements. I'm very glad to have met you." She held out her hand.

Defeated, Tyler took her hand in his own. He glanced at the three faces watching the two of them, and his face reddened.

Jade saw the frustration in his face, and she let her eyes show him that she felt the same way. He responded with a smile.

"Good-bye, then."

"Good-bye."

She looked down at her hand and then back at his face. Reluctantly he let go. Jade politely said good night to Cecile then kissed Amos on the cheek. She followed Mr. Todd out of the room.

The butler again winked at her and was about to open and close the front door then sneak her back through the kitchen when they heard a voice behind them.

"Miss Crandall!"

Jade turned back to Tyler in surprise as he hurried forward.

"Miss Crandall, I know we've just met, but do you think I could see you again?" At her worried look, he hastened to add, "I'll only be here a week, and then I must go back. Please."

Jade was silent, trying to think of some reply. How could she tell him that it was impossible? She didn't want it to be impossible!

"I'm very sorry. I'll be unavailable this week." She knew how inadequate the apology was.

"I understand." He sighed. "Let me at least see you to your carriage." Jade cast a startled look at the butler. Mr. Todd appeared ready to block the door when Cecile's voice came from the doorway.

"Oh, there you are, Tyler. Uncle Amos wishes to see you after you've brought me to my room." She glared at Jadyne. "Haven't you gone yet, Miss Crandall?"

"Just leaving. Good-bye again."

Jade turned to Mr. Todd, so he dutifully opened the door for her, and she stepped out. She wasted no time but hurried around to the back of the house. The kitchen door was locked, and she didn't dare knock. She'd have to walk home in her good slippers.

Uneasily, she faced the dark path and wished a carriage really was taking her home instead. She prayed for the Lord's protection and then started down the path as fast as she could.

The wind still swayed the branches, and the moon cast shadows over the wet, rain-soaked ground. Noises made her head turn one way and then the other. She slipped and floundered but remained on her feet.

When she reached the cottage, she stopped, out of breath, and waited for her racing heart to slow. Her feet were soaked, and while she stood there panting, she couldn't help laughing at her foolishness.

A far-away laugh echoed hers. She looked back over her shoulder at the path while a prickly feeling crept up her neck into her scalp. A dark figure of a man stood leaning against a tree! Jade scrambled to the door in her slippery shoes and threw herself inside. She quickly bolted the lock after her.

Hazel came swiftly from the other room. "Jadyne, what's wrong? What's happened?"

"There was a man in the woods." Jade still gasped for breath. At her mother's horrified look, she hastened to add, "He didn't come near me. In fact, he only laughed at me because he saw me running like a frightened rabbit down the trail." She didn't want her mother worried. "It was probably that crazy Wil Tait having a good laugh at my expense."

"Where are your shoes? Look at those slippers."

"I'm sorry. I left without them." Jade sank into the nearest chair.

"How was the evening?" Her mother still looked concerned.

"Oh, Mother, it was fun! Mr. Granville enjoyed himself so much. He gets quite lonely, you know. The people were nice, except Cecile. I don't think she knows how to be."

"Jadyne!" Hazel scolded. "And how about Mr. Newly. Did he recognize you?"

Jade smiled. "No, he had no idea who I was. I can't believe he could be fooled so easily." She saw her mother's look. "He was nice too."

"Good, because he asked Sidney to be his guide this week while he's here."

Jade jumped to her feet. "Mother, he doesn't—"

"No, he doesn't know you are related to Sidney. They met when Mr. Newly had gotten himself lost. He's offered to pay Sidney."

Jade pondered the situation as she got ready for bed. She'd warn Sidney not to say anything about his family. She almost felt she was being deceitful, but she hadn't lied to the man. She just didn't want him to know she was the maid at the Granville mansion.

She climbed in under the warm quilts and closed her eyes. Again she relived the moments when Tyler had held her hand and looked into her eyes. She sighed as she started drifting off to sleep. *Mrs. Tyler Newly...*

Her eyes flashed open, and she sat up. What was she thinking? Slowly she lay down again and considered her thoughts. Was she in love with him? A man she'd just met?

Inside the Granville mansion, Tyler's eyes were wide open as well. *Miss Jadyne Crandall*, he thought. Where had he heard the name Crandall before? He tried to remember, but it escaped him.

She was just about everything he had hoped to find in the woman he wanted to make his wife. He sat up in the bed, and his heart thundered. *His wife?* Slowly he sank back against the pillow. *His wife.* She was exactly the person he wanted for his wife. But how could he know this in just the few hours he'd been in her company?

Lord, he prayed, *show me if this is your will. Lead me in the right path.*

Chapter 11

Chicago

Jade appeared early at the kitchen door ready to go to work. The path wasn't so scary with the morning sun sprinkling through the trees. She found a man's footprints along the trail and affirmed that last night hadn't been her imagination.

But nothing bothered her today. She had a song in her heart and a smile on her lips as she said good morning to Mrs. Todd.

"Mr. Granville wants to see you right away, Miss Jade. And here are your shoes. Roland told me about the mix up at the front door. He felt badly about it."

"It was no problem, Mrs. Todd. In fact, it was rather funny, really, all our plans gone awry. I'll just put my cap on." She grimaced in the small mirror by the door. "And now I'm ready. Should I take up a tray or just go?"

"You might as well bring the tray. I've got it all ready." The cook placed the tray in Jade's arms. "Here, let me tuck that curl back in place. My, you have bouncy hair under that cap!"

Jade laughed. "It is a problem keeping it hidden. I'll see you later. Oh, Mother said to thank you for the bread. I forgot to last night. Do you think I could try making it again?"

Mrs. Todd laughed. "We can try, Jade. Now, hurry along so I can get something done."

Jade walked swiftly through the quiet mansion. The clock ticked loudly in the stillness. She tapped on Amos's study door where he always took his breakfast and entered when she heard his call.

"Good morning, Jade! I'm glad you're here early."

"Good morning, Mr. Granville," she answered cheerfully. "Did you sleep well?"

"Wonderful! Having people over in the evenings agrees with me. But that's what I need to talk with you about."

Jade set the breakfast things in order as she waited for him to continue.

"I want you to take a few days off, my dear."

Jade looked surprised.

"I will still pay you, but I'm afraid our guests might recognize you now even in your uniform."

Jade started to protest, but Amos held up his hand.

"I don't want to chance your embarrassment, Jade. Besides, there's something else I wish you to do."

"What?" Jade was perplexed.

"I'd like you to come to another dinner the night before our Mr. Newly has to leave. I'll invite the same people, and we'll finish our business then. Will you come?"

Jade was silent a moment. She would see Tyler again only to say good-bye. The thought saddened her. She had at least looked forward to working here and seeing him without his being aware of her. She looked at the old gentleman. "Yes, of course I'll come."

"Good! I wish I knew more about young Newly's other business here. Strange, he won't say much about it, only that he has to do something for the others at their camp. I wonder what it is. What's he up to?"

Jade was about to ask a question when there was a tap on the door.

"Come in," called Amos.

Tyler Newly entered the room. Jade took one look at his handsome face and knew that if she wasn't already in love with this man, she was about to be. Suddenly aware that he must not know who she was, she became very nervous. Amos felt his young friend's concern and quickly took matters into his hands.

"Good morning, Tyler. Do come in. Sit down." He motioned to the chair in front of his desk. Then he looked at Jade and said, "Would you please tell Cook to prepare a tray for Mr. Newly. He can join me for breakfast right here."

"Yes, sir," Jade spoke quietly and kept her head lowered.

Tyler's eyes darted to her when she spoke. He sighed then made a negative shake with his head.

Amos tried to hide a grin.

Jade made her escape back to the kitchen and explained the situation to Mrs. Todd.

"I'll miss teaching you to do the bread today, but I think Mr. Granville is right. That Miss Cecile is always snooping around, and she could come upon you when you weren't prepared and discover your identity. Yes, I think it's wise that you keep clear of here for a while."

"I'm just sorry to leave you with so much," said Jade. "Remember, though, when I come back, I'm learning how to make bread."

The cook promised, and Jade slipped out the back door. She pulled her hood over her hair and started down the path through the woods deep in thought.

Mr. Granville said Tyler was doing some other business that he didn't know anything about. She, too, wondered what that could be or if it was even important. She thought that Tyler should at least explain to his host what he was doing, especially if it involved Palmer. Why was he being so mysterious?

Without warning, an arm reached from the trees and grabbed hers, swinging her around. Jade let out a scream that was quickly muffled by a hand. Instantly she bit the hand and kicked the man's legs as she tried to pull free.

"Jade! Hold still! I only want to talk to ya! Ow!"

"Wilbert Tait!" Jade's green eyes flashed in anger. "Don't you ever scare me like that again! What's the matter with you?" She slapped his hand away from her arm and tried to stop the trembling the sudden fright had produced in her.

"Well, ya weren't even looking where ya were going, so I just stopped ya! Ya didn't have to scream." He looked at his hand. "And ya didn't have to bite me neither!"

"I'd bite anyone who grabbed me like that! Goodness, Wil, it was bad enough you laughed at me last night when I ran home. You didn't need to scare me twice."

Wilbert scowled. "What do ya mean last night? I was driving the carriage all night, taking them people home."

Jade looked at him, and a tiny prickle of fear shivered down her neck. She tried to shake it away and asked in a trembling voice, "Well, what do you want?"

Wilbert cocked his head to one side and said, "I seen ya come out of the house now, and I thought it would be a good time to ask ya something."

Jade waited, but as his eyes roamed her face and hair, she began to get a sinking feeling.

"I figger since we're both in the 'working class' now that maybe you and I could—"

Jade didn't wait for him to go any further. "I'm sorry, Wil, but I don't think so." She turned to leave. He grabbed her arm again.

"Don't ya start playing like you're too good for me. Besides, I've got money, lots of money. And I can get more. You be nice to me, and you and me can be just like these rich toffs we have to work for." His eyes gleamed. "I'd buy ya anything ya want, Jade." He moved closer to her, and Jade realized he was bending to kiss her.

Quickly slipping a foot behind his ankle, she pulled it forward while she pushed him backward. The surprise of her attack caught him off guard, and he stumbled and fell. She took off at a run.

She chanced a look over her shoulder to see if she was being pursued, but Wilbert was being helped up by another man. She slowed and stopped behind a tree and watched while she caught her breath.

The strange man was laughing, but Wilbert looked angry. Then the man reached into a pocket and pulled out some money, handing it to Wilbert. Wilbert took the money eagerly and shoved it into his own pocket. The two headed back to the stables together.

Jade continued home, her thoughts racing. Who was that man? Was he the one who laughed at her the night before? What was he paying Wilbert for?

Puzzling over the questions, she entered the cottage to find her mother and brother in an argument.

"You said you would be his guide. You gave your word. You can't back out now."

"Ma—"

"Don't call me 'Ma!'"

"Sorry, Mother. I just got offered a job at the grocer's. I've been trying to get that job for a month. I can't turn it down, Ma, 'cuz it will be a job I can keep for years. This cowboy fella only needs me for a week. Don't ya see? Come on, Ma!"

"Don't call me—"

"What's the trouble?" Jade intervened.

"Jadyne, why are you home?" Mother and son turned to look at Jade. "Did something go wrong?" Hazel asked, concern creasing her brow.

"No, no, everything is fine. What's this all about?"

Hazel sighed. "Sidney gave his word to Mr. Newly that he'd be his guide. Now, he wants to back out and go work at the grocer's instead. I told him a man should keep his word."

"Jade, the job at the grocer's will last longer than this guide thing. If I don't take it today, Mr. Reeves will give it to one of the other boys. And we need the money," he added stubbornly. "Besides, I can get one of the fellas to take my place with the cowboy."

Jade stared thoughtfully at Sidney. If Sid were with Tyler, he could learn what he was up to. Amos had a right to know the business his brother's partner was in. She grabbed Sid's shoulder.

"You are going to keep that job, Sid. Come on, and I'll help you make arrangements for the other." She pulled him out the door.

"But, Jade," her mother called after her, "why are you home?"

"I just need a few things, Mother. I'll be back for them shortly."

Sid scowled at his sister as she pulled him away from the house. "Come on, Jade. I though you'd be on my side," he grumbled.

"Sorry, Sid, but this is more important right now. Here's what I need you to do…"

Chapter 12

Chicago

Sid leaned against a tree at the corner and tried to appear nonchalant. He squirmed and pulled off a glove to scratch his back through his thick overcoat. His green eyes narrowed as he watched the carriages pass by.

Finally, a carriage stopped. The boy froze beside the tree until Tyler spotted him and called, "Morning, Sid. Come on. Let's get going."

Sid moved to the carriage slowly, warily watching Tyler. Playing detective around the cowboy without his knowing it wasn't going to be easy.

Tyler frowned. The boy looked like he was about to be scolded.

"Sid, I've got an appointment in half an hour. Come on!"

Sid took a deep breath and strode to the carriage. He climbed in beside Tyler on the seat and kept his head lowered, looking at the man through narrowed eyes.

Tyler looked at the surly boy. Apparently he wasn't in a very good mood this morning. "Well, Sid." He clapped a hand on his shoulder.

The boy jerked away as if burnt by a hot brand. Tyler pulled his hand back in surprise.

"Don't like to be touched, mister! Jes' keep yer hands to yerself!"

Startled, Tyler said, "Okay, okay. You don't need to act like a grizzly with a toothache. What's wrong with you this morning?"

"Nothin. Jes' don't like to be touched, that's all. Now, where ya wanna go?"

Tyler shook his head. It looked like it was going to be a long day. "I've got an appointment with Wade Pullvey. He works in his father's business somewhere north of the city." Tyler named the building.

"I know where it is. Take a left here," Sid growled.

They reached the Pullvey's establishment, and Tyler jumped down. He looked at the boy uncertainly. "You want to come in?"

Sid shrugged his shoulders in the big coat. "Ya need help finding yer way in there?"

Tyler scowled. "Look, if you don't want this job, I'm sure I can find someone else to do it."

Sid saw he was going too far; he'd better back off or he'd never find out what Tyler was up to. "Sorry. I'll come."

As they entered the building together, Tyler reached up and removed his Stetson. He looked at the boy beside him and motioned with a flick of his fingers for Sid to remove his cap. Sid clapped his gloved hand over his cap and scowled up at the man.

Tyler stopped abruptly and gave the rebellious boy a dark look. He was about to speak when the lad interrupted him.

"I don't take this cap off for nothing! Ya hear me? Nothing!" The green eyes flashed, and Tyler could have sworn there was fear behind the bravado the boy was trying to display. Remembering the tears he had once seen in Sid's eyes, Tyler's look softened.

"Sid, your father wouldn't want you to be disrespectful, would he? I know his memory is important to you, but don't forget the things he must have taught you."

The boy spun on his heel and started out the door. He was jerked to a sudden stop by a hand on his coat collar. Alarmed, he clapped his hand back on his cap as he was pulled nose to nose with a very angry Tyler Newly.

"Don't walk away from me when I'm talking to you, young man!" Tyler loosened his grip on the boy but held him with his eyes. "I'll let you keep the cap on, but," he continued when he saw the relief in the boy's face, "as long as you are working for me, you will show a little more respect. You got that?"

The lad swallowed the lump in his throat and looked into the sky-blue eyes so close to his. "I'll do what ya say, mister, 'long as ya leave me and my cap alone."

Tyler let out an exasperated sigh. The boy was going to try his patience.

"Newly, I see you found us. Is there something wrong here? Who's this?" Wade Pullvey strode toward them.

Tyler straightened up away from the hostile boy. He smiled a greeting at the businessman and introduced Sidney as his guide.

Wade's eyebrows shot up. "A guide? We can provide you with someone to show you around, Newly. No need to depend on a street orphan." He looked at Sid as though he were diseased.

"Uh, no. No thanks. Sid and I will manage just fine." Tyler slipped an arm around the boy's thin shoulders.

Sid jerked away from him and gave him a dirty look. Tyler scowled.

Wade laughed. "Well, if that's the way you want it, Newly, suit yourself. Come on. I'll show you around. *You*, stay here and don't touch anything." He pointed at the boy.

The two walked off together, leaving Sid to sit in the waiting area. Wearily, the boy slumped down into a chair and took a deep breath. His hands went to his cap again, and he tugged at it here and there to put it just right.

The minutes ticked by, and Sid spent them either chewing on his lower lip or staring into space. Tyler came back down the corridor about an hour later. He stopped a way off and watched Sidney run to the door and open it for an elderly lady. The boy even tipped the brim of his cap to her. Maybe there was hope for him after all.

"Sorry it took so long, Sid."

The boy jumped at the sound of his voice, and Tyler scowled.

Sid pulled his cap lower and mumbled, "I don't mind 'long as yer payin' me."

Tyler looked irritated with the boy and checked his pocket watch. "We've got an hour before my next appointment. How about showing me some of the sights?"

They got back into the carriage, and Sid asked, "What do ya wanna see, mister?"

"How about the lake? I saw Lake Superior once, but I've never seen Lake Michigan before."

Tyler was jovial for the next hour while Sid took him to the harbor and showed him around. The boy forgot his wariness and enjoyed showing the older man the sights. He described things with obvious pride and boyish enthusiasm. As the time got closer to Tyler's next appointment, Tyler kept looking at his watch and seemed nervous. Sid looked at him strangely.

"Are ya gettin' sick, Mr. Newly? Does being by the water bother ya?"

"No, Sid, I'm fine." Tyler rubbed his chin as they headed in the direction of his next appointment. He took off his hat and ran his fingers through his hair.

Sid inquisitively asked, "What kind of hat is that anyway?"

"It's called a Stetson. Lots of men up north wear them. Here, try it on."

Sid grabbed his own cap tightly and glared at Tyler.

"Never mind, then." Tyler sighed. Then suddenly he asked, "Do you know much about women?"

Sid's eyes widened, but he stared straight ahead. "Whatcha' mean?"

"Well, if you were looking for a wife, what would you look for in a woman?"

"I ain't lookin' for no wife."

Tyler shook his head. "I know you're not! I said *if* you were, what would you look for?"

"I ain't never gettin' married."

Tyler's voice rose. "I don't care if you don't get married! Can you just answer my question, please?"

"What?"

Sid crouched low in the seat as he saw the frustration in Tyler's face.

"Nothing! I don't know why I thought you could help in the first place. You're just a kid."

Sid was beyond curious now and just plain wanted to know what Tyler was talking about, so he said, "Well, I'd look for someone like my ma."

Tyler looked sideways at the boy as if he didn't dare try to continue the conversation.

Sid bravely went on. "My ma is pretty, but she's smart too. She knows how to be a lady, but she can still come outside and play games with me. She makes me do my chores, but she'll help me if I run out of time." He looked at Tyler under the brim of the cap.

Tyler was slowing the horse in front of an empty office building. He sat for a few minutes staring straight ahead, saying nothing.

Sid took the silence to mean he should continue. "When my pa died, my ma cried a lot, but she got busy and found us a new home, and she takes real good care of my sister and me. She said the Lord helped her know what to do."

Tyler looked at the boy and grinned. "Thanks, Sid. She sounds very nice. I'd like to meet her sometime." He looked uncomfortable for a minute and then plunged on, "Now, I'm going to need your help. I've got to find women who will make good wives."

Sid's jaw dropped, and his eyes widened. "What?"

"No, don't go looking at me like that! They aren't for me. My friends back home sent me to pick out wives for them. In about half an hour, I have to start interviewing women." He sighed and got out of the carriage. "Can you read and write?"

Numbly Sid nodded.

"Good! You can be my assistant. Let's get busy."

Chapter 13

Chicago

The building Tyler opened with a key was empty but for a couple of desks and some chairs. Another doorway led to an inner office. He sent Sid to find rags to start wiping the dust off the furniture.

Sid kept one eye on Tyler and another on the work he rushed through. Questions filled his mind, and in boyish curiosity he peppered Tyler with them. How many men? How many women? How old? Would any show up? How come *he* had to choose them? Were the men ugly? What if the women were ugly?

Finally Tyler threw up his hands to silence the boy. "I don't know! I don't even want to do this! I got 'chosen' because I wasn't there when they were choosing, and I got stuck with it."

He rubbed his hand over his face and sighed deeply. "Come here, Sid."

The boy walked to the desk and plopped down on a chair. He wiped his nose with his sleeve and looked at Tyler expectantly.

Tyler smiled ruefully. "You can probably tell that I'm nervous. Truth is, I'm scared to death. How can I possibly know who to take along with me when I go back? Sid, you said the Lord helped your ma know what to do. Do you believe in the Lord too?"

The boy nodded.

"Well, I've prayed that the Lord would show me what to do. The men at home are praying. They've been praying all winter. Now spring is here, and the time has come. Will you pray with me one more time?"

Sid nodded again. Tyler looked pointedly at the offensive cap, but the boy's hand held it in place.

"You should have some respect for the Lord, Sid."

"He understands," was the stubborn answer.

Tyler led the two of them in a prayer for guidance. "Lord, I can't possibly know who to choose for these men or what men to choose for these women. I leave it in your hands to accomplish your will. And if no one shows up, we'll accept that as your will too."

Sid looked closely at Tyler after he'd finished. He was still shocked to find the man on such a mission. "Are *you* looking for a wife too, Mr. Newly?" he asked in a choked voice.

Tyler smiled and shook his head at the boy. "No. I am not interested in finding a wife like this."

Curious, Sid asked, "Why not?"

"Well, I want time to find just the right woman, not just take my pick from whoever shows up."

Sid cocked his head to one side. "What's the 'right' woman?"

Forgetting the time and his nervousness about the coming interviews, Tyler explained, "I want someone who is a lady and knows how to act like a lady. Someone—"

"Someone rich?" the boy asked scornfully.

Tyler looked at the boy in surprise. "Not necessarily."

"Someone important?"

"Well, not—"

"Someone who thinks she's better than everyone else?"

"No!"

"Mr. Newly, ya just prayed that the Lord would do the pickin'. Maybe ya should let him pick for *you* too." Sid stomped out of the room.

Tyler looked in agitation after the boy. Why was he so upset? Sitting back down in his chair, he thought of Sid's words. Of course he wanted the Lord to do the picking! Didn't he?

He thought of Jadyne Crandall. *She is the perfect woman for me*, he thought. What if she were not the society lady she was? Would he fall in love with her if she were one of the women who showed up here looking for a husband? He pictured her in his mind again and knew in an instant he would. It wouldn't matter to him who she was or what she did. Why had that ever mattered to him before?

Sid came back into the room followed by two women. He looked sullenly at Tyler and announced, "Here's some customers for ya."

Tyler scowled at the boy. He'd have to have a talk with him about manners.

"Thank you, Sid. Sit there and write down their names, please. Then send them in one at a time, and I'll speak with them in the next room. Please, ladies, have a seat."

Sid ignored Tyler and went to sit behind the desk. He picked up a pencil and motioned for one of the women to step forward.

"Name!"

There was no answer, so Sid looked up with a frown. The young woman who stood there looked pale and frightened. Sid instantly rebuked himself for taking out his anger on the poor girl. It was that Tyler Newly he was upset with. The man thought no one was good enough for him.

The woman started to sway, and Sid jumped up and took her arm and led her to a chair. "It's okay. Take deep breaths." He watched as the woman nervously twisted her hands. "Are ya feeling better? Wish I knew where there was some water for ya, miss."

The girl smiled her thanks, and Sid realized how young she was. He returned to the desk and picked up the pencil again. "Now, can you tell me your name, please?"

The girl started to speak then cleared her throat and tried again. In a shaky voice, she said, "Hermine Wetherby."

Sid struggled to write neatly with his gloved hand. He smiled a boyish grin at the young woman. "Ya needn't be nervous, Miss Wetherby. Mr. Newly is very nice. He will see ya now." He took the paper that he had written the name on and led the white-faced woman to the door. He knocked then entered when he heard, "Come."

"Miss Hermine Wetherby," he announced to Tyler. He handed him the paper and motioned for the woman to take a chair. Under his breath, he said to Tyler, "Be nice. She's scared to death."

Tyler looked at him in surprise then whispered back, "So am I."

Sid chuckled to himself and returned to the outer room.

He settled at the desk again and looked up at the woman who was waiting. The woman looked critically at the boy at the desk.

Sid swallowed. He wiped his nose on his sleeve and called, "Next!"

The woman stood up and took the chair next to the desk. "Since I'm the only one here, I guess that means me," she said dryly. "Have you ever heard of handkerchiefs, young man?"

Sid grinned. "Yes, ma'am." He sniffed and wiped his nose again. "Name, please."

The woman's eyes twinkled. "My name is Pearl Maddox, and I think you took care of Miss Wetherby very well. She's a very timid woman I've found. We came in together last night on the train. I—"

"Sid!"

The boy jumped in his chair as Tyler dashed into the room.

"She's fainted! Miss Wetherby! She's on the floor!"

Sid ran into the room, calling, "Go see if there's a rain barrel outside. Hurry!"

Tyler ran to the door.

Miss Maddox watched with interest as she followed Sid into the other room.

Sid knelt and unbuttoned Hermine's top buttons and loosened the collar of her blouse. He picked up some papers and fanned the woman on the floor. Pearl Maddox stepped out of the way as Tyler rushed in with a bucketful of water. He was about to toss it on Miss Wetherby's face when Sid jumped up and shoved him aside. The bucket landed hard on the floor and water sloshed over its sides.

"Ya tryin' to kill the poor lady before ya marry her off? Here, give me yer handkerchief."

He took the cloth from Tyler's hands and wet it in the bucket. Then he patted Hermine's forehead and neck gently until the woman came around.

Hermine's white face turned to the towering faces above her. "Oh! I'm so sorry! Please, I'd like to leave. I never should have come." She struggled to rise.

Pearl Maddox, who had been enjoying the commotion, finally stepped in. "Nonsense, girl. You've managed to come this far. Don't back out now."

They got the trembling girl to a chair, and she said, "I don't think I can."

Sid gave Tyler a piercing look. He looked dumbly back at the boy. Sid poked him in the ribs with his elbow and nodded toward the girl with his head.

"Oh! Uh, Miss Wetherby, if you're still interested in traveling with us, we'll be glad to have you. Please meet back here at 10:00 a.m. on Tuesday for final instructions."

"Thank … thank you, sir."

Pearl reached for Hermine's arm. "I'll help you to a chair. You just wait for me, and we'll go back to the hotel together, all right?" Hermine nodded, and the two left the room.

Sid started to follow, but Tyler shut the door and studied him. "I don't think she's going to make it, Sid. Why did you push me into telling her she could come?"

Sid planted his hands on his hips and spoke in a quiet voice. "She's not going to make it to tomorrow if she doesn't get some food pretty quick, Mr. Newly. The girl's starvin'! She probably spent everything she had just to get here. And there's nothing else wrong with her. She's a good person."

"Oh? And who made you a good judge of character?"

"I can tell. That's all!"

Tyler shrugged his shoulders. "I suppose your guess is as good as mine. I'm way over my head here." He frowned. "I better give her some money to live on until we go. Here." He handed Sid some bills. "Give her this when you're alone. Tell her it's part of the deal. We can't have her fainting the whole way."

Sid took the money and grinned at Tyler. "Guess yer not as bad as I thought." And he quickly left the room.

Tyler scratched his head and returned to his desk. Immediately there was a knock, and Sid entered with Pearl Maddox.

When Sid returned to the other room, he quickly slipped the money into Hermine's hand. "Mr. Newly said this was to help with expenses before ya leave, Miss Wetherby."

Hermine looked at the money, and a wry smile warmed her face. "I take it not everyone will receive this. Just the most needy."

Sid started to protest, but the woman continued. "It's all right. I should refuse it, but I guess I really do need it. Tell Mr. Newly thank you."

Sid nodded then bent his head to copy the names onto another paper. Both looked up when loud voices followed by three women came through the door. Sid's eyes narrowed as he saw the immodest dresses and heavily made-up faces. These were not the kind of women Tyler's friends were looking for, he was sure.

"Look, Sal, only one gal here and some kid! Told you this wasn't right. I knew it." The loud whisper reached Sid.

"Shut up, Dolly! If someone will pay my way out of this city, I'll go, even if I have to pretend to marry a fellow to do it."

"Yeah, I hear there's lots of mines out there, maybe gold ones. Lots of fellows too." Giggles followed the remark.

"Shhh!"

The women headed for the desk, and Sid pondered how to deal with them.

"Kid, where do we sign up to marry these fellows?"

Hermine looked nervously at Sid and wide-eyed at the women.

Sid faced the three women with mustered politeness. He looked through the blank papers on the desk and then covered them with his arm. "I'm sorry, ladies, but the positions have been filled."

"What? All of them?"

"On the first day? The ad says the interviews will be for three days, and this is only the first one. Let me see that list!" The one called Dolly reached for the papers.

Sid snatched them up and said, "I am sorry, but we're busy here. That's all that is available."

"Well, I never!"

"I don't believe it," said Sal. "Let me talk to someone in charge."

"He's not available at this time. Thank you for stopping. Good day." Sid herded the women back out the door. There was much complaining and threatening, but the three finally left.

Sid sank down on the chair at the desk and looked at Hermine, ashamed.

"I lied," he admitted.

"I know." Hermine giggled, and Sid grinned. "And I'm glad. I wouldn't want to travel with them let alone start a town with them."

"I hope Mr. Newly agrees." Sid sobered and looked anxiously at the other woman.

"He will. He seems like a decent man. You know, he asked me if I believed the Bible." Sid was surprised. "Of course, the ad said they wanted Christian women, so I expected there would be good, upright men involved. You did the right thing."

Sid felt relieved, and Pearl came out of the office.

"I guess we both are prospective brides now, Miss Wetherby," she announced with a twinkle in her eye.

"Please, call me Hermine."

"Thank you, and I'm just Pearl. Shall we go?" She turned to Sid. "See you later, young man. Keep up the good work."

The room seemed awfully quiet after the two women left. Sid sat nervously, wondering how he was going to explain to Tyler about the three women. As the moments passed, he became more uneasy. What if no one else showed up?

The two doors opened simultaneously. Tyler looked questioningly at Sid, but the boy pointed and turned to speak to the young woman who stood beside the door. Tyler backed into the office again.

"Come in," Sid motioned to the chair beside the desk.

The woman seemed surprised to see a boy behind the desk. She hesitated. "Is this the place … is this where they need … Am I—"

"Are ya answering the ad for brides?" Sid asked.

Relieved, the woman nodded. She walked to the desk and sat down. "Who are you?" she asked curiously.

Surprised at her interest, Sid replied, "My name's Sidney. I work for Mr. Newly."

"Mr. Newly. Is he one of the—you know—one of them?"

"No!" The answer blurted out. "He's handling the business end while the others are handling the settling in end. What's yer name, please?"

"Leigh Sheldon, and I'm from Boston."

Sid wrote the name as Leigh spelled it out. He was about to get up and take her into Tyler when the woman spoke again.

"I hope he'll take me. I left my job and everything."

Sid looked at her curiously. Obviously the woman wanted to talk to someone, but he knew Tyler was waiting.

"I know it sounds foolish, but I've always wanted to get out of the city and into the wilderness. I wish I could live by a creek and see deer coming to it to drink." She clenched the bag on her lap. "I'm an orphan, you see, so there is really nothing keeping me in the city, and I do so want a home of my own."

Sid watched her as she tried to explain to him her presence there. An orphan. Her light brown hair and gray eyes could indicate any of the Scandinavian nationalities. He saw the nervousness she was trying to hide and hastened to reassure her. "Mr. Newly is really quite nice. He'll explain everything to ya. Don't be afraid."

Leigh smiled at the boy gratefully. She took a deep breath and followed him to the door.

Sid left her with Tyler then sat down again. He wondered what it would feel like to agree to marry someone he'd never met. He shuddered. No wonder these women were nervous!

He looked at the empty room. Only three so far; he wondered how many Tyler needed.

Eventually the door opened again, and Tyler led the young woman out. "Thank you, Miss Sheldon. We'll see you on Tuesday, then."

She waved to Sid on the way out; then just Tyler and Sid were alone again.

Tyler looked at the boy and shrugged. "Time's up for today. Didn't I hear someone else out here?"

Sid avoided the question. "What do ya mean 'for today'?"

"The ad we sent out said there were three days for interviews. We figured that would give plenty of time for delays in traveling for the ladies to get here. So if you don't mind helping me tomorrow?"

Sid rubbed his freckled nose. "I guess."

"Good." He seemed anxious to leave the building, and he looked preoccupied. Sid studied his face, wondering what he was thinking; then he shrugged and walked ahead of him to the door. He turned with a scowl when he heard a snicker behind him.

"What's so funny?" he demanded.

Tyler chuckled again and looked at the young boy. "I was just thinking how different you city folks are."

"Whaddya mean?"

"Well, the way you walk, for instance." He laughed again, and Sid looked wary. "My brother Abel wouldn't be caught dead walking like that."

Sid's lower lip stuck out stiffly. "What's wrong with the way I walk?"

Tyler picked up the remaining papers and put them in a leather case. "Nothing," he said innocently, "except you walk like a girl!" He laughed again.

Surprise crossed the boy's face; then he doubled up his fists and growled, "You take that back, mister. Take it back right now!"

Tyler laughed even harder at the ridiculous boxing stance Sid was attempting. He walked to the boy and said with a final chuckle while he patted his shoulder, "I'm sorry, Sid. I shouldn't have made fun of you." He chuckled again. "But, oh, that feels good to relieve the tension after those interviews. Come on. Show me some more of the city, and tell me about the Chicago fire, will you? You're not going to hold a grudge just because I laughed at you, are you?"

The boy still scowled, and Tyler pretended not to notice the way he backed away from his touch.

They returned to the carriage, and Sid reluctantly began telling Tyler about Chicago's famous fire of 1871. Then he warmed to his subject and pointed out the buildings that had been rebuilt.

"My pa said that tall one there has a metal frame. Guess it won't burn so easy."

Tyler enjoyed the narrative and tour, but he was still deep in thought about the afternoon. He nearly startled Sid off his seat with his next question.

"Sid, do you know a family around here by the name of Crandall?"

The boy swallowed, and his throat suddenly became dry. "It's a big city, Mr. Newly. I don't know everyone in it."

"Hmmm," Tyler nodded. "Just thought I'd ask."

Sid glanced at the man out of the corner of his eye. "Whatcha' want to know for?"

"Oh, nothing." He saw the boy's puzzled expression, so he explained. "I just met this woman at Mr. Granville's last night, and her name was Jadyne Crandall."

Sid looked at the toes of his boots. "So?"

Tyler laughed in embarrassment. "So … I want to see her again. What's the matter? You don't like girls?"

The lad shrugged, and Tyler noticed the freckled face redden. He laughed again. "You do too, Sid."

Sid ignored the teasing and asked, "So she's one of those rich, important people who thinks they're better than everyone else, the kind yer lookin' for, huh?"

Tyler scowled at the boy and retorted, "She is not. Well, actually, I don't know anything about her except that she's very kind and thoughtful of others and very beautiful." He spoke more softly. "It wouldn't matter to me if she were rich or poor, regardless of what you think." He stared into space.

Sid's heart was pounding, and he kept his eyes downward while he listened to Tyler. He asked, "I suppose she'd be perfect for one of the brides, then, ya know, for one of yer friends."

Tyler's head shot up, and he glared at the boy. "That's not what I had in mind. You know, this is really none of your business."

Sid tugged his hat lower. "Yer the one doin' the talking."

Tyler shook his head. One minute the boy was helpful, and the next he was irritating. "We're done for today, Sid. Let's get back to the Granvilles'. I promised Mr. Granville a game of chess this afternoon."

Sid ran into the cottage and up to the rooms on the second floor. Closing the door swiftly, the boy went and stood before the mirror. The face of Sidney Crandall stared back until in a sudden movement the cap was pulled off, and after unwinding a very tightly bound scarf, long, coppery curls tumbled down. Jade looked at herself again, and only a trace of her brother's looks remained.

She had fooled Tyler Newly for a whole day!

She went to the pitcher on her washstand and poured water into the pan waiting there. Quickly she washed off the "freckles" she had dotted on with kohl that morning. She took soap and scrubbed until none remained. Then she undressed and unwound the many layers of cloth she had used to hide her feminine curves. She took a deep breath. It felt good to move again! She quickly changed into her regular clothes and hid the outfit she had worn to be used again tomorrow. She felt a little guilty about what she was doing but quickly justified it as helping Mr. Granville. Now she needed a chance to talk to the old gentleman.

Chapter 14

Chicago

"Jadyne, is that you up there?"

"Coming, Mother!" Jade quickly tied her hair back and ran down the stairs. Again her conscience pricked her for not telling her mother about her deception, but she pushed it aside. Sidney planned to come in late and say as little as possible about his day without lying.

"Are you done already?" Her mother was surprised.

"I just needed to change, Mother. I really need to go back to the mansion now."

"Is everything all right with you, Jade? You look a little flushed." Hazel looked at her daughter critically.

"I'm fine, Mother. Shall I return these dishes to Mrs. Todd?" Jade asked, attempting to take her mother's attention away from herself.

"Yes, please, and thank her again. She's a wonderful cook."

"Okay. Maybe she'll have time to show me more of her recipes. I'll see you later."

Maybe she'd get a chance to talk to Amos Granville about Tyler too. After all, Amos had a right to know what was going on.

The walk on the path proved uneventful, though Jade couldn't help looking over her shoulder every few steps. She knocked at the back door, and Mrs. Todd let her in with a happy smile.

"How are you, Miss Jade? We sure have been missing you around here."

"Hello, Mrs. Todd. I miss you too. What are you working on?" Her nose followed the smells. "Mmmmm! You've made cinnamon rolls! They look delicious! Mother sent back these dishes with many thanks. I've never seen Sidney eat so much."

The cook beamed under the praise. She was about to answer when they heard Cecile's voice outside the doorway.

"Quick! In here!"

Mrs. Todd shoved Jade into the pantry and turned as Cecile strode into the kitchen.

"I would like one egg, toast, juice, and coffee served in my room in the morning. Where are the servants in this house anyway? I shouldn't have to deliver my orders personally." Cecile was drawn to the cinnamon rolls. "I'll take one of those too," she said as she swept out of the room. Over her shoulder, she called, "We're waiting for our coffee. Serve it in the library."

Mrs. Todd jumped when Jade placed a hand on her shoulder. "Where's Becky?"

The cook sighed. "She quit already. Stanwood scared her so badly, she just up and quit. She said she could get work elsewhere and not be spied on by the housekeeper."

"Then where's Mrs. Stanwood? You're not doing the serving yourself, are you?" Jade asked in alarm.

"Stanwood claimed she had a headache two hours ago and retired for the night." The weary woman sighed again. "I'll just get a coffee tray ready and take it in. Then I'll finish these rolls and clean up for the night."

But Jade was already in motion. "You'll do no such thing. I'll just change into Becky's uniform and cap and do it myself. You sit here and rest for a while."

She disappeared into the pantry and made the change. Becky was a little larger than she was, so she tied an apron on to hold the dress in place. Then she tucked her hair up into the white cap. She looked into the mirror by the back door and was dismayed. She looked just like Sidney again! Tyler would see that in an instant! Her eyes darted around the room searching for help, and she spotted Mrs. Todd's reading spectacles.

"Mrs. Todd, may I borrow your spectacles? I think it would help if I could hide these green eyes a little better."

The cook paused from preparing the tray and looked at Jade. "Yes, of course. That's a good idea, Miss Jade."

"Just Jade, Mrs. Todd." She put on the small, wire eyeglasses and looked at herself critically. "What do you think?" The lenses magnified her vision a little, but Jade didn't think she'd have any trouble.

"You certainly look different."

"Good!" She examined her face again and then tried holding her mouth stiff with her lips in a straight line. Yes, that was better. She'd do that. "Is this all ready, then?" She picked up the tray and backed out the door. Her sparkling green eyes clearly showed that she was enjoying herself, and she winked at the worried cook before the door swung shut.

"That poor girl thinks this is all a lark, but she'll be mortified if they discover she was the woman at their dinner party."

"Mrs. Todd?" The butler entered and looked around the room. "Are you talking to the only person who's smart enough to listen … again?"

Hettie Todd sank to a chair and laughed with her husband. "How is it that you always catch me at it, Mr. Todd?" She shook her head, and worry showed in her eyes. "That girl is going to find herself in a peck of trouble one day."

Mr. Todd nodded. "I saw her go in. I had to look twice, though, to be sure it was her." He patted his wife's back. "She'll be fine, Hettie."

Jade set the heavy tray down and began to pour the coffee and set out the desserts. She peeked at the occupants of the room as she worked. Amos Granville and Tyler were battling each other in a game of chess, and Cecile was lounging in a chair, her face dark as a black thundercloud with anger.

Jade was surprised when Cecile spoke, for her voice betrayed nothing of her expression. "Well, gentlemen," she said sweetly, "coffee has arrived. Please, put away your game and come visit with me."

Amos didn't even look up. "We'll finish here first, Cecile. Go ahead and bring our coffee to us, Becky."

Jade decided to make him aware of her presence so as not to startle him later, but the name "Jade" would not do. Tyler or Cecile might associate it with Jadyne.

She carried his cup and dessert to the tray beside him. "It's *Jane* tonight, sir," she spoke softly.

Tyler's head jerked up, and she felt his eyes on her face. She held her lips stiffly as she turned back to the serving tray, and she kept her eyes low.

Amos immediately knew it was Jade, and seeing Tyler's interest, he remarked, "It's your turn, Tyler. I think I've got you now." He turned to Jade and said with a wink, "Thank you, *Jane*. I'm sorry. I didn't know you were coming tonight. How's your husband recuperating from his accident?"

Jade nearly dropped the tray she was carrying. She saw the mischief in her employer's eye and wanted to choke him. She mumbled something in reply. *Husband indeed!*

Tyler shrugged and turned back to the game, and Amos winked again. Jade nearly laughed. She reached out to set the cup and plate on the table beside Tyler, but the cup teetered on the edge, and the plate missed altogether. Tyler grabbed the cup, but the dessert landed on the floor.

Jade was mortified. "I'm so sorry!" How did that happen? She knelt to pick up the plate, and her hand missed it. Embarrassed, she patted the floor until she felt the dish.

It was the spectacles! She thought they wouldn't affect her vision, but her perception was all goofed up. Now what should she do? She became aware that Tyler was kneeling down beside her, helping to scoop the dessert back on the plate. Her neck felt hot, and her cheeks flamed.

"Really, Uncle Amos! Your servants are quite inept. I've never seen so many mistakes in all my life. I'll tell you what. I'll take the time to train them for you. It'll make your home run much more smoothly. I'll start tomorrow." Cecile clapped her hands. "You, girl, hurry and clean this mess up and bring us—"

"I'll give the orders in my home, Cecile. And my staff needs no training from you. Well, Tyler, do I win the game, or have you come up with a move to thwart me?"

Tyler handed Jade the rest of the crumbs then brushed off his hands. He noticed the blush on the maid's cheeks and knew Cecile's comments had hurt her. Cecile, he saw, was scowling and impatient at being left alone. He turned back to the game.

Jade finished cleaning up. She found that if she peered over the top rim of the small spectacles, she could see clearly what she was doing. For that reason, as well as to hide her face, she kept her head lowered.

When she hurried back from the kitchen with Tyler's dessert, she heard Amos exclaim, "How did you do that, Tyler? I was sure I had you beaten!" He chuckled as he studied the board. "You're right," he admitted. "It's checkmate."

Jade served the dessert and returned to the tray for the coffee pot to refill the cups. She felt Tyler watching her.

"So Palmer is enjoying the rugged life up north, eh? I wonder how he looks dressed like a lumberjack." Amos smiled as he settled down with his coffee.

"I have a picture of him," Tyler said suddenly. "One of my friends likes to draw, and he made a sketch of Palmer." He jumped to his feet. "Let me get it for you."

"Nonsense, Tyler," scolded Cecile. "Send the girl for it. You've left me sitting alone all evening. Don't go running off now."

Tyler looked uncertain, and Amos glared at his rude niece. Hoping to avoid trouble, Jade curtsied and said softly, "Where would I find it, sir?"

Tyler hesitated, but Cecile pulled his arm to sit down, so he answered, "They are on my desk in the leather case, please, and thank you." He smiled kindly at the serving girl, even though with her head bent low she couldn't see him.

Jade hurried up the stairs and down the hall to Tyler's room. She pulled the dizzying spectacles off her face so she wouldn't stumble, and she knocked lightly before entering the empty room.

Tyler's things were neat and orderly. It took Jade only a moment to spot the leather case on the desk, and she crossed the room in the darkening shadows to get it. She picked it up and found another leather case beneath it. They both were the same. She recognized them from this afternoon and remembered that one had the names of the prospective brides in it. Puzzled, she wondered which one to bring or if she should bring them both to the library.

"Oh, Miss … Jane, is it?"

Jade jumped and let out a little scream. The cases fell back to the desk, and the wire spectacles dropped to the thick carpet.

"I'm awfully sorry! It's just me, Mr. Newly. Here, let me light a lamp. I realized as soon as you left that I didn't specify which case to bring, so I thought I'd come help you."

Jade froze in a panic. Her mind refused to work, and her body refused to move. She just stood staring at Tyler Newly with wide green eyes. Then, when he turned from the lamp, she dropped to her knees to search for the spectacles.

Alarmed, Tyler moved to her side. "Is there something wrong, miss? I really am sorry I frightened you."

"No! I mean, I'm all right, only …" She kept her head down. "I'm afraid I've lost my spectacles. I dropped them when you came in."

"Here, let me find them for you." Tyler knelt by her side again.

Jade felt foolish and also a little guilty about tricking him. He found the spectacles and handed them to her with a smile. She slipped them on and tried to focus through them while he picked up the case he wanted.

"Here it is." He leafed through some papers. "Well, I better get back. Thank you, miss—I mean, madam. Mr.

Granville did mention that you have a husband, didn't he? I hope he is better soon." Tyler left the room.

Jade stared after him with an uneasy feeling. She tried to shake it off as she blew out the lamp and shut the door behind her. Mr. Todd was lighting the lamps at the far end of the hall, and Jade was about to walk down and speak with him when a noise in the room across from Tyler's caught her attention.

She stood still and listened while she again removed the spectacles. There it was again. A rustling and soft foot-steps. Jade looked for Mr. Todd, but he had disappeared around the corner.

She was puzzled. No one should be in these rooms; everyone was downstairs. She crossed the hall and opened the door. The room was dark, and Jade fumbled to light the lamp. As yet she didn't feel fear, only curiosity.

"Is anyone here?" The light chased the darkness into the corners, and the shadows played hide-and-seek with her as she moved through the room. Everything appeared to be fine. The room was undisturbed as far as she could tell, and she turned to leave with a sigh of relief. A slight squeak by the window sent a sudden shiver up her spine. She turned back and held the lamp up with quivering fingers.

"Miss Jade?"

She caught the lamp that dropped from her hands, and for the second time that night, she let out a small scream.

Mr. Todd hastened to her side. "What is it, Miss Jade? What are you doing?"

She placed a hand over her pounding heart. "I thought I heard a noise in here." She paused for air. "So I came in to investigate."

Mr. Todd looked around. "Everything seems to be in order." He looked at her. "Are you sure?"

She nodded. "I thought I was, but maybe it was just my imagination. I'm sorry, Mr. Todd."

"No, it's perfectly all right. Mr. Granville is a wealthy man, and there are those who would steal from him. I'll keep a watch out for trouble, miss."

Jade was alarmed. "Have you ever had thieves here?"

"Oh, yes. Sometimes it was only one of the staff who had 'sticky fingers,' but we've even had guests here who try to take things home with them. I guess rich folks can have just as much trouble as poor ones."

They left the room together, and Jade hurried back to the library to collect the dishes. She slipped the spectacles back on before she entered, but she found only Mr. Granville present. He was staring at a paper in his hands, and Jade saw a tear slip from his eye. She hesitated, but he saw her.

"Come in, Jade." He wiped his eyes and waved to the paper he was holding. "Come see Palmer."

Jade crossed the room and peered over the rim of the spectacles at the sketch of a man fishing. He had a happy face, and the setting looked peaceful and inviting. She placed a hand on the old man's arm. "Doesn't he look like he's having a grand time?"

Amos smiled. "I'm so glad he's found happiness after his hardships." He set the paper down and chuckled at the spectacles on Jade's nose. "And just what are you doing here, *Jane?*"

Jade giggled, but she cast a glance at the door.

"Don't worry. Cecile finally was able to drag Tyler out to take a walk. I imagine they'll be gone for a while." He waited for her reaction.

Jade's lips tightened and she felt the awful, painful stirrings of jealousy creep over her. Just the thought of Cecile's hand on Tyler's arm angered her. She realized Amos was watching her, so she hastened to explain her presence.

Amos's eyes widened and he stared in disbelief at the young woman before him. "You dressed like Sidney, and Tyler didn't know?"

Jade shook her head. Then she looked down at her hands and admitted, "I guess it's really like lying, isn't it? I probably shouldn't have done it."

"It was the perfect thing to do!" Amos surprised her by saying. "By all means, go back tomorrow. If your mother must know, tell her it is at my request. Find out all you can about Tyler, and then let me know. This 'bride' business is very curious. Is Palmer getting one too?"

"I don't know. I know Mr. Newly isn't, though."

"Oh?" Amos's eyes revealed his interest. "You keep up the good work, Jade. I should have hired you to go to Philadelphia. The men there couldn't find out anything about Melvin's accident for me. Now, if I had you on the case, it would have been solved by now."

"Your brother's accident?" Jade started to question the old gentleman, but voices in the hall made them both stop and look up. Jade slid the spectacles back in place and

JADE'S COURTING DANGER | 163

resumed gathering the dishes on the tray. She said a quiet good night to her employer and passed Cecile and Tyler in the entryway without comment. She said good-bye to Mrs. Todd and promised to return soon for more baking lessons.

The back door closed behind her with a quiet click. Jade pulled her hood over the coppery curls and was about to step away from the house when her eyes caught a movement behind the stables. The cool, evening breeze chilled her, and she huddled down into her cape for warmth.

She recalled telling her mother the story of her failed attempt at baking bread, and she remembered her mother's joking comment that maybe that was what she had seen Wilbert burying behind the stables. As odd as that sounded, Jade was of no inclination to investigate anything Wil Tait did tonight. She only wanted to stay clear of him.

She made a move to leave the doorstep again but pressed herself back when another figure hurried around the corner of the house.

A woman! Jade peered into the gathering darkness and recognized Cecile Granville. She was headed behind the stables.

Now Jade was curious. She stealthily followed the woman and knelt beside a group of trees to watch her. The dark was making it increasingly difficult to see, and the voices were muffled.

Cecile's shrill tones reached Jade's ears. "Where is he?" she demanded.

Jade pulled her hood back to hear better.

Wilbert answered, "He should be here soon. Maybe he had trouble at the house."

"He'd better hurry. I'm getting cold."

There was silence, and Jade tried to see what they were doing. She was going to move closer when she heard Wilbert say in relief, "He's coming."

A man appeared around the corner and joined the other two. Jade's heart sank. Though shadows hid the face, the silhouette of a Stetson on his head was plain to see.

Chapter 15

Sand Creek

The town of Sand Creek was bustling with activity. At least, that's the way it seemed to Buck Riley. After being out in the woods with only seven other guys for company, even this quiet town seemed busy. It was his turn to leave the camp and come home for a visit and supplies. He looked around the small town with interest. This was the way their town would soon look. The now empty buildings would be filled with people coming and going about their business. He headed for Nolan's hotel. He wanted to talk to the Nolan brothers about their business operations and get ideas for running his own hotel.

He received a shock when he saw Lucy Newly working at the desk when he entered. As he stood waiting for her to look up and notice him, his heart raced. She looked so beautiful sitting there chewing on her lip as she made a careful notation on the paper in front of her. For as long as he could remember, he had been in love with her. But he had never spoken of it, for he knew she only had eyes for his brother Dugan.

Without looking up, Lucy said, "I'll be with you in just one moment." She neatly folded the papers she had been working on and placed them in a tray at the corner of the desk. "There! Now, may I help you?" She glanced at Buck then jumped out of her chair.

"Buck! Buck Riley! Why didn't you say something? How are you?" She came around the desk and threw her arms around him, startling him.

Buck held his breath as his arms folded around her for an instant. Then she backed away with an embarrassed look and a laugh. "Oh, Buck! I wish you could see your face! I'm sorry! I didn't mean to rush at you like that, but it is just so good to see you."

Pleasure flowed warmly through the man at her words but quickly chilled when she looked past him and eagerly asked, "Is Dugan with you?"

"No, sorry. It's just me this trip." He tried to keep his voice steady. "It's good to see you too, Lucy. You look very pretty," he surprised himself by adding.

Lucy was surprised too. "Why, thank you, Buck. I didn't think you noticed girls that much," she teased.

"Only the pretty ones," he replied, "like you." The last words were spoken so softly, Lucy barely heard them. The words pleased her, and a slight blush crept up her cheeks.

"What are you doing at the hotel? I thought you worked at Nolan's store." Buck kept his tone light as he watched her closely, memorizing everything about her.

Flustered at his obvious attention, Lucy answered, "I asked Mr. Nolan—Jonas, that is—if he would let me work here for Harry for a time." She laughed. "You see, Rooney has been a bit of a problem, and I needed to get away from the store for a while."

Concern lit Buck's eyes. "What kind of a problem, Lucy?"

"Oh, nothing serious. He just follows me around and asks if he can come calling and such."

"And you don't want him to?"

"No, of course not! I mean, Rooney is nice and everything, but I'm not interested in him like that. You know, to have him come calling." She babbled on nervously as Buck continued to stare at her.

Buck took a step toward her and lifted her chin with his finger. "If he does trouble you, Lucy, you just let me know. I'll talk to him."

She gazed into his brown eyes and didn't breathe again until he removed his finger. "Thank you, Buck," she said softly.

He cleared his throat and astonished them both by asking, "Can you leave for a while to have lunch with me?"

Lucy's words stumbled out of her mouth. "Well … uh … yes, I take a break about now. Uh … Gretchen usually relieves me for lunch. Uh …" She cleared her throat. "We could eat here." She indicated the next room. "The hotel dining room serves pretty good food."

"Fine."

They stood silently not looking at each other until Gretchen Nolan came in. She took one look at the young people and smiled to herself when Lucy explained that Buck was taking her to lunch.

"Hi, Buck! Good to see you in town. You here to talk to Harry? He'll see you sometime after lunch, but not too early. He likes to take a little nap, so take your time. And you, Lucy, take a little extra time too. I need to catch up on my own bookwork here. Enjoy yourselves!"

The two chose a table in the dining room and sat down. After they ordered, they both sat silent. Buck couldn't believe he was actually having lunch with Lucy, but he reminded himself that she probably just wanted to hear about Dugan.

Lucy wondered why she suddenly felt so self-conscious around Buck. Buck was like a big brother to her. He was always the most tolerable of her and Mallory's shenanigans when they were kids. She thought of Dugan. Dugan was the handsome one, the debonair one, the one she was in love with. Maybe Buck would tell her about Dugan. She opened her mouth to ask him a question, but he spoke first.

"Do you always scowl like that when you're deep in thought?"

Lucy stared at Buck. "Like what?"

He reached over and smoothed a line on her forehead. "Like you're trying to think of something to say."

Her eyes closed briefly at his touch, and she forgot what she was going to ask him.

"What have you heard from Mallory?" Buck relieved the tension with his question.

Lucy took a deep breath, and they proceeded to discuss Mallory and their other brothers and sisters, the church affairs, and the horses her father and his had bought. Their time together passed all too quickly, and Buck reluctantly returned her to the front desk.

"I'd better go talk to Mr. Nolan now." Buck looked down at the hat he held tightly in his hands. "Thank you for an enjoyable lunch, Lucy. I'll remember it for a long time." As if he couldn't stop himself, he reached over and brushed a wisp of hair from her face. "Take care of yourself."

The tender words stayed in Lucy's mind the rest of the day. It wasn't until she was getting ready for bed that night that she remembered she hadn't asked him about Dugan.

Chapter 16

Chicago

Jade waited by the tree for Tyler to come with the carriage. Her thoughts were in turmoil.

She had not gotten a clear look at any of the people the night before. She only knew for sure that Wilbert and Cecile were there because of their voices, but the third one, the man in the western-style hat, hadn't spoken. After he came, they had all gone into Wilbert's room at the back of the stables. Jade waited for as long as she dared; then she went on home so her mother wouldn't be worried.

Was Tyler involved in something with Cecile Granville and Wilbert Tait? Were the three of them planning something against Amos?

Jade shuddered in the oversized coat. She would do her best to find out all she could about the kind of man Tyler Newly was. She wasn't about to let anything happen to her old friend Amos Granville, no matter how much she liked Tyler.

There was that other man in the woods with Wilbert, she remembered suddenly. She hadn't gotten a good look at him either. Could he have been Tyler? And was he the same one who had laughed at her on the path? She struggled to remember where Tyler should have been at those times.

"You going to daydream all day, Sid?"

Jade jumped at the sound of Tyler's voice. She pulled her collar up closer around her neck, and, remembering his ridicule of her walk yesterday, she ambled in the most boyish way she could to the carriage and climbed in.

Tyler studied the silent boy beside him. "Good morning, Mr. Newly. How are you this fine day?" Tyler imitated the boy's squeaky voice.

Jade said nothing.

"Why, I'm just fine, Sidney. So kind of you to ask."

Jade rolled her eyes at the man. "Aw, cut it out, mister. I've got a lot on my mind."

"I can see that." Tyler's teasing changed to concern. "Anything I can help with?"

Jade shook her head.

"Well, remember, Sid, there's nothing the Lord can't help you with."

Jade looked at him out of the corner of her eye. He was waiting, so she gave a quick nod, and he said, "Right! Let's get going, then. Can you take me to Mr. Simonson's law office, please? He's a lawyer for Palmer Granville."

Jade nodded again and pointed out the way he should go. Remembering her disguise, she frequently wiped at her nose and whistled and did the many annoying little things she had so often scolded Sidney for doing.

She waited in the entryway while Tyler conducted his affairs with the lawyer. Tyler's words gave her food for thought. "There's nothing the Lord can't help you with." Could a man who talked like that be up to no good? Taking the advice literally, she spent the remaining time asking for the Lord's help in knowing the truth about Tyler Newly.

When Tyler returned, he asked for a continuation of their tour. Jade decided to show him some of Chicago's mansions, and Tyler was impressed as they slowly passed each elegant home.

"I still think the Granville mansion is grander." He pointed to a beautiful estate. "Look! There's actually a house with towers like Philippa said."

"Who's Phil … Phil—" Jade struggled with the name.

"Philippa. Philippa Gray. Oh, she's just a girl from my home town."

"You sweet on her?"

"That's none of your business."

"That's why ya don't need no bride for yerself, huh?"

"No." Tyler was irritated. "I thought I was sweet on her once, but I've learned something about myself on this trip and something about her as well."

"What's that?"

Tyler shrugged. "Sorry, Sid. You're too young to understand."

Jade scowled. This was one subject she did want to know more about. They drove past Jade's old home just then. She tried to distract Tyler's attention away from it by pointing out another home nearby, but he slowed the carriage to a stop.

Jade reluctantly looked with Tyler at the beautiful home. She was afraid she would feel sad at the memories it would raise, but she was relieved that she could look at the house without remorse. Her family's lives had changed, but they were still happy and safe. Suddenly, she wondered why Tyler had stopped.

"Whatcha lookin' for, Mr. Newly?"

"Mr. Simonson told me this used to belong to the Crandalls."

Jade's heart leaped. What else had Mr. Simonson told him?

"Remember I told you I met a young woman named Jadyne Crandall?"

Jade nodded. Her throat felt dry.

"Well, I asked Mr. Simonson to tell me what he knew about her. He said her father died, and her family had to move because they couldn't afford to stay here. Then I remembered where I had heard the name Crandall before."

Jade felt a tingle down her spine. *Why is he asking questions?*

Tyler continued, unaware of the white face of his companion. "Palmer had mentioned them to me. He got a letter from Amos about it." He stared at the mansion. "How could a girl who had all that ever leave it?"

Somehow Jade found her voice. "What's so important about a house?" She sniffed.

"I used to think a house was all that was important. I dreamed about building a big, grand house in our new settlement." Tyler fell silent.

Jade waited. Finally, she prompted, "But…"

"But then I saw Amos Granville in his big, grand mansion with all his servants and thought he would be the happiest man in the world. But he's not. He's lonely, and he's scared."

"He is?"

"He's afraid of dying, Sid. He doesn't know the Lord. And then I remembered Palmer. He left all this because it couldn't bring him happiness. He found the Lord instead." Tyler looked at the boy. "Then I met this girl. I found out that she knows the Lord, and I found out that she's a happy person. Then today I found out that she used to have all this, but now she doesn't. And you know what, Sid?"

"What?" Jade was astonished at the turn in their conversation.

"I finally realized what my folks have been trying to tell me for years."

"What's that?"

"That my happiness comes from the Lord no matter where I live." Tyler shrugged. "I suppose that doesn't make any sense to you, does it? I mean, it seems pretty obvious, but it was a real problem to me." He looked at the house again. "I think I'll do what my mom suggested and have my wife help me plan our house."

Jade nearly choked. "Thought ya weren't getting a bride for yerself."

"I might just change my mind if the right one shows up." He checked the time. "Hey, we better get to our office and set up."

They opened the building, and Tyler carried in his leather case of papers.

"Here are the papers, Sid." He rummaged through the case.

Jade looked around Tyler's arm at the papers in his hands. "What are those?" she asked.

Tyler pulled out the sketches. "These? These are the bachelors we're finding wives for."

Jade took the papers and looked through them. The rugged settings and the men pictured doing their work fascinated her. She was about to comment on how handsome they all were when she became aware of Tyler studying her face.

She stiffened her lip and wiped her nose. "These are pretty good. Who drew them?"

Tyler shuffled through the stack. "Ray. Uh…here he is. He drew one of himself. I bet he looked in a mirror to do it."

"What do these fellers do? I mean, this one is the blacksmith, right? What are the others?"

Tyler smiled, and with enthusiasm, he flipped the papers and told the boy about each one.

Jade listened and commented as they went through the drawings again. "You miss them, don't cha?"

Tyler nodded. "Yeah. They're a good bunch of guys." He took a deep breath and let it out slowly. "I hope bringing in these women won't change things too much."

The "boy" snorted.

"What?" Tyler asked.

"Well, it seems to me it will change things a lot. I mean, I'm just a kid, but I know married folks will probably spend more time with each other than with their friends. Everybody will be busy with their homes and stuff." She chuckled.

"What?"

"Well, all these guys get along good together. I was just wondering if all the women will."

Tyler frowned, and Jade could almost see that he wished he didn't have to bring any women back with him.

"Sid, let's go in the other room and take time to pray about our decisions today, okay?"

Jade nodded. Once again Tyler looked pointedly at the offensive cap, but Jade merely shook her head. Tyler sighed and began to pray.

"Father, thank you for showing me today that you are sufficient to meet my needs and that my happiness centers on your will for my life. May I follow the way you lead. Lead me today to make wise decisions. Bring only those women whom you choose to become wives for the guys back home. In Jesus's name, amen."

"Amen." Jade agreed. Again she felt Tyler study her face. "I best get out there and be ready," she said hastily. She stumbled out of the chair and clomped her large boots across the floor as she left.

She closed the door behind her and breathed a sigh of relief. Was he getting suspicious? She gathered up the drawings on the desk and slid them back in the leather case, but as she did so, she saw the corner of another drawing. She pulled it out.

It was of Tyler. Jade looked at the contented face and the proud stance. The wind was blowing his hair, and he was high on a hill looking over the land like a king.

The door to the street opened, and Jade slid the picture back in the case. She sat down as two women hesitatingly came forward. They both looked a little older than her. One was slim and dressed attractively; the other was plainly attired and plump. The latter hung back, and her friend had to coax her forward.

"Mornin'," Jade said in a boyish voice. "Can I help you?"

The slender woman stepped forward and pulled the other with her. "Good morning. We're here about the ad for brides. I'm twenty, and Cora is nineteen, so we're the right ages." Her eyes challenged the boy to deny it.

"Uh, well, why don't ya sit down?" Jade motioned to the chairs. "I'll just get yer names. Then you can go in to see Mr. Newly one at a time."

The woman named Cora looked frightened, and the other said, "No. We'd like to go together."

"Uh, okay. I guess." Jade picked up her pencil. "So what's yer name, please?"

"I'm Gwyneth Kent, and this is my cousin Cora Macardle."

Jade wrote the names on her list then copied them each on to a separate paper. She stood and was about to ask them to follow her when Cora spoke.

"You go first, Winnie. I'll go in when you're done."

"Now, Cora, you promised me you'd do this."

"I will. I will. I just want to do it by myself. You go in first."

"You better not run off now as soon as my back is turned."

Cora sighed. "Where would I run to?"

Gwyneth placed a hand on her cousin's shoulder. "Everything will work out fine, Cora. If they don't take you, I won't go either. You know that. We'll find jobs here in Chicago if we have to, but we're staying together until we get you settled."

Gwyneth turned to Jade and nodded, so Jade led her into the other room.

"Gwyneth Kent," she loudly announced and shut the door.

She returned to her desk and sat down. Cora Macardle twirled her gloves and adjusted her hat. Finally she stood and muttered, "I can't do this."

Jade jumped up and asked, "What's the matter?"

"I just can't, that's all. Tell Gwyneth I'll be at the hotel."

"Wait!" Jade didn't know why she was stopping the woman. She walked over to her. "Why are you leaving?"

Cora shook her head at the boy. "You wouldn't understand."

"I might."

Cora sat down again, and Jade saw tears shine in her eyes. "How can I expect some man to be glad to see me coming?"

Jade was puzzled. "What do you mean? Why wouldn't he?"

The woman laughed scornfully. "Well, even you should be able to see that I'm fat and ugly!"

Jade sat down beside her. "No, you're not. You are a bit overweight, but you look pretty," she said softly.

Cora looked at the boy sharply. "You're not a boy, are you?" At Jade's sharp intake of breath, she said, "You're a girl! Why are you pretending? What's going on here?" She looked at the closed door and started to rise.

"Wait! Please!" Jade caught her arm. "No, I'm not a boy. But please don't tell Mr. Newly. I'm filling in for my brother. He was supposed to help Mr. Newly with this job, but he couldn't make it. Really, it's very important to my brother and me that he not know we switched places." She looked imploringly at the woman.

"How old are you?" Cora asked.

"I'm nineteen."

Cora nodded. "Yes, I can see it now." She pointed at Jade's nose. "One of your 'freckles' is smeared."

Jade's hand flew to her face. Cora got out a small mirror from her handbag. "Here, let me fix it." She showed Jade her problem and gently wiped off the smear.

"I guess I shouldn't rub my nose so hard with my sleeve." Jade smiled timidly at the woman. "You won't tell, will you?"

Cora appeared to be making up her mind. "You're sure this bride business is for real?"

"Yes, Miss Macardle. Everything else is just as the ad said. Only I am phony."

"All right, then. I'll keep your secret." They both sighed, Jade in relief and Cora in resignation. "But you have to be honest with me. What man wants a fat wife?"

"But, Miss Macardle, you're not fat. Besides, there's more to a person than their looks on the outside. Take me, for example."

Cora smiled. "I'm just doing this because Winnie won't leave me behind. She's had offers of marriage that she's turned down because if she married, I would be left on my own. See, my parents died when I was twelve, and I've lived with Winnie's family ever since. Winnie and I are like sisters even though we're only cousins. In my misery over losing my parents, I turned to food, and I've just gotten larger and larger each year. Now Winnie's parents are gone, and we're on our own. Winnie is overprotective of me, I guess."

Jade pondered the problem. She looked critically at Cora Macardle. Her dark hair was pulled severely back into a bun, but the few wisps that had escaped were curly. Cora's face seemed plain at first, but the defeated look she wore made it seem so. Even worse was the dress she wore. The shapeless garment was as bad as the maid's uniform Jade herself wore. In contrast, she recalled that Cora's cousin's dress was quite elaborate and her brunette hair fashionably done. Could it be that Gwyneth didn't want competition from Cora?

"You know, Cora, I think you're probably prettier than your cousin, but you're hiding it. You just haven't wanted or needed to change. There's no reason any one of these men shouldn't be happy to have you for a wife."

Cora still looked dubious. "What kind of men are they? I mean, what are they like?"

"I don't know them, but Mr. Newly has told me about them. They're all good friends of his, and he's really nice." She held up her gloved hand and counted off. "Let's see, there's a blacksmith, two run a stagecoach, two run a general store—they're brothers—one owns a hotel, and Mr. Newly's cousin is in the lumber business with him. Oh, and one is an artist too. He drew sketches of all the men." Jade stood up to get the case.

"An artist?" Cora's eyes lit with interest.

Quickly Jade asked, "Are you an artist too?"

"Well, I—"

The door opened, and Tyler motioned for Gwyneth to precede him.

"Sid, could I see you a moment?" He waved the boy inside. Jade looked beseechingly at Cora one last time and received an assuring nod. Her secret was safe.

Tyler waited for Jade to walk into the room; then he closed the door behind her. Jade questioned him, "Whatcha' want?" She wiped her nose, gently this time.

"Sid," Tyler lowered his voice, "what's wrong with the girl named Cora? This Gwyneth woman kept insisting that she wouldn't come unless I agreed to take her cousin despite her 'handicap.' What handicap?"

Jade's green eyes flared. "There's nothing wrong with the lady, Mr. Newly. She's really interesting. We've been talking. She even likes art, so maybe yer friend that drew them pictures would like her."

Tyler was confused. "But Miss Kent said—"

Jade interrupted. "Why don't ya just talk to the lady yerself instead of listening to everybody else talk about her?"

"Sometimes you surprise me, Sid. You're wise for a boy your age. You're absolutely right. Send her in."

Jade hurried to the other room and motioned for Cora to follow her. She picked up the paper with Cora's name and announced as she opened the door, "Cora Macardle, sir."

Jade waited anxiously for Tyler to finish with Cora. Gwyneth seemed just as anxious but didn't converse with the boy behind the desk.

When the door finally opened again, they both held their breath. Tyler escorted Cora out and spoke to both her and Gwyneth.

"We'll see you on Tuesday, then, ladies. Thank you for coming." He returned to his room and closed the door.

Cora was smiling, and she winked at Jade. "That is the nicest man I've met." She spoke to both the "boy" and her cousin. "He said he prayed for the Lord to send just the right women, and he had no doubt that I was one of them." She positively beamed.

"Now, don't go getting your hopes up, Cora. We still have to find you a fellow once we get there."

Cora's face fell, and Jade could have cheerfully kicked the pretty Miss Kent. She turned and smiled warmly at Cora. "Mr. Newly's right, miss. The Lord will work things out."

Cora thanked the boy and followed her cousin from the room.

Jade was about to give up on any more women for the day when the outside door opened again. Her eyes narrowed as she watched the woman walk toward her. Her dark hair was pinned into a severe bun at the back of her head, and her plain gray dress was buttoned demurely up to her neck, but Jade was not fooled. This was one of the gaudily dressed women she had sent away the day before. There was no way she was going to let this woman trick Tyler.

She would have sent her packing immediately, but Tyler chose that moment to open his door. Seeing the woman, he shut it again and waited for Sid to bring her in. Trapped into letting Tyler interview the woman, Jade asked with feigned politeness, "Name, please?"

"Sally Smith."

Jade rolled her eyes at the unoriginal name. "Wait here, please."

She knocked and entered Tyler's room, closing the door behind her. Tyler looked up and past her. "Where's the woman I saw?"

"Listen, Mr. Newly. You can't take this next woman. Believe me. She's no lady."

Tyler frowned. "What do you mean?"

Jade swallowed and plunged ahead. "She was here yesterday with two others, and I sent them away. They—"

"You sent them away?"

Jade nodded. "Yeah. They aren't the right kind, Mr. Newly. Ya know what I mean?"

Tyler scowled at the boy. "Why didn't you tell me about this yesterday, Sid? Look, you told me to make my own judgment about Cora Macardle. I think this woman deserves a chance for an interview herself. Send her in."

"But, Mr. Newly, ya don't understand."

"Send her in, Sid." Tyler's tone brooked no argument.

"Yes, sir." The green eyes flashed their annoyance.

Jade stomped out and picked up the woman's paper. "Next!" she grumbled.

The woman rose and followed the boy. Jade couldn't help but notice how her eyes lit up at the sight of Tyler.

"Miss Sally *Smith*," Jade announced scornfully.

Tyler scowled at her, but she gave him a dirty look and slammed the door.

The minutes ticked by, and Jade became more and more agitated. Surely Tyler wasn't going to take the woman along. He wouldn't even consider it, would he?

Finally the door opened again, and Jade watched Tyler lead the woman out. Her lips tightened when she saw the woman hold tightly to Tyler's arm while she dabbed at her eyes with a hanky.

"Thank you, Mr. Newly. You don't know how much this means to me. I just didn't know how I was going to survive in this city any longer. I was near starvation."

Jade snorted impolitely, and Tyler frowned at her. *Starvation! The woman is almost as plump as Cora!*

"And this money will pay for my food and hotel until we leave. Bless you, Mr. Newly. Bless you!"

Jade rolled her eyes. *He didn't give her money too!*

The woman finally left, and Tyler walked purposefully to the desk and placed his hands on it. He leaned over and spoke to Jade nose to nose.

"If you are ever rude to a lady like that again, young man—"

"Lady?" Jade was too mad to be cautious. "She's no lady!"

"—I will take you over my knee and warm your britches." Tyler finished in a steely voice.

"And you even gave her money! How dumb can ya be?"

Tyler straightened and started around the desk for the boy. Suddenly Jade saw her danger, and with a yelp, she leaped from the chair and pushed it in Tyler's way. He stumbled and nearly fell over it, but Jade didn't stop as she made her escape to the door.

Tyler righted the chair and glared at the boy while he gathered up their papers. "We're not through yet, Sidney," he promised.

Jade glared back, but she was filled with trepidation. That was too close! "I'll wait in the buggy," she muttered.

When Tyler finally joined her, she eyed him with caution. He had cooled down somewhat but still looked explosive. Wisely, she remained silent.

When they reached the corner where Jade was to leave him, Tyler finally spoke.

"Sid, I'd like your help again tomorrow. We have all six women we need now, but I feel we should be there in case someone else arrives, especially since the ad says we will be."

Jade was about to answer, but Tyler held up his hand.

"But you must understand, Sid, that I will not allow you to be rude to these women regardless of what you may think of them personally."

He waited, and Jade finally jerked her head in acknowledgment. She scrambled out of the carriage, but before she could walk away, Tyler spoke again.

"And don't worry, Sidney. I'm not that easily fooled."

The carriage rolled away, leaving the slight girl in her boyish garb staring in bewilderment after it.

Chapter 17

Chicago

The next day Tyler and Jade made preparations for interviews should any other women show up in answer to the ad.

"Are your papers ready?"

Jade nodded her answer and scratched her head through the large cap.

"Let's take a few minutes to pray, then, okay?"

Tyler seemed in a much better mood today, as if the disagreement between them the day before had never happened. They went into the smaller room and closed the door. After a prayer for guidance, Tyler grinned at the boy and said, "Sid, there's something I need to talk to you about. You see, I know you're—"

A noise in the other room curtailed his words, and he motioned Jade to go see about it. Jade's mind raced with questions. Did he know who she was?

An attractive woman stood just inside the room holding onto the door handle as if ready to flee. When she saw the young boy come toward her, she backed away.

"It's okay, miss. Can I help ya?" Jade stopped by the desk and spoke gently to her.

"I've come about the ad, please." Her voice, though shaky, had a pleasant sound.

"Come in. I'll need your name."

There was no answer, so Jade looked up expectantly. "Your name?"

The woman swallowed and said in almost a whisper, "Melody Wells."

"Are you all right, Miss Wells?"

The woman nodded then shook her head. "I don't know if I should be doing this."

Jade looked down at her pencil. *How would I feel?* she wondered. *It must be awfully hard to agree to go to a new place and start a new life with someone you don't even know.* She noticed that the woman was cultured, and her clothes were fashionable.

"Do ya want me to take you in to see Mr. Newly?"

Melody appeared to make up her mind. "Yes. I'm ready now."

Jade announced her at the door. "Miss Melody Wells." She wondered what Tyler would do with her. He said they only needed six, and she was the seventh one.

After the woman left, Tyler came and sat down across from Jade.

"I told her she could come," he said. "I don't know why. It just seemed that I should. You know, I got to thinking maybe Buck will change his mind when all the other guys have wives and he doesn't."

"But what if he doesn't change his mind? What are ya going to do with her then? Marry her yerself?" Jade held her breath while she waited for his answer.

Tyler chuckled. "Nope. I'm not in on this deal, and I made that clear to every one of them."

Jade snorted. "What didja' do? Tell them, 'Don't fall in love with me. I'm too good for ya'?"

"Course not!" Tyler showed his irritation. "Will you quit saying that? Any of those girls would make a wonderful wife, and I wouldn't have agreed to take them if I didn't think so."

Jade muttered something under her breath about "Sally Smith."

"What did you say?"

"Nothin'."

Tyler looked at her suspiciously. "Listen, Sid, I talked to Mr. Simonson yesterday." He paused. "I know who you are."

Jade slumped down in the chair. "What do you mean?"

Tyler smiled. "It's okay. You don't have to be embarrassed. I know things have been pretty hard for you and your family and that you and your sister have to work."

Jade sat up straight. "My sister!"

Chagrined, Tyler answered, "I know I should have told you yesterday when we drove by your old house, but I didn't know how. You're Sidney Crandall, and your sister is the girl who came to the Granville mansion for the dinner party the night I arrived. Jadyne Crandall."

Jade's thoughts were in turmoil. "So you know she's my sister," she stated carefully.

"I hope you didn't mind me talking about her the way I did. I really admire you both."

He paused, and Jade wondered what he would think if he knew she was a maid at the Granville mansion. He was acting differently now than when he first arrived, but she wasn't at all sure what his reaction would be to that.

Tyler looked uncomfortable. "Uh, Sid. I'd really like to see your sister again. I didn't get to talk to her much that night, and well, I'd like to. Do you think she'd see me?"

"You sweet on her, Mr. Newly?" Her boldness surprised even herself.

"What if I was?"

"Are ya?"

"That's none of your business."

Jade scowled. "Well, she's not home."

Tyler sighed. "I thought so. She said she wouldn't be available, but I hoped … When will she be back? Where is she?"

Jade smiled. "That's none of yer business."

Again irritation crossed Tyler's face. The boy always tried his patience. "I'd like to see her before I have to leave, so if you could somehow get that message to her, I'd be grateful."

He stood. "Now, it looks like our time is up here, so let's get going before anyone else shows up. The next thing on my list to do is find a preacher."

"A preacher!"

"We need one at our town, and we certainly will need one to perform marriage ceremonies, so the guys asked me to check around for one. Where should I start?"

Jade shrugged her shoulders.

"How about your church? Maybe your pastor has some ideas."

Jade shrugged again. "All right."

They arrived at the elegant-looking building, and Tyler stepped out of the carriage. "Aren't you coming?" he asked the boy.

"Uh, Mr. Newly, I gotta go home now. My ma has chores for me."

Tyler nodded. "I guess I'm through with you for the day. Here." He dug into his pocket. "I promised to pay you, remember?"

Jade was about to refuse; then she remembered that Sidney wouldn't have, so she accepted the money. But looking through it, she couldn't help protesting, "This is too much, Mr. Newly!"

"No, it isn't. You've been worth every penny, especially when I needed help with the women. Say, can you come with me on Tuesday when I meet with all of them again?"

Jade hesitated. She didn't need to check up on Tyler Newly anymore. She was certain that he was a good man and not doing something underhanded. She was about to refuse when Cecile Granville stepped up behind Tyler.

"Tyler! Fancy meeting you here. Isn't this just wonderful! I was hoping to see you today."

"Hello, Miss Granville." Tyler removed his hat.

Jade watched carefully. What was Cecile up to? Another Granville carriage was behind theirs, and Wilbert Tait was the driver. Despite her recent decision to trust Tyler, all of Jade's suspicions instantly returned.

"Why don't we have lunch together?" Cecile exclaimed. "I can join you in your carriage and send the other home." She turned to the carriage and saw Jade. "Oh! Who's this?"

"This is Sidney," Tyler explained. "He's been my guide around the city. Sid, say hi to Miss Granville."

"How do."

Cecile inclined her head but looked distastefully at the boy. She turned back to Tyler, and her face creased into a smile. "Lunch, then?"

"I'm sorry, Miss Granville, but I still have a lot of business to do. I'm afraid I won't be able to."

"Nonsense! I'll be happy to wait for you. Besides, there are some important things I need to discuss with you. You remember … things we talked about last night."

Jade watched Tyler struggle in indecision. Finally, he said, "As you wish, Miss Granville. I'll be happy to have lunch with you."

"Good!" Cecile waved Wilbert to leave and turned to the carriage again. She saw that the boy was still sitting there. "Don't you have something else to do, boy?"

"Sid was just leaving," Tyler said. Jade almost thought she heard regret in his voice as she climbed down. As Tyler assisted Cecile in the carriage, he called, "See you Tuesday, Sid?"

She nodded, and the carriage rolled off.

Jade hurried home and changed. She wanted to talk to Amos while his guests were both away, so as soon as she looked like herself again, she rushed down the path to the mansion.

Amos was in his study when she arrived.

"Jadyne! Come in, come in!" Amos smiled at his young friend. "I can see you have some news for me. What is it?"

Jade sat down across from his desk and related the events she had witnessed the last few days. Amos listened closely.

"You say you didn't get a good look at the third person?"

She shook her head. "All I can tell you is that he wore a hat like Mr. Newly's."

The old man pondered the information. "Mr. Todd told me about the noise you heard upstairs too, and it seems we have some items missing, silver candlesticks and that sort of thing." He changed the subject. "Hasn't that young man discovered that you're a girl yet?" He eyed her with amusement.

"I thought he had." Jade laughed. "But he only figured out that 'Sid' was Jadyne's brother. He told me he admired our family."

"He's beginning to show promise." Amos smiled. "You're still coming Tuesday night, aren't you? You know he leaves the next day."

Jade looked uncertain. "I don't know, Mr. Granville. I just want things to be back to normal again where I'm just the maid."

Amos chuckled to himself. If things went the way he hoped, she'd never be a maid again.

"You plan to come on Tuesday night," he ordered. "Remember, I'm still your boss."

Chapter 18

Chicago

The days passed all too quickly, and Tuesday arrived. Jade dressed one more time in her Sid disguise. Her mother still didn't know, although Sidney told her he now worked at the grocer's. Hazel assumed her daughter was working during the day as maid.

Jade was more nervous today in her act than she ever had been. Tonight she'd be herself again in front of Tyler, and she didn't dare give anything away that would make him guess the truth now.

Tyler arrived with the carriage and picked her up. Jade noticed that he was preoccupied and nervous himself.

"How was yer lunch?" she asked.

"What?" Tyler didn't understand.

"Yer lunch." Jade spoke slowly and loudly as if he were hard of hearing.

"What are you talking about? I just had breakfast."

Jade sighed. "Yer lunch with that fancy woman!"

"Oh! Fine."

Silence again.

Jade gave him a sideways glance. "What didja eat?"

Tyler turned to her with a frown. "Sid, I've got a lot on my mind right now, if you don't mind."

"Like what?"

Tyler sighed. "Like what to say to seven women who will be traveling with me for the next week and who will in all likelihood become my neighbors and possibly even my relatives considering I have two cousins wanting to get married."

Jade nodded in understanding. "Ya don't want them to think ya don't know what yer doing."

"I know what I'm doing."

Jade nodded again. "So what are ya going to do?"

"I'm—I'm not sure yet."

Jade just nodded.

They opened the building and had no sooner set out their papers than the women began to arrive. They came in quietly, looking at each other and then not looking at each other. They waited expectantly for Tyler to begin.

When it appeared that they were all there, Tyler stood at the front of the room by the desk. Jade sat off to the side where she could see the women's faces while he talked to them. Her quick eyes noted that all the women except Melody Wells wore the same dresses they had worn for their interviews. Apparently they were not women of means, which would partly explain their presence here. Melody's dress, again, was fashionable, and it occurred to Jade that Melody could be in a situation similar to her own—once wealthy, now poor.

She perused the other faces and wasn't surprised to see the nervous tension evident on them. How frightening this must be to leave all that they once knew and venture into an unknown future with unknown future husbands!

Only Pearl Maddox seemed relaxed, and Jade recalled Tyler telling her, as Sid, that the cheerful woman had taught school for several years before deciding that life was passing her by and that she was ready to change that. She seemed undaunted by the uncertainties ahead.

As Tyler opened his mouth to speak, the door opened, and all the ladies turned to see who it was. A man entered. He was a young man about Tyler's age, Jade thought. He had on a dark suit, and a timid smile appeared on his face when he saw all the women. He removed his hat. He was of medium build and had short, dark hair. He nodded to Tyler and sat down on one of the chairs in the back.

The women still looked at him curiously until Tyler cleared his throat and got their attention again.

"Thank you, ladies, for coming. We'll be leaving first thing in the morning by train. We'll ride the rails for three days until we come to Freesburg, Minnesota. Then we have to switch to stagecoach. At a way station, we will switch to our own stagecoach that will take us to our new settlement, and you'll be able to meet the men."

The women were giving him their full attention.

"Now, my friends have instructed me to make it clear to you that you are by no means required to stay if you choose not to. We want everyone to be absolutely sure of themselves before any weddings take place. If you decide you want to return to Chicago, we'll pay your fare. Are there any questions?"

The room was silent, and Jade saw Tyler breathe a sigh of relief. Things were going well. Then...

"What if they decide they don't want us?"

"Well—"

"Will there be chaperones?"

"Uh—"

"Who are these men?"

"What are their names?"

Questions began pouring in, and Tyler stood looking bewildered by the deluge. Jade shook her head. He did *not* know what he was doing.

"Ladies, ladies, please, one at a time," Tyler protested. "I'll try to answer all your questions, but one at a time. Now, who's first?"

Three women spoke at once, and Jade laughed out loud at Tyler's exasperated expression. He heard her and gave her a dark look. Then as if he suddenly had an idea, he held up his hand for silence. Jade watched him warily.

"Ladies, my assistant, Sidney Crandall, will answer these concerns you have." He walked over to Jade and lifted her by the arm and marched her to the front of the room.

"Oh, no ya don't!" she hissed at him.

"Help me, Sid, please!" he implored. He released her in the center and went to a chair.

The women looked from Tyler to the boy. Then Cora Macardle smiled encouragingly and raised her hand. Jade immediately called on her.

"Yes, Miss Macardle?"

"Sidney, can you tell us a little about these men? We know absolutely nothing."

Jade looked to Tyler for help but could tell by the expression of panic on his face that she wasn't going to get any. She took a deep breath and walked to the desk, being careful to clomp her boots and imitate Sidney as much as possible. Removing the sketches from the leather case, she started.

First, she showed each drawing and told the women the man's name and occupation. Frequently she paused to scratch or wipe her nose, and Cora indicated her approval by a slight nod of her head.

Then, when she had gone through all the pictures, she said, "Now, ladies, don't go and start picking which one ya want right now. Ya've got the whole trip to pray about it and think about it. And when ya get there, ya need time to get to know these fellas. Maybe none of them will be right, and the Lord will lead ya back here."

Tyler was astonished at her speech, but the women were in agreement.

"You know they have to have time to get to know us too," commented Leigh Sheldon.

"He's right. We don't need to rush this," agreed Pearl.

"Now, about traveling," continued Jade, ignoring Tyler's surprise. "The train has sleeping berths that can hold two people each. There's a top bunk and a lower bunk." She had traveled on the train many times, back when money had been no issue and life was just pleasure and leisure. "You will be paired up as follows: Hermine Wetherby and Pearl Maddox, Gwyneth Kent and Cora Macardle, Leigh Sheldon and Melody Wells. Miss Smith, ya'll either have to share with another female passenger, or ya'll be alone. As far as chaperones, yer all are old enough to take care of yerselves, aren't cha'?"

The women laughed, and Tyler smiled. He came to the front again and put an arm around Jade's shoulders. She stood perfectly still but scowled at him.

"I think since Sid does such a good job at making arrangements that he should come along and be our chaperone. What do you say, Sid? I'll send you home whenever you're ready. It would be your chance to see some country."

The women clapped in approval, but Jade was clearly startled by his words. She managed to stammer, "I…I…don't think my ma would let me."

"We'll talk about it," Tyler said. Then with renewed confidence, he faced the women again. "Ladies, I would like to introduce you to another one of our traveling companions." He pointed to the man in the back. "Pastor Malcolm Tucker has agreed to be the pastor of our church."

The young man stood and said, "How do you do?"

No one knew who said it, but a whisper was clearly heard, "Wonder if he's married?"

"Whatcha need me along for?" Jade asked Tyler as they drove away.

"Sid, you're a natural with those women. I don't know how you managed it, but you settled all their questions in just a few minutes. And it would be better to have someone like you along as chaperone than just two men and seven women, even if one of the men is a preacher."

"Where'd ya find him anyway?"

"The pastor of your church introduced me to him. He's his nephew, and he just got done with his schooling. This will be his first church, but the great thing is, he's always wanted to work away from the big city. Worked out pretty well, huh?"

"*Is* he married?"

Tyler frowned as he shook his head. "No." Then he laughed. "But remember, we've got one extra along."

Jade muttered, "Yeah, he and Sally Smith would make a great pair."

Tyler leaned toward him. "What did you say?"

"Nothin'."

"Look, Sid. I'll talk to your mom if you want and explain everything. I'll even travel back with you to make sure you make it okay."

Jade's eyebrows rose under her huge cap. "Why would ya do that?" she asked suspiciously.

"I got my reasons." Tyler refused to say more.

Jade shook her head. "I'm sure I can't, Mr. Newly, sorry."

Chapter 19

Chicago

Hazel watched with interest as her daughter rushed around the small cottage preparing for Amos's dinner party. For some time she had been suspicious of her daughter's behavior, so today she had gone up to the Granville mansion to speak with her, only to find that she wasn't there.

Mrs. Stanwood had been the one to inform her.

"Your daughter has been given several days off, Mrs. Crandall. We have replaced her with someone more efficient, and quite possibly she won't be needed in the future."

Hazel ignored the slight and replied, "Then I should like to talk to Mr. Granville, please."

Mrs. Stanwood pulled her already stiff back even straighter. "Mr. Granville is not in the habit of receiving visitors from the back door! Good day, madam." She was about to close the door, but Hazel walked in and passed her without a word.

Mrs. Todd pushed open the swinging doors and entered the kitchen. At the sight of Hazel, she exclaimed, "Mrs. Crandall, how nice it is to see you, ma'am. How are you and young Sidney?"

"We're fine, Mrs. Todd. Thank you for asking. Can you tell me where Mr. Granville is right now?"

The cook took no notice of the glowering looks the housekeeper was giving her. "Of course, Mrs. Crandall. He's in his study. Mr. Todd will be happy to announce you."

She led the way through the swinging doors, and Mr. Todd greeted them both pleasantly and took Hazel to the study.

Amos was delighted to see her. "Hazel, come in." He saw her stern expression. "I can see you have something important on your mind."

"I'd like to know where my daughter is, Amos. I was under the impression she worked for you."

"She does. She does. Let me explain."

A lengthy hour passed as Amos answered her questions and reassured her. At the end of his explanation, Amos folded his hands and looked at her calmly. Hazel studied the older man's face. She was shocked by what he had told her, yet he seemed happily content with the situation. She suspected he had more up his sleeve that he wasn't sharing with her.

"She's been dressing like Sidney and running around the city alone with this man?"

Amos chuckled. "Your daughter is quite an amazing woman, Hazel, and don't forget, even though it was her idea, I encouraged it."

"Are you unsure of Mr. Newly?"

"I'm interested in knowing anything that pertains to Palmer. The wealth of our family is always threatened by those who endeavor to take it away. You know what I mean. If Edmund hadn't been so trusting of others, you would still be wealthy today. He was cheated by people who befriended him, and he would never think ill of anyone."

Hazel nodded wearily. "I know. I was uneasy about things, but I never questioned his judgment."

"So you understand that even though I'm pretty sure of this young man, I like to check out all possibilities."

"But why use Jadyne?"

Amos smiled. "Now you're going to think that I'm a meddlesome old man. Those two young people are in love with each other, Hazel. No, don't go looking shocked! They don't even know it themselves yet. I wanted to give your daughter a chance to be with Tyler and get to know him without him knowing it. My guess is that he'll propose to her tonight and ask him to join the other brides he's taking back."

Hazel was stunned.

"Think about it. Jadyne could start a new life up north without the social snobbery of the city holding her back.

She would be happy there. Maybe you and Sidney should think about going yourselves."

"Amos, you're going too fast!" She shook her head in bewilderment. "I don't know what to think of all this, but I do know I can trust your judgment. And if this is what the Lord wants for Jadyne's life, then I'm all for it. My job now is to go home and pray for her."

The old man shook his head. "You really think that will help, don't you?"

Hazel smiled. "When are you going to believe it, Amos?" she said softly. "You've got all this money, but you're still not content, are you? I've told you before; your happiness will come when you accept the Lord as your Savior."

"I know you believe that. Young Newly has been telling me all about it too. You know he said Palmer accepted his religion."

"It's not a religion, Amos. It's a relationship with Christ. He becomes your constant companion and guide. With him on your side, what is there to fear?"

Chapter 20

Chicago

Jade was announced by Mr. Todd and welcomed into the parlor by Amos's smiling face. As before, the same people were assembled for the evening's dinner party.

Her heart thumped erratically under the emerald satin of her gown. Her copper curls trembled, and her hands felt damp with nervousness.

"Miss Crandall, how delighted I am to see you again! Where have you disappeared to?" Wade Pullvey took her hand and led her to a corner of the room, where he kept her monopolized until dinner was called. At first she was surprised at his attention, knowing that he knew all about her financial and social status, but she reminded herself that had any of the "social set" been present in the room, she was sure Wade's attention would have been elsewhere. This was a flirtation, nothing more. She was aware of Tyler's eyes on her and of Cecile's efforts to keep Tyler distracted.

Amos decided to put an end to Wade's dalliance. "Mr. Newly, please escort Miss Crandall. Perhaps, Wade, you would assist your mother, and Cecile, please do me the honor." He held out his arm and then motioned for the Simonsons and the elder Pullvey to follow.

Jade smiled with relief into Tyler's eyes. *Finally!* she thought as her hand was tucked into his arm. His face reflected the sentiment.

"Miss Crandall," he spoke quietly. "I need to talk with you privately this evening."

She inclined her head, and as he gazed at her, she hoped fervently that she had scrubbed off all the "freckles" from her nose. He seemed not to notice any, for he said, "You look very beautiful tonight."

"Thank you, Mr. Newly." Her quiet, cultured voice was a far cry from the raucous tone she used to imitate Sidney. She couldn't help the small smile that appeared on her face at his politeness and attention, so different from his treatment of the boy. She recalled when he grabbed her by the collar and threatened to warm her britches!

Amos arranged the seating exactly the same as before, but after Tyler's simple prayer of thanks, Wade clapped Tyler on the shoulder.

"My turn to sit between the ladies, Newly. You had both of them last time."

Reluctantly, Tyler changed seats. As the new maid began to serve, Cecile immediately turned all her attention on Tyler, and Wade put all his effort into charming Jade. Amos couldn't help chuckling to himself at the two miserable yet polite young people. Finally, as the meal came to a close, he gave them some relief by claiming everyone's attention.

"Tyler, my lawyer and I"—he indicated Lee Simonson— "have gotten together this week, and we've made a few legal decisions that will affect Palmer."

The lawyer nodded at Tyler.

Amos continued, "I want you to take some important papers back with you for Palmer to sign. He can keep them in his possession until he decides to return for a visit or else I'll send someone to retrieve them for me."

Tyler nodded. "That's fine, Mr. Granville. I'll be happy to deliver them for you."

Lee Simonson shook his head. "I don't like it, Amos."

Tyler looked at him. "Is there a problem?"

The lawyer shifted in his chair to face Tyler. "Amos wants to sign all the papers before he sends them. I just don't think that's wise."

Amos smiled. "I'm getting old, Lee. Who knows if I'll be around before Palmer gets back here? I want this business taken care of now."

"But, Amos, not your will!"

Cecile's head shot up.

"Especially my will. Palmer's a lawyer too. He'll know how to handle it."

"I still don't understand the problem," said Tyler.

Lee turned back to him. "If Amos has already signed his will and sends it with you, you would be responsible for it until it was handed to his brother. He left an opening for Palmer to write in his particular wishes before he signed." The lawyer shook his head. "Obviously he trusts you very much to send an incomplete but signed copy of his will in your care."

"You mean you're worried that I might alter or add to Mr. Granville's will?" Tyler's voice was hard.

"No, not you necessarily." The lawyer looked Tyler in the eye. "But someone else could, if they got a hold of it."

"That won't happen, sir," Tyler looked at both men. "I give you my word."

Amos nodded in satisfaction, but Lee Simonson still looked unconvinced.

"Gentlemen, I thought you promised not to talk business tonight," Mrs. Pullvey protested.

"You are right, Elizabeth, and we won't any more. Let's retire to the library, shall we?"

The evening passed quickly, and Jade's face ached from smiling at Wade's inane remarks while her teeth were clenched in frustration. Cecile overdid herself in claiming Tyler's attention. She kept a hand on his arm, and whenever he tried to excuse himself, she pulled him back with a laugh and a protest. Jade would gladly have boxed her ears.

Finally the guests began to leave. The Pullveys waited good-humoredly for Wade to finish his lengthy good-bye to Jadyne. Then the Simonsons left, and Jade reluctantly made ready to depart. Amos rose from his chair.

"Cecile, would you mind seeing me to my room? I'm afraid I'm getting weary in my old age."

Cecile scowled at her uncle. "I'm sure your butler would be of greater assistance, Uncle Amos. Besides, Tyler and I had a few things to discuss yet."

It was Tyler's turn to scowl, but Amos intervened. "No, I need to have a word with you, Cecile." He stepped over to Jade. "Good-bye, my dear. Thank you for coming." He leaned over to kiss her cheek and whispered, "Meet me in my study in half an hour."

Jade looked at him in surprise, but she nodded her head in agreement. She and Tyler watched as Amos left the room with a reluctant Cecile beside him.

Tyler turned to Jade. "Finally! I thought I wouldn't have a chance to speak with you. I think Wade and Cecile had a conspiracy against us."

Jade smiled, but her nervousness suddenly returned.

Tyler took a deep breath and plunged on. "Miss Crandall, I have to leave tomorrow, and even though our time together has been short, I want to ask you something…something very important."

Jade held her breath.

"I really have enjoyed being with you, and I don't know if your brother has told you about working for me or not, but I have gotten to know him too and like him immensely. I know I don't know you very well, but I'm sure about this." He took her hand and held her gaze. "I would like to…to…ask you to…to…"

Their eyes held, and though Tyler's clearly showed her that he was in love with her, he finished lamely, "To write to me."

Jade blinked.

"*Write* to you?"

"Tyler, thank you for waiting for me." Cecile breezed into the room. She glared at Jade and at their hands held together. "Haven't you left *yet*, Miss Crandall?"

Jade withdrew her hand from Tyler's. "I'm just leaving, Miss Granville. Good night. Good night, Mr. Newly."

"Miss Crandall, wait. I'll see you out."

"There's no need, Mr. Newly. Have a pleasant trip." She left the room, and Mr. Todd helped her out the front door.

Once again Jade rounded the mansion and entered through the kitchen door. Mr. Todd was waiting for her with a conspiratorial grin on his face.

"Mr. Granville instructed me to take you to his study as soon as the coast is clear, Miss Jade." Clearly he enjoyed the subterfuge.

Jade smiled absently at the butler as she removed her cape and prepared to wait. She felt confused and hurt. *Write to him?* Surely Tyler was going to say something else; she saw it in his eyes. Was it because he saw Cecile coming? Or did he back out for a different reason?

Jade's self-esteem was shattered. What would she have said if he had asked her to marry him? She sighed. She would have said yes. Now she didn't know what she would say if the opportunity came again.

In a glum mood, she followed Mr. Todd to the study. The butler looked one way then another as he opened the door and let her in. He winked with mischief, and Jade managed a weak smile in return.

Amos was waiting at his desk. "Jade, come in. You were splendid this evening! I hope Wade Pullvey wasn't too much of a trial for you." He saw the girl's depressed features. "What's wrong?"

Jade pushed her brooding thoughts aside. "I'm sorry, Mr. Granville. I'm fine. What was it you wanted to see me about?"

The old gentleman studied her face. "Did you and Tyler have a chance to talk?" he asked.

"Yes, we did. We talked while you and Cecile were gone."

"And … ?"

Jade squirmed in her chair. "And he asked me to write to him."

Amos frowned. "Write to him?" he repeated. He had thought Newly could do better than that. Maybe he had misread the man. "You know," he continued, watching Jade closely, "I'm worried about him having all those important papers with him and having to watch out for— how many?—seven women besides? He's going to have his hands full."

Jade sighed. "Yes, he even asked me, I mean Sidney, to come along and help him."

Amos's eyes lit up. "That's an excellent idea, Jade!"

Jade looked at her employer in puzzlement.

"Don't you see? If you went along, you could help me keep an eye on those papers and really make sure Palmer was all right."

Jade frowned. "I thought you trusted Tyler."

"I do. I do. But he's going to need help, Jade. By thunder! I wish I could go myself. But since I can't, you can be my eyes and ears and let me know exactly what's going on."

Jade pushed the idea around in her head. She would be able to see more of Tyler, even see this new settlement. The idea fascinated her.

Chapter 21

Chicago

Jade hurried along the sidewalk in the early morning fog to the train station. Her large bag banged against her legs with every step. She wondered how much stuff her mother had packed for her.

Surprisingly, when Jade told her mother that Amos Granville wanted her to go north for two weeks to handle some business for him, Hazel had agreed to send her. And when Jade hesitatingly told her that she would be disguised as Sidney, her mother had frowned but answered, "Amos told me about your masquerade. I don't know what this is all about, but I trust Amos to be doing the right thing. If he thinks this is wise, I will agree. But, Jadyne, this deception will catch up with you, and when it does, you may not like the consequences."

There were so many more warnings her mother could have made. Given Jade's reduced status in society already was one thing, but to run the risk of losing her reputation completely by taking this trip was another. Had there been more time to contemplate her actions, perhaps Jade would have backed out and asked Mr. Granville to send someone more capable to help Tyler. Perhaps she would have realized that she would never be able to undo what she was about to do. But as it was, Jade thanked her mother with a hug and assured her she would be careful.

She was late. The train was already waiting, and she could see Tyler standing with Malcolm Tucker and a group of women. He was looking over their heads as if searching for someone. She came up behind them and grabbed his sleeve.

"Mr. Newly."

Tyler looked down at the boy, and his face broke into a grin. "Sidney! I've been looking all over for you! You decided to come!"

"Yep. My ma said I could come."

Tyler suddenly looked past her. "Is your sister—"

"My family stayed at home. We already said good-bye."

"Oh."

"Whatcha' waitin' for?" She looked around at the faces. "Where's Miss Macardle and Miss Kent?"

"That's what we're waiting for." Tyler sounded impatient. "Look, I'll go get your ticket, Sid, and maybe by then they'll be here. They better hurry."

The women stood nervously, looking around. Jade had the impression that they would leave if given half a chance. They were shivering in the cold morning air, and their faces looked white and scared. Only Pearl Maddox and Sally Smith seemed cheerful. Then, without warning, Hermine Wetherby began to crumple to the ground.

"Oh, dear! There she goes again." Pearl grabbed for Hermine and held her while Malcolm Tucker rushed to assist her. He picked the fainting woman up in his arms and looked around for something to do with her.

"Why don't you put her on the train?" Jade suggested. "In fact, why don't you all get on and wait for Mr. Newly there? It would be warmer and drier."

"That's an excellent idea," said Leigh Sheldon.

The women agreed with a measure of enthusiasm, and they all helped the pastor with his burden.

After they had gone, Jade waited, shifting the heavy bag from one hand to the next. Finally, she set it down and sat on it. She jumped up when she saw two women scurrying toward the train.

"Over here!" she called.

Cora and Gwyneth turned at her call, and with relieved faces they hurried toward her.

"I'm sorry we're late, Sidney," Cora said between gasps.

"We wouldn't have been, but Cora got cold feet. Honestly, Cora, it's too late to back out now," Gwyneth admonished her cousin.

"It's never too late," Jade spoke softly. "But you'd regret it all your life if you didn't at least give it a chance." Immediately after speaking the words, Jade realized how true they were for herself as well.

Cora nodded at Jade, and some of the fear left her face.

"Where are the others?" asked Gwyneth.

"They just got on the train. Go right up there. I'll wait here for Mr. Newly."

A young woman standing nearby turned sharply to look at Jade. She was wearing an attractive dark-blue traveling suit complete with a fashionable hat. Jade returned her look with curiosity. The woman seemed about to approach Jade, but just then Jade saw Tyler coming.

"Over here, Mr. Newly," she called.

The woman's head jerked in the direction Jade was looking, and with an excited scream, she yelled, "Tyler Newly?"

Tyler stopped and stared at her, and Jade scowled as she watched the woman run to Tyler and throw her arms around him.

Tyler looked equally surprised as he met Sid's eyes over the woman's hat.

"Tyler! Ty, you don't know me, do you?" The woman held onto both his arms as she laughed at his puzzled expression.

Suddenly Tyler's face registered recognition and shock at the same time.

"Mallory? Mallory Riley?"

The lovely woman laughed out loud, showing beautiful white teeth.

Jade's teeth were held clenched together as a wave of jealousy swept over her. Who was this woman?

"Mal, what are you doing here?"

"I'm on my way home, Ty. I'm all done with being 'refined' at that nonsense ladies' school. What on earth are *you* doing here?"

Jade could have sworn Tyler was afraid of nothing, but suddenly he looked very frightened indeed. After an uncomfortable space of time, he looked uneasily at the lovely woman and said, "It's a long story, Mal. You're not on this train, are you?"

Mallory laughed again. "Okay, Ty. What are you up to? Lucy and I could always tell when you boys were about to get yourselves in trouble."

"All aboard!"

Tyler looked quickly at Jade. "Sid, where is everyone?"

"They're all on the train, Mr. Newly. Yeah, even the last two made it." She answered the question before he could ask.

Mallory again looked at the boy, and a strange expression crossed her face. "What is going on, Tyler?"

"Let me help you with those bags, Mal. Come on, Sid. The train's going to go!"

They boarded the train and moved through the coach. The group was on one side of the car, and Malcolm called to Tyler, "Here we are, Tyler. Miss Wetherby fainted, so we had to get her on board."

Tyler seated Mallory and said, "I'll be right back after I take care of a few things."

Jade was undecided. She didn't know if she should follow Tyler, who looked like he was trying to escape from this beautiful woman, or stay and find out who she was. Mallory decided for her.

"Sit down, Sid. Tell me what's going on."

Jade sat down across from Mallory, but she wasn't sure how much to tell. Tyler might not like it.

The train started moving with a jerk, and Jade became uncomfortable under the woman's stare, which traveled from her large boots to her oversized coat to the cap that nearly touched Jade's nose.

Finally Mallory spoke, but her voice was low, and she leaned forward so only Jade could hear.

"All right, who are you?"

"My name's Sidney, miss."

"No, it is not. I want to know your real name, and I want it now, or I'm telling Tyler his little friend is a girl dressed up like a boy."

Jade's mouth dropped open, and she stared in horror at Mallory. "How did you know?"

Mallory's expression was unreadable. "I'm something of an expert. Now talk."

"My name's Jadyne Crandall—Jade. But please, miss, Tyler must not know. He mustn't!"

"Why not?"

"It would take too long to explain now. Please trust me! I'm only trying to help him."

Mallory's eyes narrowed as she thought. "Okay, for now I will let that be. Tell me what Ty is up to. Quick!"

"What do you mean? Who are you anyway? What a minute! Riley! Are you related to Dugan Riley and … and … Buck?"

Mallory nodded. "They're my brothers. Now, hurry and tell me before he comes back."

Jade swallowed hard. "Well, Miss Riley, Tyler came to Chicago to do business for Palmer Granville and for their new town. But...but he's bringing back these women to be brides for his friends."

"*What?*" Mallory nearly rose off her seat. "Which ones? Do you know which friends?"

Jade nodded. The woman's reaction startled her, but she supposed it was somewhat of a shock. "There's your brother Dugan but not your brother Buck. He didn't want one."

Mallory stared at her with disbelief in her eyes. "Go on."

"And there's two brothers...Ralph and Ray something."

"Tunelle."

"Yes. And...a...a...blacksmith."

"Bernie."

Jade nodded again. "And two more brothers, Michael and Gabriel...."

Mallory sank back in her seat. "Trent."

"What, miss?"

"Their last name is Trent."

Jade was frightened by the woman's white face. "Miss Riley, are you all right? I'm sorry. This must be quite a shock for you."

"You're sure *Michael* asked for a wife?"

"He's on the list."

Mallory put her head down. "All this for nothing," she murmured.

"Excuse me?"

Mallory shook her head at Jade and set her lips firmly. "I was hoping Michael Trent would finally see me as a woman instead of a tomboy." She laughed in scorn. "I even went to this fancy ladies' school and everything. Now I find out he'd rather marry someone he's never even met instead of me." She turned to stare out the window.

"I'm sorry," Jade said quietly.

Tyler finally rejoined them. As he sat down beside Jade, Mallory shot her question at him, "Which one of them are you marrying, Ty?"

Tyler scowled at Jade. "I see Sid has been talking."

"I made him. Ty, what are you thinking of? Is everyone in on this?" Mallory threw her anger at him in her voice.

"It wasn't my idea, Mal. The guys had it all planned last fall. They've been praying about it for a long time now."

"Praying! Oh, sure. They say, 'Lord, I want this. Give it to me.' And then off they go and do it because God must want them to. He's answering their prayers."

"Mal, you know better than that."

"What do our parents think of it?"

Tyler dropped his eyes. "We haven't told anyone yet."

Mallory gave him a disgusted look.

"Mal, look. We're not forcing anyone to stay. The women have agreed to come out and meet the guys, and the guys want a chance to meet them. There aren't that many women in our area, Mal. You know that's true."

"What about the ones who are there? What about Lucy, Ty? You want to break her heart when she finds out you brought back someone for Dugan?"

"Dugan?"

"Lucy's been in love with Dugan since we were kids."

Tyler was astounded. "Did Dugan know that?"

"Would it matter? Michael has known for years how I feel, but look." She pointed to the women. "He'd rather have someone he's never seen before."

Tyler's eyes roamed over her feminine attire with interest. "Maybe he should look again. He's never seen you look like this before."

"And is that why he should suddenly fall in love with me, Ty?" Mallory stormed. "Because I look better now? Don't you see? I'm the same person I was, and I always will be." She yanked the attractive hat off. "I was stupid enough to think these things might make a difference, but now I know that they won't. And I don't want them to. He just never will be interested in me, the real me, so I might as well face it." She stood and swayed with the train. "I suppose you finally decided Philippa was good enough for you." She marched away and found an empty seat away from all of them.

Jade watched Tyler out of the corner of her eye. She was shaken by the fact that Mallory had seen through her disguise so easily. She wondered how much longer she could fool him. She gave out a yelp as Tyler slapped her sharply on the knee.

"Goodness, Sid! You're going to have to toughen up if you're going to be out in the wilderness. We ought to find you a Stetson like mine and get rid of that city-looking cap."

Jade's hands flew to her cap. "Told ya once, mister. This cap stays."

Tyler laughed. He looked uneasily at the back of Mallory's head several seats away. "Think she'll cool down?"

Jade followed his gaze. "She's yer friend's sister?"

"Yes. Our parents are great friends, and we all kind of grew up together. I sure feel bad about hurting her like this, but Michael made it clear to me he wasn't interested in her."

"What was she like before? I mean, she said she never dressed like that."

Tyler grinned. "She was nearly always wearing buckskins or her brother's pants. She rides and hunts and outdoes most of us fellas, Michael included. I guess Michael figured like the rest of us that she wasn't ever going to grow out of it."

Jade coughed and squirmed in her seat. "Well, I'm just a kid, and I don't really care much what a girl looks like, but seems to me, she's better lookin' than all them women yer taking with ya."

Tyler was surprised. "You know, I think you're right. It's funny because at first I didn't know who she was, but now I can see clearly that she's the same girl that dressed like a boy. I wonder what Michael will think of her."

"Who's Lucy?"

Tyler rubbed his face with his hands. "There's another problem. How was I supposed to know Lucy was interested in Dugan? This is getting more and more complicated. I told those guys I didn't want to do this."

"So who is she?"

"She's my sister."

Jade nodded in understanding. "So is Philippa good enough for ya now?"

"No! I mean, yes—I mean, no!" Tyler struggled with his words. "She's good enough, but she's not for me. I found the one I want."

Jade swallowed nervously. "Who?"

Tyler smiled at the boy. "Let's just say I'll be traveling back to Chicago with you because I left behind some unfinished business."

Jade felt herself grow warm all over. She smiled secretly.

Chapter 22

Sand Creek

Lucy looked up from her desk and absently watched for activity out the window. Sand Creek was quiet today.

A tall, dark-haired man strode down the street and entered the telegraph office. Lucy's heart picked up its beat. It was Dugan!

Hastily she set her "Out to Lunch" sign up and dashed out of the hotel and across the street. She slowed her steps and gracefully entered the small office.

"Hello, Lucy," the man behind the counter said. "Funny you should come by just now. I've got a telegram for your family from Tyler. Here it is."

"Lucy! Hi!" Dugan smiled at her. He held a telegram in his hand too.

Lucy's heart fluttered at his smile. It always did when Dugan smiled. "Why, Dugan! What are you doing in town?"

"Guess it was my turn finally." He laughed. He waved the telegram. "Ty sent us one too. Looks like he'll be here soon. I can hardly wait. What does yours say?"

"My what? Oh!" Lucy looked briefly at the message. "He just says he'll be back soon, but he's going straight to the settlement instead of stopping at home." She frowned. "That's a shame! We haven't seen him in a while. Why is he doing that?"

Dugan grinned. "We ordered a lot of stuff from the city. I guess it's easier to just haul it straight there than go through Sand Creek."

"Oh." She smiled sweetly at him. "We've missed you, I mean, all of you out there."

"It's been great there, Lucy! Soon Gabe and I will start our coach line, and we'll be in and out of here more often."

"That will be wonderful, Dugan."

"Well, I gotta go. I've got lots to do before Ty gets home." He tipped his hat to Lucy and left.

She stared after him deep in thought. The telegram in her hand gave her an idea. Her folks had been talking about taking the family out to Tyler's settlement for a visit. Maybe they could meet him there when he got home from Chicago. Wouldn't he be surprised? Would Dugan be glad to see her there?

Strangely, it was Buck's face that flashed through her mind. Was Buck the one she hoped would be glad?

"Dugan!"

The brown-haired man stopped suddenly and looked around. Philippa Gray called to him again as she approached.

Dugan waited impatiently and with a measure of caution. He had never cared for Philippa's snobbish manner. Fortunately, she had always left him and Buck alone. They weren't in her "class."

"Hello, Philippa. What can I do for you?" he asked politely.

Philippa twirled her parasol and gave Dugan a smile.

"I couldn't help overhear you talking with Lucille. Tyler will be home soon?"

Dugan was disgusted at her eavesdropping. "He'll come when he's ready."

Philippa ignored his rudeness. "Now, Dugan, you know how close Tyler and I are. Why, we're practically engaged! I just want to know when to expect him in Sand Creek so I can give him a warm welcome."

"He's not coming through Sand Creek. Gabe and I are picking him up with our new coach at the way station near Freesburg."

"Thank you, Dugan." She walked away with a satisfied expression.

Dugan groaned to himself as he rode out of town. Philippa's look meant trouble for someone, and he was afraid that someone was Tyler.

Chapter 23

Train

The monotony of riding the rails evidenced itself soon after Tyler bought the ladies their lunch of sandwiches from the train vendor. The ladies, now that they were committed to the trip, began asking questions about the settlement but mostly about the men. He was finding it hard to keep up with them.

Mallory Riley surprised all of them when she moved to Tyler's side and said, "Maybe I can be of some help."

Tyler questioned her with his eyes.

"I owe you an apology, Ty," she said quietly. "It was wrong of me to judge you or the fellows just because they chose wives in this way. You were right. If they prayed about it, and the Lord answered, who am I to tell them they're wrong? Please forgive me."

Tyler answered by giving the lovely girl a bear hug. Jade grinned at Tyler and Mallory, this time without feeling a trace of jealousy.

"Maybe you shouldn't give up, Mal," Tyler said in her ear, but she just shook her head.

She faced the women and explained. "Ty and I grew up together. My name is Mallory Riley, and one of your prospective husbands is my brother Dugan. I have another brother at the settlement named Buck, but Ty tells me he's not getting married yet. Let me see … what can I tell you about my brothers?" She went on to describe Dugan and relate some of his childhood to the listeners.

Jade listened in fascination as Mallory told the women things about each of the men to help them understand and like them. She also told about each one accepting the Lord as their Savior and how important he was in their lives.

Malcolm Tucker also listened closely to the descriptions of the men he would be pastoring. Jade noticed that he still sat with Hermine and watched out for her comfort and needs quite carefully.

Tyler relaxed and listened to Mallory as she did a better job than he ever could of describing the men. She told the women little things like the color of the men's hair and eyes, things he didn't even know but things that seemed very important to the future brides. He laid his head back and closed his eyes.

"I say, is this seat taken?"

Tyler's eyes swung open, and Jade turned from Mallory to see the man who sat down beside Tyler. She frowned. Something about the man bothered her. It was almost as though she knew him from somewhere. Amos's warnings about the papers Tyler carried came back to her, and she decided she better be on guard.

Mallory finished her descriptions with Michael Trent. Jade wondered if she was the only one who saw the change in her face and heard it in her voice. Mallory told about Michael then finished with, "They are the nicest bunch of men I know, and they deserve the best, but they're no angels. They fight and squabble with each other, and they can get as moody and cantankerous as a black bear with a sore paw. And when my brothers haven't shaved for a day or two, they look almost like a couple of bears."

She kept the ladies laughing and talking, and the time flew by. The porter eventually entered their coach and lit the lantern. He went from berth to berth and prepared the sleeping quarters for the night. Mallory was assigned to share with Sally Smith.

Jade hadn't given the nights a thought until Tyler spoke to her.

"Sid, I don't know what arrangements there will be for you. I got your ticket at the last minute. Let me see about it."

Jade's eyes opened wide in concern, and she saw Mallory look at her curiously.

Tyler returned from talking to the man in charge. "It's okay, Sid. I was going to share with Malcolm, but he said he'd bunk with someone else so you can take the top bunk in my berth. I better keep an eye on you, or your ma and sister will be pretty upset with me."

"Uh … no, it's okay, Mr. Newly. I'll just sleep in one of the seats," Jade offered.

"But, Sid—"

"Excuse me, sir, if you have a spare bunk, I'd gratefully take it. I got on at the last minute too, and they were filled up." The man who sat beside Tyler spoke up. "That is, if the boy doesn't want it."

Jade looked at him suspiciously, and it was then that she noticed the western hat he had set beside him.

"I changed my mind," she blurted. "I'll take it."

Mallory regarded her with surprise, but she said nothing.

Tyler shrugged his shoulders at the man. "Sorry." He moved out of the way as the porter prepared the berth.

Mallory grabbed Jade's arm and pulled her to a quiet end of the car. "I think you better tell me just what you're up to, whatever your name is."

Jade sighed. "It's Jade. Listen, I don't like this either, but I know who that man is, the one with a hat like Tyler's. Well, I don't know *who* he is, but I know where I've seen him before. He was at the Granville mansion talking with Cecile and Wil Tait."

Mallory looked thoroughly confused, so Jade explained as best she could about the papers and Mr. Granville. "The man was in the woods with Wil once too. He paid Wil money. And my mother saw Wil bury something. I'll bet he's the one stealing from Mr. Granville."

Mallory rubbed her forehead. "And you think he's after these papers?"

Jade nodded.

Mallory digested the information. Finally she spoke again. "How old are you?"

"Nineteen."

Now Mallory was surprised. "I thought you were thirteen or fourteen! You're older than me!" She watched Jade closely. "Why are you so interested in helping Ty?"

When the freckled face before her reddened, she said, "You're in love with him, aren't you? Does he know? Wait a minute. How could he know? He doesn't even know you're a girl."

Jade hesitated to answer, but finally she said, "I think he's in love with Jadyne Crandall, but he thinks I'm her brother."

Curious, Mallory asked, "How does he know Jadyne—I mean, you?"

"I attended Mr. Granville's dinner parties as myself, and we ... talked. Of course, I was also there as a maid, but he doesn't know that."

Mallory held up her hand. "I don't understand any of this any more." She shook her head. "I think the best thing to do is to tell Ty who you are and why you're here. Then you can warn him about this man."

Jade's head was shaking back and forth vigorously before Mallory finished speaking. "No, Miss Riley, I can't do that! Not yet! Don't you see? I've gotten things so messed up already with my disguises that he will never believe me. He'll despise me."

A moment of silence passed.

"Okay, okay." Mallory agreed. "But if I think it becomes necessary to tell him, I will."

Jade nodded.

"Pull that cap lower, and don't smile so sweetly," Mallory commanded. "Those lips are a dead giveaway. And for goodness' sake, get in your bunk before Tyler goes to bed!"

Chapter 24

Train

Jade took Mallory's advice and excused herself early for the night. She would have to watch the man with the hat carefully. She had to help Tyler protect Mr. Granville's papers.

As she waited for the porter to finish her berth, she stared absently out the door into the next car. A man in an expensive-looking black suit and hat was talking animatedly to the dark-haired woman beside him. She seemed bored with the conversation and turned her head away from him.

Jade's throat constricted. The profile of the woman was clear for a moment. Then she faced forward, and again Jade could see only the back of their heads.

Cecile Granville? Why would she be on this train?

Jade decided to get a better look. Maybe she was wrong. She opened the door and went into the next car. She passed the couple without looking at them and sat down in an empty seat. After a few moments, she got up and headed back.

It was Cecile! There was no mistaking it. She glanced at the rich-looking man beside her and almost gasped out loud. *Wil Tait!*

She hurried back to her own car and the berth that was now prepared.

Wil Tait! Why was Mr. Granville's groom dressed like a wealthy gentleman and sitting with his boss's niece?

Jade's head spun. Tyler needed to know. Those two and the man she saw that night were probably after Mr. Granville's papers. Of course! Cecile had heard about them at the dinner party. That was it!

But how could she warn Tyler? He didn't know that "Sid" knew anything about his important papers. She could mention seeing Cecile and Wilbert. "Sid" saw them in front of the church with Tyler that day.

Calming down at last, she opened her bag and stared in dismay at its contents. Her mother had packed dresses and petticoats and all her frilly things. Jade shook her head. Obviously her mother didn't like her dressing like a boy. What if Tyler Newly looked in her bag!

At the top of the neatly folded clothing Jade saw her small Bible. She lifted it out and opened it. A paper was placed in the book of Galatians, whether on purpose or accident Jade wasn't sure, but as her eyes scanned the familiar verses, she read, "Be not deceived; God is not mocked: for whatsoever a man soweth, that shall he also reap."

Thoughtfully she put the book away and climbed into the bunk fully clothed. What was her mother trying to tell her? That her deception would have lasting repercussions? Jade sighed deeply as she turned to the wall and pulled the blankets over her head. After this trip, she would never pretend to be someone else again!

Mallory talked quietly with Tyler before they too retired. She was endeavoring to give Jade the time she needed.

"Mal, you're quite a girl. I really appreciated your help today." He laughed. "I guess I didn't need Sid along to take care of the women after all."

"There's something else, isn't there, Ty? Something more than bringing brides home. What are you up to?"

"Why do you say that?"

"Because I know you too well. You're acting differently. What's going on?"

Tyler laughed again. "If you don't think interviewing seven women and making arrangements to bring them back is enough to make me act differently, then there's something wrong with you."

Mallory just watched him. "Okay, but I'll find out. I always do."

Jade heard Tyler fumble around in the curtained berth as he prepared for the night. She remained quiet, and soon she could tell he was asleep. What would her mother think of her now?

The night wore on, but Jade was restless. She dozed on and off, uncomfortable in her clothing, especially the tightly wound cloth. She turned from side to side.

She was drifting off again when she heard a small sound above the noise of the train. Her eyes blinked open, and she lay still, staring into the darkness wondering what it was that had disturbed her. She had become accustomed to the steady clacking of the train on the rails and the creaks and groaning of the swaying cars. She could still hear Tyler's even breathing, so she knew it wasn't him.

Her eyes were adjusting to the darkness, and she moved them without turning her head. Her breathing was shallow, and as she listened, she could hear her own heart beating.

In the next instant her head was up, and in the dark a man dove out of the curtained room.

"Tyler!" she screamed.

Tyler scrambled to get out of his bed, and Jade heard a loud thud then a groan. She peered over the side of her bunk and made out Tyler's form. He appeared to be struggling with a blanket. She jerked her head back as he came to his feet.

"What is it, Sid? What's the matter?"

Footsteps thundered down the passageway, and sleepy voices muttered and grumbled. A porter called through the curtain.

"What's going on? Mr. Newly, is there a problem?"

"Are you all right?" Tyler asked quietly.

Jade nodded her head then realized he probably couldn't see her. "Yes."

"The boy must have had a nightmare," Tyler spoke quietly to the man. "Sorry to disturb everyone."

He turned back to the bunk and spoke to Jade in a quiet voice. "What happened?"

"There was a man in here. When I lifted my head, he ran off. I don't know, but I think he was going through yer bags," she whispered hoarsely.

Tyler knelt and felt his bags. Jade could hear him fumble with the catch.

"They seem fine. I think yours is opened, though. Shall I light a lamp?"

"No! I don't have anything valuable. Just close it."

"Well, try to go back to sleep, Sid. We'll check into it in the morning."

Jade heard Tyler settle back into his bed. Suddenly she heard him laugh softly. She listened, wondering what was funny.

"Do you even *sleep* with that cap on, Sid?"

Jade awoke with a start as she heard the porter's call. Uncertain about getting out of the bunk, she peeked over the side. Tyler was already gone. With as much haste as possible, she climbed down and prepared herself for the day. How she wished her mother had packed some of Sidney's things! She strongly suspected that her mother had neglected them on purpose in order to get Jade to stop masquerading.

At least she could repair her "freckles" and repin her hair. She moved speedily and had the cap firmly back in place in moments. Now she had to find Tyler and somehow see if the papers were really safe.

Tyler was in the next car with Malcolm. Jade stood back and studied him a moment. His sandy-blond hair and blue eyes made him stand out from the other men on the train. Oh, how she longed to have him see her as a woman again! She looked down at her boyish garb and knew she had to mentally prepare herself to approach him as Sid and not as Jadyne with her love for him showing in any way in her face or her demeanor. Jade moved with the rocking train and dropped down beside him on the seat.

"There you are, Sid. Did you finally get some sleep last night?"

Jade nodded. She wanted to talk to him about it but not in front of the pastor.

Malcolm rose just then, and Jade noticed that his attention was fixed on the doorway. Hermine and Pearl came through, and Malcolm hastened to assist them to a seat.

"Tell me about last night, Sid. Just what did you see?" Tyler turned his full attention on the boy.

"I heard a noise. I don't know what it was even. I waited, and then I saw a movement, and I sat up. A man rushed out, and then I yelled for you."

"Did you get a good look at him?"

Jade sighed. "No. It was too dark, and his back was to me. Did ya check all yer stuff? Was anything missing?"

"Everything was in order. How about yours?"

She nodded.

"Well, I reported it to the porter, and he's alerted the train staff. It was probably some petty thief."

"There's more."

Tyler leaned toward her. "What?"

"Remember that fancy lady that took ya to lunch?"

Tyler's brow puckered. "Miss Granville?"

"Yeah, that's the one. She's on this train, and her driver is with her."

"Where did you see them, Sid?"

She pointed. "In the car after ours. They were there last night anyway, and Mr. Newly?"

"Yes?"

"The driver was wearing pretty fancy clothes, and he didn't look like a groom at all."

Jade waited while Tyler sat deep in his thoughts. Finally he spoke, "Thanks, Sid. I'll keep an eye on them. How about you just stay away from them, though, okay?"

The next two days of train travel passed slowly. Boredom set in, and the women complained of aching bodies and the need for a bath and a good night's sleep. Jade silently echoed their sentiments whole-heartedly. There were no more incidents at night, and Jade was exhausted from trying to stay awake and keep watch. She saw no more of the suspicious man or Cecile and Wilbert.

It was the afternoon of the third day when Tyler gathered the women together to explain the next step of their journey.

"We'll rest and clean up in Freesburg before taking the stage. I've reserved rooms at the hotel, and I'm sure a hot meal will be available for our supper."

A feeling of anticipation came over the group, and Jade smiled at Mallory with pleasure. She didn't notice the man with the western hat sitting at the back of the car.

"Tyler, if you don't mind, I think I'd like to stay with your group and go to the settlement. After all, one of these ladies will be my sister-in-law. I'd like to know who she is." Mallory requested.

Tyler understood, but still he questioned her. "Are you sure, Mal?"

"Yes. By the way, where'd you find that Sally Smith?"

"Why?"

Mallory shook her head. "You're going to have your hands full keeping track of her. Haven't you noticed? She's always in a different car talking to strangers."

"Once we're on the stage, it will be easy to keep track of everyone. I'm glad you're here, Mal." Tyler squeezed her hand.

Freesburg

There was a great deal of commotion trying to sort out baggage and the supplies Tyler bought in the city. The women clambered for their belongings, pointing and giving Tyler directions on what to do with them. Finally, in desperation, he turned to Mallory and Sid.

"Take the ladies to the hotel and get them settled. I'll finish here. I have to send a load to Sand Creek to pick up later, and I need to check at the telegraph office. Here, Sid, take these leather pouches with you to my room, okay? I'll join you all for supper as soon as I can."

Jade hurried after Mallory and the others. The small town of Freesburg fascinated her. Never had she been in so small a town, having lived in the city all her life. The train station seemed to be the main hub of the community, and she could see that the edge of town was at the end of the street. Only a few houses were beyond, scattered here and there in the trees.

The boardwalk echoed their footsteps as they walked to the hotel. Jade looked from side to side at the buildings that made up the main street. After the train station, there was the telegraph office and the grocer. Jade peered into the window as she passed. No, it wasn't just a grocer; she saw clothing and tools and even furniture. She slowed as she stared in amazement at the variety of goods displayed.

She pulled herself away to catch up to the women. A saloon, a livery, and blacksmith completed that side of the town. She looked at the other side as they crossed the soft, muddy street. The women held their skirts and grumbled, but Jade just clomped through it in her boots. She continued her inspection. Another saloon competed for customers on this side. Next to the hotel was a bank, and farther down was a building she wasn't sure of, maybe the town meeting place. Beyond the main street she could see houses and … barns?

She caught up to the others and saw the same incredulous looks on some of their faces. No wonder the railroad stopped here and went no farther. She wondered what the new settlement was like if it wasn't as far advanced as this.

A commotion on the street caused her to turn while the others entered the hotel. A stage was just coming into town. Jade watched with interest as people came out of the buildings to see who was on the coach.

There were only a few occupants. Jade was amused when a young woman descended and opened a frilly parasol even though the sun was now setting. She was obviously proud of her up-to-date fashions, but Jade smiled to herself. Even though the woman was better dressed than the other women she had noticed in the small town, she was way behind the city fashions. Even Jade's simplest dresses were more fashionable than hers.

As Jade turned her back on the interesting town to enter the hotel, she felt a hand on her arm, and she looked up past the brim of her cap.

"Let's take a little walk, shall we?" The man from the train blocked her way as he gripped her arm tighter. She opened her mouth to protest, but she saw the small gun in the hand under his coat.

"No, wait!" she cried. Alarm filled her as he pulled her off the boardwalk and in between the buildings.

"Quiet, kid! We're just going for a walk."

The gun was pressed into her side as the man pulled her along. Apparently the man expected no further trouble, but Jade had been playing the part of a boy too long. With an angry growl, she jabbed her elbow into the man's ribs. Then as he doubled over, she kicked him in the shins with her heavy boots. She turned and ran back to the street as fast as she could, but she never saw the person who reached out and grabbed her; she only felt a stinging blow to her head and saw blackness fold over her.

Chapter 25

Freesburg

Tyler finally sorted out the luggage that belonged to the women and had the porter set it aside for pickup by the stage.

He also organized his purchases for a future delivery. When he completed those tasks, he headed to the telegraph office, all the while trying to watch the other passengers who got off the train. He wasn't too worried. Freesburg was a small enough town that if he missed the three he was looking for now, he'd find them again.

There were two messages. One was from Gabe and Dugan; they were waiting in Sand Creek to meet Tyler and his group at the way station as soon as he sent word. Tyler nodded in satisfaction. The sooner he was done with this "delivery," the better. He was anxious to return to Chicago and finish some more important business.

The other message gave him a shock. It was from Amos Granville. An attempt had been made on his life, and he was warning Tyler to be extremely careful.

Tyler stared at the paper for a long while. This answered questions both Palmer and Amos had, and he realized Palmer's life was probably in danger too. The sooner they got to the settlement, the better.

As if his haste now could get them there faster, he hurried to the hotel. A woman rose from a chair as he entered.

"Tyler!"

Startled, he turned, and his heart sank at the sight of Philippa Gray tapping her closed parasol in her hand.

Her features hardened. "Why, Tyler, I thought you'd look happier to see me than that!" Quickly, her tone turned charming. "You've been away so long. I've missed you. I just had to come meet you."

Tyler was amazed but not fooled by her transformation from anger to coquettishness. Too many times he'd seen Philippa flare up over some little thing and then act sweet as sugar the next. Before, he'd admired what he thought was self-control; now, he only saw her trying to cover up the real her.

"Hello, Philippa. Yes, it has been a long time. Will you excuse me? I have some things I must see to."

He moved to the desk and left Philippa fuming as she stared in disbelief at his dismissal of her.

Tyler got his room key and was making inquiries of the clerk when Mallory descended the steps and approached.

"Hi, Mal. Did you get everyone settled in?"

She nodded and smiled. "They'll be keeping the hotel staff busy. I think every one of them has ordered hot water for baths. I—"

"Mallory Riley!"

Mallory turned in surprise to the angry girl behind her. "Philippa. What are you doing here?"

"So that's what's going on!" She glared at first Tyler and then Mallory.

Tyler was disgusted at the expression on Philippa's face. "What are you talking about, Philippa?"

"Here I wait for you in that two-bit town to come back and get me out of there, and you take up with this ... this—"

"Hold on right there, Philippa! I never told you I'd come back for you or anything of the sort."

"You!" She spat at Tyler. "You were the only one in that rotten town who had any hopes of getting enough money to get away from it. We were going to be rich when you got your inheritance. We were moving to the city and build a fine house. And then you go off with *her*!"

Tyler and Mallory stood shocked to silence by Philippa's ravings.

Tyler spoke gently to the angry woman. "Philippa, I never promised you any of those things. You've dreamed them up in your head. I like Sand Creek, and I like our new settlement, and I plan to build a home there and live, but not with you. I'm sorry."

Philippa's face hardened even more. "I'll get out of there without you and your money, Tyler Newly. You just see if I don't." She turned and marched up the stairs.

"Whew!" Tyler breathed a sigh of relief when she was gone. "I never knew she had planned all those things about us. Honest, Mal, I never led her to believe I felt like that about her."

Mallory nodded in understanding. "I know. She's always gotten everything she wanted. I suppose she just expected to get you too. And your money."

"What money?" Tyler laughed.

Mallory just smiled at him. "Say, do you know where Sid is?"

Alarmed, Tyler asked, "Isn't he with you?"

Mallory frowned. "He was. I thought he came into the hotel with us and went to a room. I was so busy sorting out the women's rooms; I didn't pay much attention to him."

Tyler turned to the desk clerk. "Did a young boy, about this tall, with a … a … large cap pulled down over his eyes come in and get a key?"

The clerk leaned on the counter and drawled, "No, sir. Only people's come in so far is you and her"—he pointed to Mallory— "and that loud woman that just went up, and all them other women you're paying for rooms for."

Suddenly Tyler noticed the group of people standing around them watching and listening to all their business. Apparently the townspeople weren't used to this much excitement. Philippa's loud speech had drawn their attention, and now they'd have something to talk about for weeks.

Tyler felt his ears redden as the people looked at him curiously. The clerk's declaration that all the women were with him didn't help.

"There was one other fella, but he was tall, and he said he was a preacher," the clerk informed him.

"No young boy, though? You're sure?"

"I'd know if there was, mister."

Tyler pulled Mallory through the people to the boardwalk out front. The evening was setting in, and in the shadows Mallory could see the worry on Tyler's face.

"What is it, Tyler? What's going on?" she asked anxiously.

"Sid may be in trouble. I should have watched more closely! I just didn't think they'd try anything here!"

"Who, Ty? Who are you talking about?"

"And they tried to kill Amos too. I didn't think they'd go that far!" Tyler looked up and down the nearly empty street. "They can't be far. Mal, take care of the women. See to everything for me, okay?"

"But what's happened to Sid? What on earth are you talking about—someone trying to kill someone?" Mallory was trying to sort out Tyler's jumbled words.

"I've got to find her, Mallory. I've got to! If anything's happened to her, I'll—" And Tyler took off for the livery.

Mallory peered into the darkness where he'd gone. "What's—" Then her eyes widened. "*Her?*"

Chapter 26

Chicago

Amos could hear Stanwood's commanding tone clearly from the partially open door of his bedchamber. He felt helpless, a prisoner in his own bed by the wound that grazed his side from Hunter's attempt on his life. In a younger, stronger man the wound would seem minor, but in a man of his years, extreme caution was being taken to prevent any complications.

There she goes again! Amos listened to the sarcasm Stanwood used in criticizing the new maid's efforts. Why hadn't he paid attention before to how cruel and demeaning the woman was? He wondered now what kind of treatment Jade had received from the housekeeper. He tried to muffle his groan as he switched positions, but the nurse in the chair nearby the bed immediately stood and adjusted the covers around him. He scowled at her, but she made no response and her expression remained unchanged as she returned to her chair.

When will she get here? He thought again for the hundredth time.

Then Stanwood's voice rang out once more, and Amos's lips tightened at her words.

"I told you downstairs, Mrs. Crandall, that Mr. Granville is not receiving visitors and certainly not visitors who arrive at the back door." Her voice rose higher. "How dare you enter uninvited into the private quarters of his house! I shall call for a constable immediately to have you removed from the premises," she screeched.

"You do that, Mrs. Stanwood." Undaunted, Hazel Crandall knocked on the partly opened door. "Amos?" she asked softly.

"Come in! Come in!" Amos tried to raise himself up on the pillows, but the nurse was right there to push him gently back. Her stern features and strong hands were no match for the frail man, and he succumbed once again, but not without issuing his own command.

"I will speak with Mrs. Crandall in private." He dared the woman to argue with him by giving her a fierce scowl. The nurse eyed him speculatively then appraised Hazel as she stood, waiting, an amused smile almost hiding the concern in her eyes.

"I shall give you five minutes. Then he must rest," she instructed the visitor.

"Thank you." Hazel walked to the bed and placed a hand on Amos's arm. The amusement left her as soon as she saw the pale face on the pillow.

"Oh, Amos! I came as soon as I got word that you had been shot and that you wanted to see me. How are you?"

"Sit down, my dear. I'm sore but I'm going to be fine according to my doctor. However…I…I am *not* fine!" His expression pleaded with Hazel to understand.

Hazel pulled the nurse's chair closer to the bedside and reached for her old friend's hand. "You've faced death now, and you realize you're not ready. Is that it, Amos?"

Amos squeezed her hand and nodded. A moment passed while he composed himself then he spoke.

"When I lay there, shot, bleeding, waiting for help to come, I kept hearing in my mind the things that you and Jade and Palmer and even young Newly have been 'preaching' to me. And I argued with myself. I thought, 'But God will see how good I've been and how much money I've given to the poor and how respectable I am.' But then I remembered you saying, 'When will you know you've done enough? What if your goodness isn't enough?'" He paused and drew in a shaky breath. "I can't afford to not be sure about something as permanent as death, Hazel. I need to know for sure that God is going to accept me."

Hazel had tears in her eyes by the time Amos had finished speaking.

"I'm so happy to hear you say that, Amos!" She dabbed at her eyes and drew a small Bible from her bag. "Let me share with you what God says about our goodness. Here it says that 'all our righteousness is as filthy rags.'" She flipped some pages. "And here in Ecclesiastes, 'There is not a just man upon earth that doeth good and sinneth not.'

"Like I've said before, you can't expect your good to outweigh your bad as a measuring tool to get you into heaven because even your good is of no value in God's eyes. His Son Jesus Christ is the only good, perfect being, and it is *his* goodness that God sees. Because he was without sin, the Lord Jesus Christ was able to go to the cross for you, Amos. He took your sin for you—*became* sin—so that your sin would never more be a hindrance between you and God. Do you see that?"

Amos was watching Hazel with rapt attention. They were both startled when the nurse entered the room.

"Time to rest." Her voice brooked no argument. But she wasn't prepared for the vehement response from her patient.

"Leave!" he commanded. "I'll call you when I need you!"

The nurse, though shocked by his shout, began to shake her head.

"Please." Hazel rose and walked over to her. "We need more time. It is of upmost importance."

"Yes!" growled Amos from the bed.

The nurse looked between the two and noticed the Bible in Hazel's hands. Lowering her voice she said, "He's not going to die, you know."

"We need more time," Hazel repeated softly.

After a moment, the nurse nodded and left. Hazel returned to her chair and resumed their discussion as if the interruption never happened.

"So you see, Amos, Christ's death took care of your sin. His resurrection proves he is capable to overcome death and can offer life to us—eternal life with him in heaven. The key to accepting this is faith. I don't mean just believing that these facts are true; I mean that you must believe that the Lord Jesus Christ did this for you personally and accept by faith this gift to you." She turned to her Bible once again.

"Titus 3:5 says, 'Not by works of righteousness which we have done, but according to his mercy he saved us.'"

Tears flowed from Amos's eyes as he gripped Hazel's hand again. Several moments passed without either of them speaking; then Amos cleared his throat and began. "Thank you, my dear. Thank you for being so patient with me while you waited for me to understand and put my pride away and completely, humbly accept Jesus Christ as my Savior. I will trust him by *his* work on the cross, not my supposed goodness, to be my assurance of eternal life." He wiped at his eyes and chuckled. "God had to almost kill me to get me to become his child."

Hazel reached over to hug her dear friend and they talked together for a while longer before she reminded him that he needed more rest.

"Yes, send that bossy nurse back in." Amos grinned triumphantly. "I have something to tell her that might actually put a smile on her face! Say, I can hardly wait to tell Palmer ... and Tyler ... and ... and we need to let Jadyne know. I may even tell old Stanwood."

Hazel glowed with happiness as she left Amos. She could hear his excited voice talking to the nurse. *Thank you, Lord,* she prayed. *Please protect Jade and Tyler and the others now that Hunter has shown his evil intentions.*

As she walked back to the cottage she made up her mind. Entering the small home, she called, "Sidney! Sidney, where are you?"

Her red-haired son appeared in the room, eating an apple.

"Get our bags, Sidney. We're going to find Jadyne."

Chapter 27

Freesburg

Jade woke with a nauseous feeling. Her head ached, and she felt a lump through her cap. She lay still, gathering her thoughts and trying to remember what happened to her.

She had been running away from the man in the western hat. She winced as she remembered the blow she had received. So someone was with him and helped him. Now, where had they brought her?

Slowly she got to her knees. The dizzy, nauseous feeling waved over her again. She waited for it to pass then rose up onto her feet. Her head pounded, and she closed her eyes against the pain. She stood quietly waiting for relief, and while she waited, she realized where she was.

It was a barn or a stable, her nose told her. Now that she was more aware, she could hear the snorting of horses and smell the hay. She blinked to adjust her vision, and the pounding in her head receded a little.

She put out her hands until she found something solid. She was in one of the stalls. She felt along the edges, stumbling in the dark as she went until she found the opening. Now she could see the grayness of the outdoors between the boards and cracks of the walls. She headed toward the outside wall, hoping to find the doorway to get out of the barn, when a door creaked open behind her, exposing her in its light.

"Hunter! That kid's awake, and he's trying to leave!"

Jade scrambled to the wall in hopes that there was a back door to escape by. She was jerked back roughly by her shirt collar, and she made a strangling noise until she was released.

"I told you to watch him!"

"Will you shut up, Cecile! Give me a hand, will you? Ouch! Get some rope or something."

The man called Hunter twisted Jade's arm behind her back. She cried out, and he snarled, "Kick me again, and I'll break it!"

Cecile joined them. "I can't find any rope. It's too dark in there." She grabbed Jade's other arm to pull her along.

They struggled forward in silence until Jade's boot caught on the corner of the water trough, which was strategically placed under the barn's eaves. She fell forward, and her momentum carried Cecile along with her. Struggling to keep her balance, Jade pulled back sharply and shoved Cecile to the side. A splash and a scream followed as Cecile fell in the trough. Jade heard the man laughing on the other side of her.

"Quit your screeching, Cecile. Someone might hear you." He kept a firm grip on Jade as he helped the shivering woman from the icy water.

"I'll kill him!" Cecile yelled.

Hunter laughed some more. "Not yet you won't. I need some answers first. Come on. Let's get to the house. It's a good thing no one is living here at the moment."

Jade looked around in the gray light. There were no other homes nearby, and she couldn't see the town when she turned her head in all directions.

"Looking for something?" Hunter pulled her to the house while Cecile sloshed behind them muttering threats at the boy.

They entered the house, and Hunter pushed Jade into the corner and made her sit on the floor. The only furniture were two chairs and a table on which a lamp with a blackened chimney dimly illuminated the room. The leather pouches Jade had carried were there, and papers were strewn across the table.

Jade took a good look at the man named Hunter. He was the man from the train, the one she saw with Cecile and Wilbert behind the stables, and the same one who gave Wilbert money. *Hunter*. Suddenly she remembered. He was Cecile's brother, Amos Granville's nephew.

"I'm freezing to death, Hunter. Light the stove while I get changed, and hurry up about it." She glared at Jade and spoke through chattering teeth. "I'll give *you* a little swim before we leave and see how you like it."

Wisely, Jade said nothing. She pulled the cap down tighter and her collar up higher around her neck. Somehow she knew she would be in worse trouble if Cecile found out who she really was.

"Where's Tait?" Hunter asked Cecile. "He should have been here by now."

"I told him to get an extra horse and meet us in an hour, but it's been over that, so he probably got lost. How did you find out about this place anyway?" Cecile spoke from the next room in a shaking voice.

"I asked at the saloon if there were any places for sale around here." Hunter coaxed a flame in the stove and fed it some of the sticks from the pile left next to it. "I don't know. Tait seemed squeamish about you knocking the kid out. Think we can count on him?"

"He wants the money, doesn't he?"

"He's been useful. I couldn't have sneaked into the mansion to steal the stuff otherwise. And he kept it hidden well too."

Cecile returned in dry clothes and stood shivering by the small fire while her hair still dripped down her back. "So is the will in there?" she asked eagerly.

"All kinds of papers are here, so it has to be. I just haven't found it yet. Isn't it nice that old Uncle Amos is going to leave all his money to his dear niece and nephew?"

Hunter sat down at the table and began looking through the pouches while Jade watched with concern. Tyler hadn't entrusted the important papers to *her* care, had he? Surely he had safeguarded them better than that!

"What are those pictures of?" Cecile leaned over Hunter's shoulder for a better look.

"Cecile! Your hair is dripping on everything! Move!"

"Oooh! Look at these men, will ya? What's Tyler doing with these pictures? Here's one of him too." Cecile picked up the drawing of Tyler. "He's handsome, but not rich enough to suit me. Of course, I'll have enough money for both of us once we find that will."

"Take your picture and go fantasize over there. These papers are all wet now." Disgusted, Hunter shuffled through them. "Lists, names, I don't see any of Uncle Amos's papers here. What's this?"

He pulled a paper out of the bundle and read it with interest.

"Hey, Cecile. Wasn't that girl who was at Amos's dinner parties named Jadyne Crandall?"

"Why?" Cecile scowled.

Jade kept perfectly still, but her heart doubled its beating.

"Here's a paper full of information about her: name, age, address. Say, she's the one staying in Uncle's gardener's cottage. You know, the girl Tait is crazy about. I saw him get knocked down by her in the woods once when he got too fresh." He laughed.

"So? What's Tyler want with information about her?"

But Hunter's expression had changed. "Listen to this. She works for Uncle Amos as a maid." He looked questioningly at his sister. "Why would he have her come to his party if she was his maid?"

Cecile swung around to face her brother. "I remember her now! She was working the first day I came. She fixed my hair that day then showed up at the party that night as a guest. What's Uncle Amos trying to pull anyway? Is she some kind of spy?"

"There was a maid who nearly found me in the guest room one night. I was taking the silver candlesticks. If the butler hadn't shown up, she might have spotted me behind the drapery."

"Why does Tyler have this information about her? Are they both working for old Amos?"

Hunter scanned farther down the page. "Says here she has a brother about twelve years old named"—he looked at Jade— "Sidney."

Jade's heart thumped and her eyes were wide with fear. Why did Tyler have all that information about her? Where did he get it? From Amos?

Hunter stood and walked over to her. "Isn't it interesting that your name just happens to be Sidney too? I heard Newly call you that on the train. Are you one of Uncle Amos's spies too, Sidney?"

He reached down and grabbed Jade's collar. She tried to roll away from him, but he blocked her movements. He jerked her to her feet.

"Well, Sidney, if you work for Uncle Amos, then you know where his papers are." Hunter crouched down and stared nose to nose with Jade, but she kept her eyes lowered and her lips, though trembling, she tried to hold firm.

"So, you're going to tell us—Hey!"

Jade's eyes darted to his face, and she tried to back away from the look in his eyes, but he still held her collar firmly.

"What is it, Hunter?" Cecile stood up.

"This is no boy!" Hunter's hands combatted with Jade's as he pulled off her cap and scarf and ripped open the buttons on her huge overcoat. "She's trussed up like a turkey!" He laughed. Ruthlessly, he pulled pins out of her hair while she gasped in pain, and the snarled mass of copper descended to her shoulders.

"Jadyne Crandall!" Cecile spat the words.

"So you and Newly are in on this together! We were probably set up, Cecile. Newly knew I'd try to get the papers from the boy, so he set him up as bait. We've got to get out of here. Now!"

"What about the will?"

"We'll get it, but not here."

"What about her?"

"She's coming with us for now."

"Why? Just get rid of her! She knows our plans."

"I can use her for bargaining with Newly, you idiot! Now go get the horses from the barn."

Cecile glared at her brother. "I'm not going out there by myself. You go!"

Hunter was exasperated. "I can't trust you to guard her. She'd get away from you in a minute and run for Newly. Here, take the lantern if you're such a chicken, but go!"

Cecile grumbled as she threw a shawl over her wet hair. She picked up the lantern and headed out the door.

Darkness filled the room as soon as the lantern and Cecile were gone. Jade's arm was growing numb under Hunter's tight grasp. She tried to pull free, but he yanked her toward him and locked his other arm around her, twisting hers until she gasped in pain.

"You're not going anywhere, Miss Crandall." Hunter's voice was quiet but steely. "Imagine. The girl I followed in the woods and hoped to have time to pursue lands right here in my arms. It's like a gift from heaven."

His fingers began working the snarls from her hair. The pulling brought tears to her eyes, but she didn't let out a sound. Somehow she had to get away from him. She squirmed in his arms, but Hunter's grip tightened and he grabbed a handful of her hair and pulled her head back. Jade gasped in pain, and his mouth crushed down on hers.

She fought him then. She fought and kicked, and when his head pulled back, she took a deep breath of air and let out a piercing scream. His hand clamped down on her mouth and nose, and she struggled to breathe. Then he swung her in front of him as the door burst open and crashed into the wall.

A dark figure dove through the doorway and hit Hunter and Jade on the legs. They fell together, and Hunter's hold was broken. Jade rolled free and gasped for more air while the two men struggled in the darkness.

They rose up in the black room, and Jade heard the thud and smack of punches hitting flesh and bone. The scuffling of boots and grunting as they exchanged blows told her they were moving toward the glow of the small stove. There was a crash, and she saw sparks and coals scatter on the floor, and she heard one of the men yell out in pain.

The door of the stove hung crookedly, and the red coals illumined the figures. With a glad cry, Jade recognized Tyler and knew she had to help. She got to her feet and stumbled over an overturned chair. Picking it up, she lifted it over her head and waited until the men broke apart; then she threw the chair with all her might at Hunter's head. The resounding crack and groan followed by a tremendous thud as he hit the floor told her that her aim had been successful.

Tyler brushed the chair off the fallen man and lifted him by the shirtfront to deliver one more punch. Hunter slumped to the floor, and Tyler stood awkwardly, taking in deep breaths of air. He started to turn to Jade but swung about as another man ran into the house.

"Mr. Newly? Is everything all right? We got the woman in the barn while she was getting the horses. She scratched the sheriff, and he's ready to make her walk back to town he's so mad. Are you all right, sir?"

"I'm fine, Dawson. I … believe that's … Hunter Granville you'll find there." He pointed to the crumpled man. "Put him over a horse, will you?"

As the men were talking, Jade dropped to the floor and frantically searched for her cap with her hands. She just found it when Dawson asked, "Is the boy okay, Mr. Newly?"

"I think so, Dawson. We'll be right out. You go on ahead."

The man named Dawson dragged Hunter out the doorway; then Tyler turned around. Jade was struggling to stuff her hair up into the cap for lack of pins. She could see Tyler's outline in the dark room with the glowing coals behind him.

"Are you all right?" he asked, and she heard the tremor in his voice.

With a small cry, Jade ran to him and threw her arms around him. His arms came around her uncertainly, but as she hugged him tighter, he pressed her closer to him while he gently pulled the cap off and released her hair once more.

She felt him kiss the top of her head, and with her face pressed against his shirt, she asked in a muffled voice, "How long have you known?"

"Forever," he whispered.

She pulled back slightly and looked up into his shadowed face. "Really? From the first?"

"Well, no." He pulled her close again. "But I knew before we left on the train. Remember, I have two brothers at home about Sid's age. They're a lot different than you."

"But why didn't you—"

They both turned as a lantern bobbed by the window and in the doorway. Jade pulled away and stepped a little behind Tyler as the man with the lantern looked at them curiously.

"How's the lad, Newly? Is he hurt?" He caught sight of Jade then and exclaimed, "Oh ho! So it's not a lad. Well, I can see you two are busy. We'll just go on ahead of you. Here, you may need this." He set the lantern down and winked at Jade as he left.

"Thanks, Sheriff. I'll talk to you in the morning."

Tyler turned again to Jade, but she backed away, and her hands fumbled and flitted over her hair nervously. He held out his hand to her and waited.

The light suddenly made Jade bashful. She looked down at her attire and felt her snarled hair. She was disheveled and in need of a bath and very much aware that she looked frightful. She glanced at Tyler, but he only watched her without speaking, giving her time. Then with an exclamation, she stepped quickly to him.

"You're bleeding!"

"Am I?"

"Yes, here." She pulled a handkerchief from her pocket and pressed his temple. As she came fully into the light, he saw that her lip was bleeding as well.

His voice was tight. "He hurt you, didn't he?"

Jade touched her mouth. "He ... he ..."

"I know. I saw from the window. I'm sorry I wasn't here sooner." He gently touched her lips with his thumb while his hand cupped her chin. "I love you, Jadyne."

She smiled softly. "Jade."

His eyes returned the smile warmly. "Jade, a precious jewel." He bent down and gently brushed her lips with his. "Will you become my wife, Jade? Your mother has already given me permission to ask you."

Jade backed away, nearly tripping on the broken chair. "*My mother?*"

Tyler laughed softly. "After I met you at Amos's that first night, I found out all I could about you. When I realized it was you dressed like Sid, I didn't know what to think, but Amos filled me in."

"*Amos?*"

"I think he's been matchmaking behind our backs and at the same time keeping tabs on our business. He used you to find out about me, and he let me in on your family's hardships so I wouldn't betray your identity." Tyler shook his head. "When I first came to the city, I must have sounded money and power hungry. He was testing me to see if it would matter to me that your family was no longer wealthy."

"Does it?"

"I would want to marry you if you were the wealthiest or poorest woman in the world, Jade." He looked uncomfortable for a moment. "I don't have much to offer. I don't even have a house yet, and I've seen what you've had. It scares me to think I can never provide all that for you."

Jade started to protest, but Tyler held up his hand.

"I've also seen the cottage you're in now." He shook his head. "I'm not sure we'll be able to start out with anything as elaborate as that even. I may only be able to provide you with a small cabin this year. But if we work together, I know we can make a home that will give us happiness because our love went into it."

Jade's eyes glowed as she watched Tyler's face.

"Of course, you haven't answered my question yet," he said pointedly.

"You really want to marry me?" she asked. "Even though I've been trying to fool you with my disguises?" She looked at the papers on the table. "You even knew I was the maid, didn't you?"

Tyler nodded. "Before Amos would tell me anything, I had Mr. Simonson hire someone to find out about you for me. When I learned that you were actually working for Amos, I confronted him about you."

"Why?"

"I had to know how to find you, Jade. I wasn't about to leave that city without asking you to marry me."

"And you even talked to my mother?"

He nodded. "She was wonderful! I told her everything about me and the settlement. I promised her I'd return with you, or 'Sid,' and marry you there, if you'd have me. Which, by the way, you still haven't told me." He held his breath while he watched the confusing emotions flit over her face.

Then her eyes looked steadily into his, and she answered, "I think I fell in love with you the first afternoon I saw you. I was the maid at lunch, and I watched your face as you told Amos about Palmer accepting the Lord."

"You were the maid then?"

"You never really looked at me or any of the servants at first." She smiled.

"I was acting on what I thought was good advice," he admitted sheepishly. He waited for a few moments longer while they looked at each other. "Do you love me enough to marry me?"

"Yes, Tyler, but do we have to wait until we get back to the city?"

He laughed and held out his arms. She rushed to him again, and they held each other for a long time. When, after a tender kiss, he finally released her, Jade laughed nervously and said, "I never imagined I would be proposed to in an abandoned house, wearing boy's clothes, and in need of a bath and a comb."

"You're beautiful," Tyler stated, and Jade knew he meant it. "We better get you back to the hotel. I imagine we'll have a lot of explaining to do to everyone."

Jade picked up her cap. "Mallory knows, and so does Cora. They guessed right away. I wonder how many people I really fooled."

Tyler gathered up his papers and put them back in the leather pouches. Then he blew out the lantern and asked, "Why did you pretend to be Sid? Amos said it was your idea in the first place."

Jade squeezed Tyler's hand in the darkness. "I guess I wanted to find out as much about you as you did about me."

They went outside and saw that the sheriff had brought out the horse from the barn that Jade must have been on to get there. She suddenly remembered the reason they were there.

"Tyler, how did you know to come here?"

He helped her mount after a quick kiss. "Amos's groom, what's his name? Tait? He found me at the sheriff's office and told me all about Hunter and Cecile. He said when they knocked the boy out, he wanted out of the deal. He said he was supposed to meet them here. I don't know how long it would have taken us to find you without his help."

"Wil isn't really bad like they are. I think he just hoped to get paid a lot of money."

"Well, he's headed back to the city on tomorrow's train. He said he would tell Amos about letting Hunter into the mansion to steal things. I think now we can trust him."

"I'm glad. And I'm glad the papers are okay too."

Tyler chuckled as they walked the horses on the moonlit road. "There were no papers, Jade."

"What?" She stopped her horse and stared at him.

"Amos and I set up the bait for Cecile. You see, Amos suspected foul play in his brother's death—you know, Cecile and Hunter's parents. His investigators didn't find anything to suggest that their accident was anything but an accident, but he wasn't sure. When Cecile showed up and things turned up missing, Amos began to suspect that Hunter was working with her to get his money. We thought up the business about the will to tempt them to make a move."

Jade was incredulous. "You and Amos were in this together?"

Tyler nodded. "It was Hunter who looked through our things on the train. I was awake the whole time watching him. By the way, you look beautiful when you sleep."

Embarrassed, Jade exclaimed, "That's another thing! If you knew who I was, why did you insist on sharing a berth with me?"

"I couldn't let you share with someone else, could I? And I certainly wasn't going to let you sleep out in one of the cars alone. I promised your mother I'd take good care of you."

"And when did you talk to my mother?" Jade couldn't help being sidetracked.

"The night after Amos's dinner party, just before we left. I went to the cottage after your light was out and spoke with her then."

"She knew. That's why she packed my dresses," Jade mused.

"Anyway, back to Hunter. I was hoping he'd steal some papers then so I could accuse him and have him arrested here in Freesburg."

"But I scared him off."

"You scared me right off the bed!"

Jade laughed. "But now they're in jail and will be sent back to Amos?"

"They'll go back to Chicago, and Amos will press charges for thievery and attempted murder."

"*Murder?*"

"I got a wire from Amos when we arrived here. Someone, he believes it was Hunter, shot at him just before the train left, and Amos is fairly certain that Hunter and Cecile had something to do with their parents' 'accident.'"

"Is he all right?" Jade asked anxiously.

"According to the telegram, he's recovering fine."

Jade shuddered again at the thought of Hunter kissing her. He had tried to kill Amos!

"It's okay now, Jadyne." Tyler moved his horse closer to hers and touched her arm. "He'll be fine. He's a tough old gentleman."

"Remember what you said about him being afraid of dying? He's not saved. What if he had been killed?"

"I guess we can just thank the Lord he's been given another chance. I've been praying for his salvation ever since I met him. He reminds me of how Palmer was, trying to earn his way to heaven."

They talked quietly until they reached the hotel. Tyler helped Jade down from her horse, and she slumped wearily against him.

"You're exhausted. Here." He picked her up in his arms and carried her up the steps.

Mallory hurried out as soon as she saw them. "Finally! I was going crazy waiting for word that you had found her…him…" She saw Jade's hair was loose, and she grinned at Tyler. "It's about time you two stopped pretending."

"Meet the future Mrs. Newly, Mal."

"Congratulations! Mind if I say I'm not surprised?"

Jade's arms circled Tyler's neck, and she spoke quietly to him. "Maybe I should go in on my own two feet, Ty."

He shook his head. "I'm not putting you down until I get you to a room. Mal, where's Jade sleeping?"

Mallory opened the door and led the way. "She's sharing with me. There are no bunks in this hotel." She pretended to glare at Tyler.

On the way past the surprised clerk, Mallory ordered hot water to be brought up for Jade's bath. When they reached the room, Tyler set Jade down gently but didn't release her. He looked pointedly at Mallory, and she said in a disgusted voice but with a smile on her face, "Okay, I'll be in the hallway, but hurry, Ty, the poor girl can hardly stand up."

The door closed, and Tyler pulled Jade close to him again.

"As soon as we get these women to the settlement, I want to take you to meet my family. Then we'll go back to the city and get married. I was thinking, do you think your mom and Sidney would move out here with us?"

Jade smiled and hugged him. "Oh, Tyler! Wouldn't that be wonderful?"

He smiled at her pleasure. "I love you, Jadyne Kathleen Crandall, soon to be Newly."

"You do know all about me," she said as she raised her head to kiss him good night.

A knock on the door brought them reluctantly apart. Mallory poked her head in.

"Time's up, Ty. Now, scoot and let me take care of her."

Tyler squeezed Jade's fingers. "I'll see you tomorrow. Night, Mal, and thanks." He gave her a kiss on the cheek then shut the door behind him.

Mallory looked critically at Jade. "You've been through a lot by the looks of you, and you smell like a barn! Want to tell me about it while I fix your bath?"

Freesburg

Mallory tiptoed out of the room the next morning and left Jade to her sleep. She descended the stairs and stepped into the hotel lobby and was immediately face-to-face with Philippa Gray.

"I saw him come out of your room last night, Mallory," Philippa hissed.

"What are you talking about, Philippa?" Mallory asked quietly. She stared down the other woman until Philippa's eyes darted away.

"He won't amount to anything anyway. I've found a real gentleman, someone with style, someone who appreciates me." Philippa laughed scornfully. "But don't think you took Tyler from me. I could have had him if I wanted." She began tugging on her gloves. "I'm leaving for Chicago today. I've sent a wire to my mother, and I've let her know about you and Tyler, so you can forget about trying to get away with your infidelity. The whole town will know. My mother has been wanting to get back at yours and Tyler's for years. Now she can!"

"What did you say to her?" Mallory's face had reddened, and she was trying to control her temper.

"I have to leave now, Mallory." Philippa crossed to the door and took the arm of a distinguished-looking man. "I'm ready now, Wilbert. I'm so excited to see your big city with you." The couple walked out of the hotel with Philippa's parasol twirling behind them.

"What's Philippa doing with Wil Tait?" Tyler asked Mallory as he came up behind her.

"Who?"

"Wil Tait. He's Amos Granville's groom."

"His what?"

"Groom. You know, he works in the stables and chauffeurs Mr. Granville and his guests."

Mallory started to laugh. She looked after Philippa, who was twirling her parasol as she clung to Wilbert Tait's arm, and she laughed harder.

"What's so funny?"

Mallory gasped and caught her breath. "Philippa is going to Chicago with this 'distinguished gentleman of style who appreciates her.' Wait 'til she finds out who he really is."

Tyler grinned. "Well, maybe she'll come back with an appreciation for what we have here at home after she's seen the city. She needs some reality in her life. Everything has been a dream for her." He turned back to Mallory. "Is Jade up yet?"

"No, Tyler, and don't go disturbing her. The poor girl is exhausted. I bet she didn't sleep a wink on that train, what with watching for trouble and sharing a berth with you. That alone would give a girl nightmares!" She ducked as Tyler feigned a punch at her. "Hey, where is everyone? Have all the ladies come down already?"

Tyler sighed deeply. "I have some good news and some bad news."

Mallory's eyebrows arched up.

"The good news is that Malcolm and Hermine decided to get married."

Mallory smiled and nodded. "It looked like that might happen all right."

"Malcolm spoke to me early this morning. The poor fella was feeling guilty about taking one of the women away from the men at the settlement, so I asked him, 'Do you want one of them to marry her, then?' He looked so horrified. I had to laugh. I sent them off to the town's preacher to get married before we leave. He can't really perform his own ceremony, you know."

"So that's where everyone is. What's the bad news?"

Tyler gave her a sheepish look. "I don't know if you'll think it's such bad news," he admitted. "Sally Smith is leaving on the train."

"Good news!" declared Mallory.

"Yeah, well, I know Sid, I mean Jade didn't want her along, and I guess you didn't either, but I was hoping to give her a chance at a new life." He shrugged his shoulders. "She left with some man from town."

Mallory just gave him an I-told-you-so kind of look.

"Well, something else we have to consider here is that we're now one bride short." He let the words sink in.

Mallory shook her head. "No, I made my decision. No longer will I chase after Michael Trent. If he is so willing to marry someone he doesn't know when I've been under his nose all these years, then he'll never want me thrust on him this way. And goodness! I wouldn't want him to *have* to take me. What kind of marriage would that be? No, you can get the idea of me being one of your silly brides right out of your head."

Tyler rubbed his chin. "You're still coming to the settlement, aren't you?"

"Yes, I'll come. Ty!" Suddenly she grabbed his arm. "Lucy and Dugan could still get together!"

Tyler looked doubtful. "Mal, Dugan never has said anything about Lucy. In fact, of all the men, he was one of the most eager to get a mail-order kind of bride."

"The fool! I'll have to have a talk with him once we get there."

Chapter 28

Sand Creek

The main street of Sand Creek was already bustling with activity when Michael rode in. He saw at least six people. A record. He had stopped out at the farm first to see his parents; now he was going to catch up to Dugan and Gabe and ride with them to the way station to meet Tyler. He wasn't busy at the settlement at the moment, and he convinced himself and the others that he was needed here. Of course they all thought of reasons why they should come too, but Palmer put a stop to that.

"You have plenty to do to get ready before they come, and if you don't have enough work on your own things, I can give you some of mine," he told them. "Michael should go and order the rest of the supplies we need anyway. Besides, it's his turn."

The others grumbled good-naturedly and threatened Michael not to take the prettiest girl before they had a chance. But he was hoping to do just that.

He spotted his brother Gabe and Dugan Riley outside Nolan's mercantile. They were lounging on the bench, and it looked like they had a bag of penny candies they were busily devouring. Michael shook his head.

"You two look like you're playing hooky from school," he said as he swung down from his horse.

"Mike! What are you doing in town?"

"I'm checking up on you two to make sure you bring back what you were sent for."

"Ha! See, Dugan. He wants first pick!"

"Oh, I'm not worried about first pick. Once the women get a look at you two, they'll be relieved to see a handsome lumberjack like me."

The men laughed together, and Michael stuck his hand in the bag and helped himself to their supply. They visited for a while; then Gabe said, "I'll go check at the telegraph office again to see if Ty wants us to leave yet."

Dugan stopped him. "Bud is going to kick you out if you bother him anymore this morning. He said to wait until he lets us know. Now, sit down!"

"I wish Ty would hurry up and get on that stage," Gabe complained.

As if wishing made it possible, Bud stepped out of the telegraph office and signaled to the men. They jumped up together, and it became a race to see which one of them made it across the street first.

"You have news, Bud?" Gabe asked nonchalantly.

The balding man scowled at the three. "This just came in. Now maybe you'll give me some peace today."

Gabe grabbed the message Bud held out and eagerly read its contents. "Time to go, fellas. Let's get our coach and horses and move!"

"Hold on!" Bud held up his hand. "Have any of you seen Mrs. Gray yet this morning? I have a message for her too."

"I assume it's from my daughter." Violet spoke from behind the men. Quickly the three removed their hats.

"Good morning, ma'am."

"Morning, Mrs. Gray."

"Ma'am."

She accepted the message, and as she read it, her face whitened. The men awkwardly tried to excuse themselves, but she stopped them with her hand.

"I think you gentlemen will find this most interesting." Violet's voice was bitter and hard.

They turned back to her and politely waited although they were anxious to be on their way.

"It seems that your friend Tyler Newly has decided to make your sister Mallory"—she looked directly at Dugan— "his mistress."

The three men appeared thunderstruck, and Dugan's face darkened in anger. "I don't much care for your accusation, Mrs. Gray. You know that is not true."

"My daughter is not a liar, Mr. Riley. She is so heartbroken she has gone on to Chicago to recover herself." Her eyes were hard and her features no longer pretty. "Your two families have disgraced themselves in this community. And you God-fearing, religious people." She sneered.

Dugan took a deep breath, but Michael clamped a hand on his shoulder.

Gabe planted himself in front of Violet. "Tyler and Mallory have done nothing wrong, Mrs. Gray. I'd stake my life on that."

"Do what you want, young man. The fact is, my daughter saw them in the same hotel room in Freesburg. Ask them to explain that." She turned on her heel and strode purposefully down the boardwalk.

"She's going to spread that story all over Sand Creek," growled Gabe.

"Come on. Let's go," commanded Michael.

Dugan watched the back of the angry woman. "It's not true. It can't be."

Chapter 29

Freesburg

Jade stepped into the hotel lobby, hoping she had enough courage to face the next important moments. She was dressed in a traveling suit her mother had packed for her, a dark-green, full-skirted dress that tucked into her waist. A short jacket of the same color and a stylish matching hat completed her outfit.

She had pinned her freshly cleaned hair into a cascade of coppery curls that dangled in orderly disarray to her shoulders. Her eyes, no longer hidden by the huge cap, reflected the color of her garments, and the very faintest of freckles crossed her nose. She bit her soft lower lip in nervousness as the group of people waiting there looked at her curiously. She prayed for Tyler to quit staring and to cross the room to her.

They had decided the best thing to do was to tell the others the truth right away about her masquerade and go on from there. She held her breath as Tyler finally reached her side and took her hand. He turned to the women and Malcolm.

"Ladies, I have an announcement to make before we leave on the stage. First of all, let me congratulate Pastor and Mrs. Malcolm Tucker on their marriage." He extended a hand to the red-faced preacher and shook his heartily. "May God bless your lives together in his service."

He turned back to Jade with a smile and took her hand again. "Now, I would like to introduce you to the future Mrs. Newly, my bride-to-be, Miss Jadyne Crandall."

Mallory grinned and jumped up to give Jade a big hug. Cora winked at Jade, and the others smiled timidly at her.

Tyler looked down at the floor for a moment then spoke again. "Miss Crandall may look a little familiar to you, and there's a good reason for that."

Jade swallowed and felt Tyler's hand tighten on hers. The women were studying her features curiously. She saw one or two shake their heads.

"Jade has been with us the whole trip, but you have known her as my young helper Sidney."

There was a general intake of breath, and all eyes again studied her. Melody, Pearl, and Leigh looked impressed, but Jade saw disapproval cross Gwyneth's pretty face. A unanimous question of *why* was evident on all their faces.

"Before you start asking a million questions, let me explain," Tyler said. "Miss Crandall was working with me in an effort to apprehend some thieves who followed us from Chicago. No—" He held up a hand. "They were not after any of your belongings but rather some important papers of mine. I am happy to say that last night the thieves were put into the Freesburg jail, and they will be sent on their way back to Chicago today. Miss Crandall's disguise was an important asset in catching the culprits."

There was silence for a moment while this news was digested. Mallory grinned at Jade, and Jade felt herself smiling in relief that it was over. She heard Melody say, "Well done!" And Leigh and Pearl added their approval.

"But you shared a berth on the train!" Gwyneth's shocked voice lay open Jade's worst fears. She glanced at Tyler and saw his mouth set. He made to answer, but Cora intervened.

"Of course, Winnie, don't you see? That would have to be part of the act to catch the robbers. Oh, I think it is all very exciting! You did such a wonderful job, Miss Crandall. I'm sure not even your own mother would have recognized you. You'll have to tell us all about it on the way."

"And congratulations to the two of you!" Malcolm now extended his hand to Tyler, who took it with a grateful, "Thanks."

"Yes, congratulations! When's the wedding?"

As the women surrounded Jade with good wishes and questions, she felt she could finally release her pent-up breath. She returned their smiles with genuine warmth, and when Cora was near enough, she whispered a heartfelt, "Thank you!" in her ear.

The stage was finally ready to leave. It turned out that Hermine, the blushing bride, was an excellent rider, and she chose to ride horseback beside her new husband. Adequate food and rest plus being in love seemed to have renewed her strength. Mallory caused a slight stir when she donned her buckskins to ride.

"It's the most comfortable way I know," she explained. "Besides, I'm home now. I can wear what I want."

And Tyler would also ride alongside the coach.

"If I would have known I could ride horseback instead of in the coach, I would have dressed differently," Jade told him.

"I like the way you're dressed just fine," Tyler answered with admiration glowing in his eyes. "But you can change at the way station and ride after that if you'd like. I know I'd like it."

So Jade entered the coach somewhat reluctantly along with Cora and Gwyneth. Melody, Pearl, and Leigh sat across from them, and they were ready to go.

The rocking coach bounced along over the rough roads, and the spring sun shone warmly on the budding countryside. The ladies visited pleasantly among themselves. They seemed to accept Jade as one of them, due mostly to Cora's genuine friendliness. Gwyneth avoided speaking directly to Jade, but the others ignored her rudeness. Presently Jade became drowsy, and despite the jouncing of the coach, she slept.

She awoke with a start when Melody tapped her on the arm. "I'm sorry to disturb your rest, Miss Crandall, but we're nearly at the way station. Mr. Newly just called to us as he and Miss Riley rode on ahead."

Jade thanked her and straightened her stiff neck and back with a groan. "Please, all of you, call me Jade. It's short for Jadyne."

The ladies smiled, and everyone began straightening hats and adjusting jackets. Gwyneth leaned out the window then quickly pulled her head in and exclaimed, "There's another stage there, and three men are waiting beside it!"

Immediately the women strained to get a look at the men. Leigh poked at her hair nervously, and Cora yanked her coat together and began buttoning it with shaky fingers. Jade hid a smile as she assured Melody that her hat was indeed on at an attractive angle.

The coach rolled to a stop, and Jade watched with interest as Tyler swung off his horse and then turned to help Mallory down. He had a huge grin on his face, and he said something to Mallory that made her laugh. His hands were still on her waist when one of the three men, the tallest one, clamped a hand on his shoulder and spun him around.

Tyler spoke with delight. "Michael!" But the tall man cut off his words with a punch to the chin that sent Tyler sprawling in the dirt.

"Michael!" yelled Mallory. "What did you go and do that for?"

Tyler sat up and gingerly touched his jaw. His face was a puzzled mixture of anger and amusement.

Michael looked at Mallory. "Get on your horse. We're going for a ride." His voice was tight and low.

"What? Are you crazy or something?" She looked at Dugan and Gabe, who appeared just as astonished as the rest of them.

"Either get on your horse, or you're riding with me." Michael's expression was dark and angry.

"I'm not going anywhere with you, Michael Trent. What's the matter with you, anyway?" She glared back at the man.

"Fine!"

Michael grabbed Mallory and threw her up on his horse. Before she could scramble off the other side, he grabbed the reins and mounted. Then he spurred the horse away at a gallop.

Tyler stared after them in disbelief. "What was that all about?" he questioned Dugan and Gabe. The two men grinned at each other and helped Tyler get up.

Gabe said, "I think I know, and I think I'll tell you, but first, don't you think we better help these nice ladies out of the coach?"

Mallory stopped struggling as the horse raced down the trail; she was too experienced a rider to upset a horse running at a gallop. Presently Michael reined in the horse as they stopped by the river.

Mallory was prepared. As soon as the horse stopped, she slipped off its back and started walking with an angry stride back to the way station. Michael's long legs overtook her, and he planted himself in front of her. She stopped and then moved sideways and marched on. He blocked her again. The maneuvering went on until Mallory threw up her hands.

"What? What do you want? Why are you acting like this?"

Michael crossed his arms and leaned over to look directly into her face. "What's going on between you and Ty?"

"Me and Ty?" Astonishment flooded her face.

"Yes, you and Ty. Tell me the truth."

"The truth about what? What's wrong with you, Michael?"

He threw his arms wide and began pacing in front of her. She watched him, and the beginnings of understanding appeared on her face.

"What have you heard?" she asked cautiously.

Michael stopped again. "Violet Gray got a telegram from Philippa," he said in an accusing voice.

"Oh!" Mallory was beginning to see. She noticed a large rock nearby and sat down.

Michael followed her. "I see you know what I'm talking about."

"Maybe. I'm not sure. You better fill me in a little more." A tinge of anger shaded Mallory's words.

"Did Philippa see or did she not see Tyler come out of your hotel room?" Michael demanded.

"I guess she did," admitted Mallory.

Michael grabbed his hat off his head and raked his fingers through his hair. He slapped the hat against his leg, startling the peaceful chirping of the nearby birds. Bluntly, he asked, "Are you his mistress?"

Mallory jumped to her feet, and the birds flew out of the bushes with a screech. "How dare you think such a thing, Michael Trent! How long have you known Tyler and me? All our lives! You know the kind of man Tyler is, and I had hoped you knew me better than that." She glared at him. "Of course it isn't true!"

"But what—"

"Philippa Gray is a snobbish, jealous person. She would twist anything to her advantage." Mallory paused to catch her breath. "Ty was in my room saying good night to his bride-to-be. I was the chaperone, you might say."

Michael was shocked. "Bride-to-be? You mean, Ty is marrying one of the women?"

"She wasn't one of *your* mail-order brides, Michael. Don't worry. There's still one for you," she said bitterly. "Can we get back now?"

"Mal, I'm awfully sorry. It's just that—"

"Forget it, Michael! You know, I would expect this kind of behavior from Dugan or…or…Buck, but not you. Why the big-brother act all of a sudden?" She was still angry at his accusation.

"Well, I—"

"I mean, it's not like you've ever cared about me, so it must be Tyler. Why didn't you drag Tyler out here to scold? You could have punched him some more."

"Mallory, listen—"

"I want to go back." Sudden tears sprang into Mallory's eyes. She sniffed and brushed them away with the back of her hand. Michael gently took her arm.

"Leave me alone, Michael." She pulled away and started walking back again.

Michael caught her easily, and he looked into her tear-stained face. "I'm really sorry for what I said, Mal. You're right. I do know better, but will you let me explain something to you?"

Mallory sniffed again, and Michael pulled out a handkerchief for her. She took it without looking at him. "What?"

Michael released his hold on her and took a deep breath. "When Mrs. Gray told us what Philippa's message said, I felt like I had been kicked in the stomach. I didn't want to believe it, but my mind kept asking, 'What if it's true?' I tried to convince myself that I was feeling this awful pain in my gut because of Tyler, but it was more than that."

Mallory twisted the wet handkerchief in her hands as she listened, wide-eyed, to Michael.

"I didn't talk much to the guys on the way here, but I did a lot of praying. I asked the Lord to show me why I was feeling the way I was. I couldn't understand it.

"Then I saw you and Ty come riding up. You looked almost like a boy in those buckskins, but you were mighty pretty with your hair all braided like that and flying out behind you. You had a smile on your face." Michael paused, finding it difficult to continue. Mallory waited in uncertainty.

"When I saw Tyler holding you, and you were laughing together, something cracked inside of me. I couldn't stand the thought of you with anyone but me. I guess what I'm trying to say is … I love you, Mal." He turned to look at her.

"You *what?*"

"I love you. I think I have for a long time."

"Michael." Mallory closed her eyes for a moment and put out a hand to hold him away. "When I heard you sent for a bride, something in me died. I had an awful struggle with myself until I finally gave it over to the Lord. He gave me peace and the ability to accept the fact that you didn't want me. Now … now you've turned everything upside down again. I don't know what to believe anymore." Her hand dropped.

Michael took a step closer to her. "You can believe me when I say I love you, Mallory, and I want you to be my wife. I can't believe I was such a fool not to know before! Do you think you could learn to love me again?"

Mallory looked carefully at Michael and saw the truth in his eyes. Tears filled her own again. "You don't know how long I've waited for you to love me," she whispered.

His finger came up and caught the tear that ran down her cheek. "Could you learn to love me, Mal?" he asked again.

"I guess I never stopped loving you, Michael. I loved you enough to give you up."

He drew her close, and her arms went around him. "I always thought of you as a little kid, but now I see you're a beautiful woman, despite that outfit," he gently teased.

Mallory laughed up at him, but her laughter faded as she saw she was about to be kissed for the first time. Michael's lips gently touched hers. Then he pulled her close and kissed her again. When he released her, they stared at each other in amazement.

"You're definitely not a little kid anymore," he said.

The others were sitting down to a meal when Michael and Mallory opened the door of the way station. All heads turned to them, and Mallory felt her face grow hot. Michael put his arm around her and walked purposefully to Tyler. He held out his hand.

"I'm really sorry, Ty. Please forgive me."

Tyler winked at Mallory. "I guess you had a good reason, Mike. Is there anything the two of you have to tell us?"

Michael grinned at his cousin. "Everyone! Mallory has agreed to become my wife."

Gabe rose from beside Leigh Sheldon at the table and slapped his brother on the back. "After all this, you picked old Mal anyway, huh?"

Dugan reached for his sister and embraced her. "Best to you both," he said as he shook Michael's hand. "But I don't envy you getting outrode and outshot by your own wife. You know my sister!"

Jade watched the good-natured teasing and saw the way Michael flung his arm around Mallory's shoulders.

She frowned slightly, but Mallory looked enraptured, so she also rose and opened her arms to the happy woman.

"Oh, Jade! Only God could have worked out a mess like this one," Mallory said softly in her ear.

Tyler stepped in next for his hug, and the other women and Malcolm and Hermine offered their wishes to the happy couple. Gwyneth's remark was heard by a few, "I guess he's no longer on the list."

"There's still enough left for all of you." Tyler laughed. He then introduced Jade with a great deal of pride to his best friend, and the meal resumed.

Jade liked Michael Trent. She watched him look lovingly at the buckskin-clad woman beside him. He looked relieved and happy at the same time, and yet Jade saw another emotion there that bothered her. He seemed … resolved.

As soon as they were finished, Tyler said they needed to get ready to leave. The baggage had to be transferred to Dugan and Gabe's coach. They would travel until nightfall and stop at a cabin along the way where arrangements had been made with the older couple living there to board them for the night.

Tyler brought Jade her bag. "You did say you would like to ride with me," he said hopefully.

Smiling, she quickly went to change into a split skirt for the ride. She hurried back outside and found that Gabe had elected to take her place in the coach.

"I figured I could get to know you ladies better on the way, and I can tell you heaps of stories about all the other fellas." He grinned most handsomely as he helped each lady inside. Jade noticed with a smile that he made sure he sat beside Leigh.

Dugan growled, "Well, get aboard, then, you ladies' man. But remember, we switch places soon."

The entourage headed out. Michael and Mallory took the lead riding side by side like a finely matched pair of steeds. Malcolm and Hermine followed with their horses close together. Next was the coach, and Jade smiled as she heard the ladies giggle at some outlandish thing Gabe had just said.

"Happy?" Tyler asked as he reached for her hand. They rode far back in the rear to avoid the dust, and Jade was thankful for the privacy. She nodded as she smiled at the man who would soon be her husband.

"More happy than I have a right to be after all my deceit," she teased. Then she grew serious. "My life has taken so many turns in this last year that I'm having trouble keeping up. My father dying, the loss of our money, becoming a 'working girl,' dressing like a boy, and now engaged to be married and live here in this beautiful country." She gazed with pleasure around her. "The Lord has always been with me, though, gently pushing me along."

For the remainder of their ride they got to know each other better, discussing any topic that came up. It was a time they needed after their whirlwind weeks in the city. Jade felt at peace and confident about the man she had agreed to marry.

The cabin came into view, and the coach and horses halted. Dugan, who was now riding inside, climbed out and helped each of the ladies down. Jade watched carefully to see if he had decided on one of them yet. She wasn't sure, but Melody seemed nervous, and Dugan became tongue-tied around her. Jade caught Mallory's eye and they smiled, although there was a hint of sadness in Mallory's face.

"I don't know how Lucy will take it when she finds out about this," she whispered to Jade. "She's as crazy about Dugan as I am about Michael."

Jade stretched her stiff muscles. "Remember, Mallory, the Lord worked things out beautifully for you. He can take care of your friend too."

"My friend is going to be your new sister. Don't forget."

A slow smile crossed Jade's face. "That's right. I guess I better be praying for her too."

The elderly couple welcomed the travelers with a hot meal. The ladies were to spend the night inside the cabin, and the men would take the barn. Jade felt sympathy for the newlywed couple as they took a short walk to say their good nights.

A partial day of travel the next day brought them to Dugan and Gabe's first way station where, in the future, people riding the coach would spend the night. A large rustic cabin was up, and corrals were ready for when they would start their regular routes. Dugan and Gabe and their wives would share the home until Gabe's station was ready on the other side of the settlement between it and Norris.

Gabe's choice of a bride seemed clear as he proudly took Leigh on a tour of the new way station. She seemed equally delighted, and Jade couldn't help thinking along with the others, *One down, four to go.*

"Don't tell me your town, or settlement or whatever you call it will be as primitive as this!" Gwyneth's pretty face had a sour, disagreeable expression.

At the words, concern creased Tyler's forehead, and Gabe's excitement deflated into insecurity. Eyes skimmed their surroundings once again as Cora glared at her cousin in irritation.

Surprisingly, it was the fashionable Melody who put things back in perspective. "I don't think I've ever seen such a beautiful place! Look at that sun blazing on the far hill, and I can hear the river gurgling somewhere back there making me want to explore."

Dugan's attention was fixed on Melody as she turned to the log cabin.

"A person could do a lot with curtains and tablecloths and pictures here and there," she continued. "And it's so peaceful after living in the city." She avoided Dugan's eyes.

"That's what I like," Leigh joined in enthusiastically. "This is exactly what I dreamed of seeing when I decided to come out here."

Jade breathed a sigh of relief, and Cora smiled at the women in apology for Gwyneth's words. Gwyneth was still unconvinced.

Pearl said good-naturedly, "I think any place is what you make of it, and no doubt a lot of work awaits us if we're starting a town in this wilderness. I don't know about you, but it sounds exciting to me." Her eyes twinkled in anticipation.

"Me too," Cora's words were barely audible, but Jade heard them and gave her arm a squeeze.

The men insisted on preparing the noon meal for the ladies. Then they all readied themselves for the remainder of the journey with a spirit of anticipation. They were ready to go in record time. Malcolm's prayer before they left further heightened their desire to be on their way. "May you lead our steps today, Lord, as we cross the doorway into our futures in this new community of pioneers. May we be used of you to further your gospel and share in your love. In your Son's blessed name, amen."

Michael and Mallory again raced out in the lead, and the others picked up the pace in an effort to hasten their arrival. Tyler voiced some new concerns to Jade.

"I never thought how rustic and simple our way of life would seem to ladies from the big city."

"Gwyneth's opinions are her own, Ty, not those of the majority. You heard them. Pearl and Cora are eager to see the settlement, and as far as Leigh and Melody are concerned, they would have just as soon stayed at the way station."

"And you?" Jade heard his uncertainty. "How could you ever live like this after all you've known?"

Laughter rippled from Jade's throat. "I share Melody's feelings. This is the most beautiful country I've ever seen! And, Ty, living with you will bring me more happiness than living in any mansion or palace could."

Love shone on Tyler's face. Suddenly he pointed ahead. "There it is, Jade!"

Chapter 30

The Settlement

It was late in the afternoon when they reached the settlement. Tyler led Jade ahead of the coach so they would arrive first. Jade quickly scanned the area, taking in the new buildings with their fresh white lumber. It was small but larger than she had pictured from Tyler's description. She tried to listen as he pointed out various sites, but her attention was fastened on the men waiting on the boardwalk in front of the hotel.

The older man with silver in his hair she recognized as Palmer Granville. He rose from the bench on which he had been waiting to greet the visitors. Coming down the steps, their hair neatly combed and faces shining from a good scrubbing, were two men who looked like brothers. Jade nodded. Ralph and Ray Tunelle. *Which one is the artist?* she wondered.

Another man stood waiting for the coach to come to a halt so he could assist the ladies out. His muscular, brown forearms were crossed in front of him, giving him an appearance of nonchalance, but Jade noticed the tight expression on his face. *The blacksmith, Bernie Riggs, no doubt.*

"Mallory?"

Jade turned to see a lean, dark-haired man come from the doorway of the hotel with a surprised look on his face.

"Buck!" Mallory didn't wait for Michael's help but leaped from her horse into her brother's arms.

"Mal! When did you get back? What are you doing here?"

Tyler reached to help Jade down while Mallory rattled off her explanations to her brother in an excited, breathless voice. Buck seemed stunned, but he took Michael's extended hand, who then grinned and again flung his arm around Mallory's shoulders.

"You sure you can handle this wildcat, Mike?" he asked in mock concern.

Dugan stopped the coach with a loud, "Whoa!"

Tyler took Jade's hand, and Malcolm and Hermine joined them to watch.

Bernie stepped forward and reached for the door, but it burst open, and with a wide smile Gabe descended first. "Howdy, boys! Nice of you to come meet me like this." He turned his back on them, and Bernie watched in frustration while Gabe helped the women out of the coach.

"Welcome to our town, ladies!" Gabe said with flair. "Let me introduce you to the founding fathers."

The ladies stood by him uncertainly while they cast shy glances at the men.

"This here's our blacksmith and a very good friend of mine, Bernard Riggs. We call him Bernie."

Bernie opened his mouth to speak, but Gabe brushed past him. Pointing to the two on the steps, he announced, "Meet the proprietors of our general store, *and* they're brothers as well, Ralph and Ray Tunelle."

The two nodded their heads and looked bashfully at the women.

"Now, this here's Mr. Palmer Granville. He kinda takes care of all of us. Keeps us in line, you know."

"Welcome back, Gabriel. The place has been quiet without you." Palmer shook the younger man's hand while Leigh stifled a laugh.

Undaunted, Gabe strode over to Buck. "And last, but not least, Dugan's older brother, Buck. But don't fancy him, ladies, because he's too scared of women to get a wife." Jade saw Buck's ears redden.

Tyler took over. "Thank you, Gabe, for your kind words." He approached the women. "Let me introduce the ladies now. Miss Leigh Sheldon—"

"Sorry, fellas. She's mine." Gabe held out his hand to Leigh, and with pink cheeks and a smile, she took it.

Tyler was surprised, but Jade only smiled. From the corner of her eye she had been watching Dugan, who was still seated on the top of the coach. He had been casting furtive glances at Melody, and as Tyler turned to introduce her, he rubbed the palms of his hands on his legs nervously.

"Well, congratulations Gabe and Leigh." Tyler recovered from his surprise. "Next is Miss Melody Wells."

Ralph Tunelle took a step forward. "How do you do—"

Suddenly Dugan jumped down from the coach, startling everyone. Jade hid a smile behind her hand.

"Uh—Miss Wells," Dugan stumbled over his words, and Ralph looked at him strangely. "I was wondering if you … if you and me … if …"

"Yes, Mr. Riley," Melody answered smoothly. She slipped a hand through his arm and smiled sweetly at him. "I'd love to get better acquainted with you."

"You would? You will?" A grin broke across Dugan's face, and he gazed into her face until Tyler cleared his throat. With dazed expressions, the two of them moved aside.

Two down, three to go, thought Jade as Buck Riley's reaction caught her attention. He seemed stunned and almost angry with his brother. She wondered why. Then she noticed Cora fidgeting, her eyes downcast, and she felt her nervousness as strongly as if it were her own. *Cora's the best one of all of them,* she thought. *Surely one of these men will see that.*

Tyler continued. "This is Pearl Maddox."

Pearl's eyes sparkled as always as she spoke a greeting and looked at each of the men. Tyler moved next to Gwyneth.

"Miss Gwyneth Kent."

Gwyneth tugged at her gloves. Her lovely features weren't unnoticed by the men, and Ralph again took a step forward to welcome her, but she merely said, "How do you do?" without even looking up.

"And Miss Kent's cousin, Cora Macardle." Now Gwyneth's eyes flashed up, and she watched closely for the men's reactions. Cora looked as if she wanted to hide behind something; her hands twisted nervously. Welcomes were expressed by the men, and Tyler moved on to the Tuckers.

"This will be our new pastor, Malcolm Tucker, and his new bride of—what's it been, two, three days?—Hermine Tucker. Malcolm, that's the church down there on the corner, and I guess until we get a house built, you and Hermine will stay at the hotel. Is that satisfactory?"

"That will be great, Tyler. Thank you." He turned to the others. "I'm looking forward to sharing God's Word with all of you, and I see no reason why we can't enjoy the Lord while we work together on a house."

He spoke the right words, and the men shook hands and welcomed him with sincerity. Here was a man who was not afraid to roll up his sleeves along with the rest of them.

Then Tyler reached for Jade's hand again, and with pride in his voice, he said, "And I want you all to welcome *my* future wife, Miss Jadyne Crandall."

Recognition lit Palmer's eyes at the name while the others whooped and cheered. Tyler took the teasing in stride; he deserved it after saying he wouldn't be taking a bride.

Buck spoke up. "Let's get you all settled here in the hotel. We've got the rooms ready, but you ladies may want to fix them more to your liking. We aren't the best at such things. Bernie and me, uh ... Bernie and *I* have been working on a supper for everyone, so we'll ring this bell here when it's ready."

The ladies thanked him, and the men reached for their luggage and led them into the hotel. Palmer stopped Jade.

"Miss Crandall, I'm happy to meet you. I knew your father years ago. I'm very sorry about his death."

"Thank you, Mr. Granville." Jade appreciated the sincerity in his words. "It's a pleasure to meet you too. Your brother often speaks of you."

"How is Amos?" Palmer asked with a smile.

Tyler joined them. "There's a lot to tell you, Palmer. Perhaps we could talk while the ladies are resting. I'll see you later." He squeezed Jade's hand.

Jade found Mallory waiting for her upstairs.

"Let's share, okay? Leigh and Melody are sharing, and so are the cousins. Pearl's in that room," Mallory rattled on. Jade saw Hermine open a door down the hall and claim it for her and her husband.

"Look at that bed!" Mallory laughed at the rumpled blankets. "Those boys never could make a bed properly, but isn't it sweet that they tried? Buck was sure surprised about Michael and me, wasn't he? I'm going to go down and see what they're making for supper." The excited, buckskin-clad girl headed for the door, but Jade jumped in front of her.

"No, you're not, Mallory Riley. You're staying right here, and you're getting ready for supper."

"What? What do you mean 'get ready'? We don't dress up for supper here like they do in the city."

"You're going to today." Jade prodded Mallory back and gently pushed her to sit on the bed. "Now, are your dresses in here?" She opened Mallory's bag.

"Those are city dresses, Jade. I won't need fancy stuff like that here."

"This is exactly what you need." Jade held up a lace-trimmed, light-blue gown. The neckline had a modest dip, and the skirt was full. She pulled out a white shawl next.

"Jade, really, I don't think you understand our lifestyle here."

"I understand that although Michael Trent looks at you with love in his eyes, he still treats you like a little girl or worse yet, like 'one of the boys.' I think it's time you showed your future husband just what he's getting."

"But, Jade, don't you see? Michael loves me just the way I am. It's what I had always hoped for, but when it didn't happen, I went to the city to try and change. Now I know I don't need to change. Isn't that wonderful?"

Jade pressed her lips firmly together. "Yes, I see your point, Mallory, but I want you to do this as a favor to me, sort of an experiment. Dress up tonight and see Michael's reaction. After that, you can make up your own mind."

Mallory was about to protest again; then she shrugged her shoulders. "I guess it would be kind of fun to surprise Michael."

Jade turned to hide her smile. She would be sure to be on hand to witness Michael's surprise and no doubt Mallory's as well.

The women had time for a short rest before they washed and changed. Jade helped Mallory pin her hair in a becoming style, twisting a braid around her head like a crown. Then, she fished a tiny mirror from her bag and showed Mallory the results of her work.

"I don't know, Jade. I look more like I'm ready for my wedding than just for supper! I'm glad you're all dressed up too, or I'd feel really silly."

"Oh, I'm sure the other ladies are dressed up too," Jade replied. "This is a pretty special occasion, our first meal all together."

The bell rang then, and the loud clamor seemed to proclaim the impatience of the ringer. Jade felt an urgency to see Tyler, but she forced herself to walk calmly to the stairs so that Mallory would do the same.

They were the last to come down. Jade could see Hermine and Malcolm talking with Tyler, and the other women were being entertained by Palmer while the men hurried about to set the food on the table. Tyler excused himself when he saw Jade, and his eyes showed his approval of her yellow dress. He caught sight of Mallory behind her, and his eyes widened.

"Good evening, ladies. May I escort you to the dining room? You look beautiful," he whispered in Jade's ear. She smiled her thanks then heard him whisper something to Mallory and receive a giggle in return.

They started into the dining room and met Michael coming out. Michael walked past them, and Tyler stopped, the two women on his arms. A curious look came over Mallory's face. Jade watched with suppressed mirth as Michael looked at the gathered women with slight irritation. She could swear he was even counting them. Finally Michael stepped to her side.

"Miss Crandall?"

"Please, call me Jade."

He nodded. "Jade, have you seen—" His words broke off suddenly, and Jade saw him staring openmouthed at Mallory.

In an innocent voice, she asked, "Have I seen whom, Mr. Trent?"

Absently, slowly, he answered, "Michael," while he placed a hand on his chest.

Tyler coughed to cover his laughter, and Jade couldn't help the smile that broke on her face. Mallory seemed unsure of herself as Michael continued to stare at her. But finally she asked, "Is there something wrong, Michael?"

"No. There's nothing wrong," he answered. "Not one thing." A slow smile started on his face, and Mallory returned it. He moved to her side and extended his arm in a gentlemanly fashion. They passed Buck and Dugan, who had also stopped to stare at their sister in amazement and who continued to stare even as Michael held out a chair for Mallory and seated her as regally as if she were a queen.

"Time to eat!" Ralph called as he came from the kitchen with a platter of sliced meat. The others extended arms to the remaining women, and soon they were all seated.

Malcolm was asked to lead in prayer, and then the meal began. Jade was satisfied by Michael's courteous behavior to Mallory. She kept an eye on the others and speculated what other couples might form. Buck was on her left, and Pearl and Bernie came next. Across from her were Mallory and Michael, then Dugan and Melody and Gabe and Leigh. The next table held Malcolm and Hermine and Palmer. Cora was between Gwyneth and Ray. Ralph sat down beside Gwyneth.

Jade noticed Tyler cock his head to one side as if listening. The other men also appeared to hear something.

"What is it, Ty?" Jade asked.

"Someone's coming. Sounds like a wagon. I'd better go check." He excused himself and left the room. Michael followed him out.

Soon voices were heard outside, and everyone at the table watched the door to see who had come.

The door burst open, and several people came in, all talking at once. Tyler appeared to be hugging them all. At the sight of the tables full of people watching them, the group was silenced.

A moment or two passed, then a young boy spoke up. "Where did all these women come from?"

Beside her, Jade heard Buck utter one word under his breath, "Lucy!" Jade noticed a girl about her age looking intently at Dugan, who was whispering something to Melody.

"Lucy!" Mallory jumped up and ran to hug her friend.

"Mal! You're home!" There was gladness in her voice, then, "What's going on here?" she asked in a quieter tone, but it still reached Jade's ears.

Questions flowed and explanations were offered. It was some time before Jade found herself beside Tyler, being introduced to his stunned parents.

Sky stared at Jade in shock, so Russ spoke first. "We're very happy to meet you, Miss Crandall."

"I know how surprised you must be," Jade spoke mainly to Sky. "Tyler and I have only known each other for a couple of weeks, and already we've decided we want to marry. But we're both sure of the Lord's leading in this area of our lives."

The uncertainty in Sky's face began to fade. "I never should have let Violet upset me. I knew things weren't like she said." She opened her arms, and Jade was welcomed to the family.

The meal had grown cold, but the men made an attempt to salvage it, and once again they sat down to eat. This time the Newly family was included. Jade had only briefly been introduced to the rest of Tyler's family, and now she noticed Lucy's consternation as she sat beside Mallory.

However, it was not due to Jade and Tyler's announcement, she was sure. Lucy simply appeared dazed. Dugan seemed blissfully unaware of Lucy's furtive glances as he smiled and talked quietly with Melody. Only Buck, seated beside Jade, seemed tense as he watched Lucy.

Then without warning, Lucy rose from the table and left the room. Sky looked after her daughter in concern, and Mallory started to follow her, but Buck jumped up and was out the door after her before any of the others. Jade met Sky's worried eyes, and quietly Jade said, "I have a feeling that … well, let's just say that I think things will work out fine."

Buck followed Lucy across the empty street to the benches in front of the Tunelle Brothers General Store. She slumped down on the seat and put her head in her hands. Carefully he sat down beside her and searched for something to say. There was almost anger in him at Dugan for causing her this pain.

In a choked voice, he said, "I'm sorry, Lucy."

She jumped as he spoke.

"It's okay, Lucy. It's just me." Buck caught her arm before she could run.

"Let me go, Buck. I want to be alone."

Buck shook his head. "Dugan's a fool, Lucy. He never saw the treasure you are."

"Dugan? Dugan seems happy enough."

Something in her tone caused Buck to search her face. "You're not angry at Dugan?"

Lucy pulled her arm free and turned away from him. Hot tears stung in her eyes.

Buck stood up slowly and silently asked the Lord for the right words while his heart picked up its beating and his mouth turned dry. "If you're not angry at Dugan, then why did you leave the dinner?"

Lucy crossed her arms in front of her.

"Lucy?" Buck touched her arm, but she shrugged him away. "Why did you leave?"

In a fury, she turned to face him. The hot, angry words burst out. "I would have expected this of the others!" She stepped forward, and Buck took a step back in surprise. "I can see Gabe and Ray and Ralph 'ordering' brides!" She moved again, and again Buck retreated. "I can even see

Bernie, and yes, I can even understand Dugan doing it. But *you*!"

"Me?"

Lucy continued to advance. "You!" Buck backed into a post, but Lucy kept coming. "I thought you would be different, Buck! I thought you had some sense. But no! You're just like them! Why don't you get back to the future Mrs. Riley? She'll be missing you by now."

Her nose nearly touching his, Lucy glared in rage at Buck. He was leaning back due to her onslaught, and the face that had been registering astonishment at her words suddenly broke into a huge grin.

"How dare you laugh at me, Buck Riley! You should be ashamed of yourself! You all should!"

Buck straightened up suddenly, and this time Lucy was forced to take a step back. Sternly, he said, "You don't think I should take a wife?" He now stepped forward, and Lucy backed up. "You think I should live alone all my life?" He tried to keep his face stern as he forced Lucy to back up more.

"I think—" Lucy began, but Buck ignored her.

Her back touched the store building, and Buck placed one arm on either side of her, making her a prisoner.

"Let me tell you something, Lucille Newly. I would already be married if a certain young woman hadn't made me believe all these years that she cared only for my brother."

Lucy's mouth dropped open.

Buck's tone gentled. "I didn't 'order' a bride, Lucy. There's never been anyone else for me but you."

"But—"

"I never let you know because I knew you thought you were in love with Dugan."

"But…I…really wasn't," she stated in a slow, matter-of-fact manner.

Buck shook his head. "No, not really. But you are in love now?"

Lucy nodded.

"With me?" he persisted.

She nodded again.

His arms went around her then, and he spoke into her hair. "Finally!" Then a moment later he teasingly asked her, "How would you like to help me run a hotel?"

Russ Newly, standing in the shadows, never heard his daughter's answer, but he knew what it was by her response as she lifted her face to be kissed. He slipped away silently. He couldn't be more pleased. Buck Riley had always been a favorite of his, and although Buck would never know, Russ had been aware of his feelings for Lucy for quite some time.

Russ returned to the hotel and took his place beside Sky. At her questioning look, he smiled reassuringly. "I think Lucy will have something to tell us really soon," he said quietly.

The meal progressed, and Sky and Russ were happily impressed with their son's choice of a future mate. Jade was charming, and she even handled the teasing of the younger boys.

Abel and Rex were attempting to outdo each other in gaining Jade's attention. Story after story kept the meal merry with laughter as they told tales on their scowling brother. Tyler's menacing looks didn't deter them, but Russ finally put his foot down and signaled to the boys that enough was enough. Abel couldn't resist getting in one last word.

"You might wanna get cotton for your ears, Miss Jade. You never did hear anything so awful as the sound of Ty snoring."

Sky exclaimed, "Abel!" in a horrified voice, but Jade only laughed.

"I know what you mean, Abel. I could hardly sleep on the train."

Dead silence followed her words, and every eye in the room turned to the couple whose faces were rapidly turning crimson. Sky again looked uncertain when she saw the guilty look on their faces.

Jade's hand went to her mouth as she realized the scandalous thoughts of the others. She looked beseechingly at Tyler for help. He chuckled, and then quickly he related their adventures in a practical manner with a touch of humor. His audience cast many a curious glance at the beautiful woman beside him and tried to imagine her dressed as a boy about Abel's age. Sky shook her head in amazement, and Russ nodded his approval. Jade breathed a sigh of relief.

Supper was nearly over when Buck walked in alone and approached Russ. A few whispered words, a nod from Russ, a quick handshake, then Buck left again only to return a few moments later with Lucy by the hand.

"May I have your attention, please?"

Jade felt Tyler reach for her hand, and she shared a smile with him as they listened to Buck's announcement.

"Lucy has agreed to become my wife," Buck said simply, but there was no mistaking the pleasure and pride in his voice.

Of all gathered, Mallory seemed the most unprepared for the news. "Lucy?" She pulled her aside after the congratulations had subsided. "Are you sure? You're not just doing this because—"

"I'm sure, Mal. Buck and I had lunch together awhile back, and since then I knew I didn't really love Dugan. I couldn't love one man and think all the time of another."

Over Mallory's shoulder, Dugan's face unexpectedly appeared. Mallory stepped aside and watched her friend's face carefully.

Dugan seemed uncomfortable as he spoke. "I'm really happy for you and Buck, Lucy. It will be great to have you for a sister." His meaning was clear, and Lucy wished she had seen it earlier. Dugan had never thought of her as anything other than a sister or a friend of his sister's.

Smiling, she replied, "Thank you, Dugan. I'll try not to be as pesky a sister as Mallory has been."

They all laughed together, and Lucy saw the relief on Dugan's face. What a bother she must have been to him!

"Melody is very pretty. I hope you will both be happy," she said sincerely.

"At least as happy as we'll be," Buck added as he slipped an arm around Lucy's waist and shook his brother's hand. He had witnessed their exchange and felt proud of Lucy and thankful that the Lord had straightened everything out for all of them.

Sky spoke to those still seated at the table with her. "If I would have known when we left home that two of my children and two of my nephews and three of my best friend's children would all be getting married, I—"

"You would have gotten here sooner," Russ finished for her.

Chapter 31

The Settlement

Jade hummed happily as she swung a shawl over her shoulders and added some finishing touches to her hair. She could hear the muffled sounds of voices and laughter in other parts of the hotel as the couples went about their business after breakfast. It was five days since their arrival in the settlement, and Tyler was finally going to show her where their house would be built.

He had wanted to do it sooner, but with his family there and so many things going on, they just hadn't had time. The Newlys were still there; they would stay for some of the weddings. Jade shook her head as she thought of the crowded hotel. The Newlys took up another three rooms: Russ and Sky in one room, the boys in another, and Lucy, Dorcas, and Emma in a third. Buck wasn't charging any of his guests, of course, and the indefatigable man was working every moment to make sure of their comfort.

But Jade wondered what he would do if he got some real guests. There were only a few rooms left.

Gwyneth's sharp voice drifted in from the hallway, and Jade frowned. Gwyneth hated everything about the rustic town, and she didn't care who knew it. Now she was insisting on going back to the city, much to the relief of the remaining bachelors, but Jade knew Cora didn't want to leave. It was beginning to look like Ray was interested in the shy, pretty woman, and Gwyneth was outraged, for none of the men displayed that type of interest in her.

Jade briefly closed her eyes and sent a prayer heavenward, asking God to give Cora enough backbone to stand up to her cousin and live her own life. She smiled, knowing that God was able to work out every detail.

"Thinking about me?"

Her eyes flew open. Hunter Granville stood before her, the closet door open behind him. His city clothes were dirty and torn, and his face showed several days growth of whiskers. His eyes were half crazed, and he was poised to pounce in any direction she might move. Jade's sharp intake of air warned him that she was about to scream, and he threw himself forward and clamped his hand over her mouth.

Jade struggled, and her heels hit the floor with loud thuds. Hunter lifted her up and tried to keep the flailing legs and feet from kicking him. He threw her on the bed and held her while his hand closed over her mouth and nose. In a hissing voice, he spoke in her ear.

"I will let you breathe as soon as you stop struggling."

Jade kicked and strained against him more violently as her lungs cried for air. She was becoming frantic, and her eyes pleaded with him.

Hunter removed his hand, and she gasped in the needed air; then his hand closed over her face again. This time she was ready, and Hunter jerked his hand away in pain as her teeth left their mark and drew his blood. Her scream was cut off by Hunter's fist. Pain slivers flew through her head, and blackness followed.

Tyler paced outside the hotel on the boardwalk. Finally he and Jade were going to get some time alone. Since they had arrived in the settlement, they had been surrounded by people night and day. He was happy his family had come and that they had a chance to meet Jade and get to know her, but they didn't seem to realize that he and Jade needed to get to know each other too. They would be leaving in two days to go back to Chicago for their wedding, and Palmer had agreed to accompany them as chaperone and to see his brother Amos as well. It seemed they were never to be alone.

Today was going to work out, though. Tyler took a deep breath and couldn't help the grin that appeared on his face. He had it all planned. Mike and Mallory were going to ask Russ for advice on their lumber business. That would take care of him. And Buck and Lucy were going to keep Sky busy with wedding plans and advice on the hotel business. His younger brothers and sisters were a problem, but Cora, bless her, had stepped in and asked if they would like to have their portraits drawn. She and Ray were going to work on them together, so that took care of them.

Tyler leaned against the rough lumber pillar. He was becoming impatient. If Jade didn't hurry, they would never escape before someone saw them and demanded their attention. He was eager to show her the place their home would be built. A home. Not a big, fancy house he had once thought so important but a home shared by people who loved each other. A home they would build together.

He was about to turn and go into the hotel looking for Jade when he noticed a wagon and riders coming. His first thoughts were, *Oh, no, more distractions to keep us from getting away,* but as he squinted to see who it was, he recognized the Rileys: Hank and Randi, and their younger sons. There were two other passengers in the wagon whom Tyler couldn't make out, but he hurried to the door of the hotel and called, "Buck! Your folks are here!"

The wagon rolled to a stop, and Hank and his boys reined in their horses. Tyler walked over to help Randi down, but he stopped in surprise when he saw Hazel and Sidney Crandall smiling at him from the wagon.

"Mrs. Crandall! Sidney! What are you doing out here?"

Hazel laughed as she got down with Tyler's help. She rubbed the aching muscles in her back. "I'm wondering that myself, Mr. Newly." She gave him a penetrating look. "What is my daughter wearing these days?" she asked, and although Tyler heard the humor in her voice, he also saw the worry on her face.

"Well, soon she'll be wearing a wedding ring now that you're here. With your permission, of course."

"I assume that means she's dressed like a proper young lady again, not a hoodlum. Whatever did you see in her, Mr. Newly?"

"Call me Tyler, Mrs. Crandall. And if you don't mind my saying, I see a lot of her mother in her."

Hazel laughed.

"How are you, Sid? Boy, there are going to be some confused ladies around here when they see you!"

Sidney grinned at Tyler. "Good to see you again, too, Mr. Newly. Like my hat? The Rileys gave it to me."

Tyler nodded appreciatively at the Stetson on his young friend's head. "Guess you needed a new one since your sister ran off with your old one, huh?"

"Yep," Sidney agreed. "I like it a lot too." He jumped down from the wagon and stood beside his mother. "Mind if I take a look around?" he questioned Tyler.

"Sure, go right ahead."

"Okay with you, Ma?"

"Don't call me—oh, go on." Hazel and Tyler both laughed as Sid followed Jethro and Parker Riley down the street.

"Where is Jadyne, Tyler?" Hazel was anxious to see her daughter.

"She's inside the hotel here. What a surprise she's going to have when she sees you! Oh, hello, Palmer. Have you met Mrs. Crandall, Jade's mother?"

Palmer Granville stepped off the boardwalk and removed his hat. There was obvious pleasure in his expression. "Mrs. Crandall, I'm very pleased to meet you. May I extend my condolences on the death of your husband? Edmund was an old school mate of mine."

"It's nice to meet you also. I've heard much about you from your brother Amos, and Edmund mentioned you often." Hazel suddenly clapped her hands together. "I'm glad you're here! Now, where's Jadyne? I have some wonderful news that you all must hear together."

"I'll send someone up for her." Tyler looked around and spotted Lucy being hugged by Randi and then by Hank. "Buck must have told his parents their news," he said to Hazel. "He and my sister Lucy are getting married." He waited a moment. "Lucy! Lucy, come here, please."

Lucy extracted herself from her future in-laws and left Buck to finish explaining to them about their upcoming wedding.

"What is it, Ty?" She looked curiously at Hazel, but clearly her attention was on what Buck was saying to his family.

"Lucy, this is Jade's mom, Mrs. Crandall, and Jade's brother Sidney is over there." He pointed. "Would you go up and tell Jade I'm ready to go, but don't tell her who else is waiting down here. We want to surprise her."

"But, Ty," Lucy began; then she saw the suppressed excitement in Hazel's eyes. "Sure, Ty." She hurried off.

Michael and Mallory hurried up the street, and Mallory embraced her parents and started talking excitedly while Michael stood slightly behind her. Hank and Randi looked from one to the other with stunned expressions.

"It would appear that there is more news for the Rileys," Hazel commented with a light laugh.

"Mallory is their daughter," Palmer explained, "and Michael Trent is Tyler's cousin." He nodded. "They've decided to get married too."

The Rileys were speechless at first as Mallory and Michael related their story. Then mayhem broke out as they all began talking at once. Hazel watched in amusement, but her eyes kept going to the door of the hotel.

"You must be very anxious to see her," Palmer commented beside her.

"Mr. Granville, if only you knew! I watched her leave dressed as a young boy to go into a wilderness alone with a young man I only briefly met." Hazel stopped for a breath. "I spent most of my time praying for her, especially after Amos was shot. Then just before we left news came about your niece and nephew and I learned that Jadyne had a part in their capture. I could wait no longer. I had to come. Yes, I'm anxious to see her."

"Did you see Cecile and Hunter?" Palmer asked, and Tyler waited for the answer.

"No, Amos plans to meet with them. What a sad thing for all of you. I'm so sorry." She placed a hand on Palmer's arm.

Palmer laid his hand over hers. "Thank you, Mrs. Crandall. I only hope that somehow, through all of this trouble, I can lead Amos to the Lord. I—"

"She's not up there!"

Palmer's words were cut off by Lucy as she ran down the steps.

"Ty, I checked every room. No one saw her leave. I even looked in the kitchen and dining room."

Worry threaded its way into Lucy's voice, and Palmer tried to allay her fears. "I'm sure she's around somewhere. Tyler, you said she was going to meet you here?"

But Tyler was headed up the steps. He called over his shoulder, "Buck! I need to check Jade's room. Something's not right here."

Buck turned from his family, and noting the concern on the faces around him, he hurried after Tyler. They reached Jade and Mallory's room together, knocked, and went in. Tyler looked all around. Everything seemed to be in order, but the uneasy feeling that started when Lucy said no one saw Jade leave refused to go away. He crossed to the open window and looked out at the back side of the hotel. Suddenly he called to Buck.

"That ladder laying down there! Buck, look!"

Buck joined him at the window.

"See the holes in the dirt below this window? Somebody used that ladder to get in here!"

"Who?" Buck was perplexed. "Who would break in here?"

But Tyler was running out the door before his question was finished. Buck raced after him, and they passed the startled group in front of the hotel at a run. As they rounded the corner of the building, the others quickly followed, shouting questions.

"Wait here! I need to check for tracks." Tyler moved on.

"Tracks? What is he talking about? What's happened to Jadyne?" Hazel reached for Sidney who had returned to see what the excitement was all about and held on tightly to her son.

Hank Riley followed Buck and Tyler and quietly watched and listened.

"Here's a man's prints." Tyler circled the area until he came to the holes left by the ladder. His mouth tightened as he pointed to a smaller set of tracks nearby. He looked carefully around and then came back to the small tracks. "They're only in this spot."

"He carried her down the ladder then set her down," said Hank. He, too, pointed to the small footprints. "She didn't move because she's probably been tied up." He indicated the man's maneuvers by following his prints. "He set the ladder back down and then picked her up again and headed that way, toward the hills."

Hazel Crandall rushed to the men despite Palmer's efforts to hold her back. "Who, Tyler? Who did this? Who took Jadyne?"

Tyler scanned the surrounding tree-covered hills. "I don't know, Mrs. Crandall, but I'll find her."

Tyler squinted in the morning light. Something, some light, flashed briefly.

"What is it, Tyler? Where?" Hazel searched in the direction Tyler was staring.

"Why don't you come inside with me, Mrs. Crandall?" Palmer gently took her arm. "We'll let the men—"

Suddenly Palmer jerked backward, pulling Hazel with him so that they both fell to the ground. A whine and echoing report of a rifle almost instantly followed. The people standing in the open area dove for cover while the three men pulled Palmer and Hazel to the side of the building.

"Palmer! Are you all right? Look! He's bleeding. I think it's ..." Tyler scrambled to open the older man's coat. "Here, it's here, high up on his chest." He pulled a cloth handkerchief from his pocket and pressed it on the bleeding wound. "Mrs. Crandall, are you hurt?"

Hazel silently shook her head while she stared at the blood oozing through the white cloth on Palmer's chest.

"I have to go get Jade, Mrs. Crandall." Tyler spoke slowly as if to a small child. "I'm going to leave you in the care of my mother and Randi Riley. Try not to worry. I think it's safe to say that we know who has Jade now. Hunter Granville is the only one who would try to kill Palmer." He turned to the man beside him. "Buck, you coming?"

Tyler and Buck left at a run for the barn behind the hotel while Hank and Randi and the others gently picked up Palmer and moved to the front of the hotel. In a matter of minutes, the other men were preparing their horses and waiting for Tyler's instructions. Randi and Sky began caring for the wounded man while the other ladies surrounded Hazel and Sidney with comforting words. Malcolm and Bernie prepared to stand guard in case Hunter returned, and they sent the younger Riley boys to the upstairs windows to be lookouts.

Bernie caught Sidney's eye. "We could use you at one of the windows, young feller," he instructed.

"No!" Hazel held her son back.

"I gotta help them, Ma." Sidney pulled away and ran for the stairs.

"He needs to feel useful right now," Pearl explained to the distraught woman. "And so do you. Let's go heat water for Mr. Granville, shall we?"

In a daze, Hazel followed the other women to do their tasks.

At the corral, Tyler spoke rapidly to Buck, "You know that area pretty well, don't you?"

At his friend's quick nod, he continued, "Circle around from the north, and I'll take the south. Whatever you do, make sure Jade's out of the way first."

As the others gathered, they split into teams and headed out. Michael and Russ went with Tyler, and Hank and Dugan joined Buck. Ralph, Ray, and Gabe started straight up the hill using the thick tree growth for cover.

Lord, please help us find her quickly, Tyler prayed as he spurred his horse forward.

Chapter 32

The Cave

Jade trembled with a mixture of fear, rage, and shock. *He killed Palmer,* she kept repeating to herself. *Mother was there. And Sidney!* She relived the moment she saw Palmer thrown backward with her mother. She saw them both fall to the ground; then Hunter had shoved her onto his horse again and had ridden fast and hard to get away from there.

She must be dreaming. Her mother and Sidney! What were they doing in the settlement? How did they get there?

She looked at Hunter in the dim light from her place inside the cave. He was staring out the entrance and studying the hillside below them. She shuddered as he laughed in delight and slapped his thigh. *He enjoys this,* she thought. *He enjoyed shooting Palmer, and he's looking forward to another opportunity to kill.*

Hunter crossed to her and leaned his rifle against the wall of the cave. He put his hands on his hips and smiled at her as she, still bound and gagged, shivered in the cool air.

"You see now, don't you, Jadyne, that I always get what I want?" His eyes were bright and wild looking as he undid the handkerchief around her mouth. "Uncle Palmer is out of the way, just like I planned. And if old Uncle Amos doesn't cooperate, you'll be next. You're my ace up the sleeve, dear girl. Uncle Amos will do anything I want so long as you are safely returned." He laughed. "At least as long as you are returned." He cupped her chin in his hand. "You are a very beautiful woman, Jadyne."

His face came closer to hers, and she glared at him with eyes no longer filled with fright. A fierce anger overtook her, and she spoke in an icy voice. "You lay a hand on me, and they'll hang you." Each word was spoken slowly and distinctly.

Hunter stopped at the look in her face and the tone of her voice. Then he laughed again. "My dear girl, I've already killed a man. What more can they do to me? Ah, but they would have to catch me first, wouldn't they?" He straightened up and looked at the cave entrance again. "These country yokels are too dumb to figure out where we are. By morning we'll be far from this place." There was daring and pride in his voice, and Jade knew he believed himself invincible.

"Maybe you can run and hide and get away with it for a while," Jade spoke to his back, "but you'll be found, you'll be caught, and you'll be punished eventually."

He looked back at her with an amused grin. "You think so, Jadyne? You'd like that, wouldn't you?" He crossed to her side again and sat down while he began untying her bound wrists. "I've only been caught once, my sweet, and that was when you were involved. You'll pay for that, you know."

Jade rubbed her tender wrists but made no comment. She watched him warily.

Hunter continued, "And as you can see, I got away. I always get away." He moved closer to her.

"You can't run away from God." Jade felt calm as she spoke, for she was reassured of the Lord's watch over her. Silently, she prayed for the right words to say.

"God?" Scorn filled Hunter's voice, and his face was incredulous. "Tell me, Jadyne, do you believe in God?"

"Yes, I do," she answered.

"A God who loves you and cares for you and watches over you? That kind of God?" Hunter persisted.

"Yes."

Hunter pushed his mocking face right up to hers. "Then why are you here, Jadyne? Why did your loving God let you get kidnapped by an evil man like me? Doesn't seem to me that he's doing a very good job taking care of you."

Jade held her back straight and her head high. With Hunter's nose only inches from her own, she answered calmly, "My God always knows exactly where I am and what's happening to me. Have you read any of the Bible, Mr. Granville?"

Hunter sat back with a laugh. "Only when I was forced to."

"Have you ever heard of Joseph? He was sold by his own brothers into slavery. He was away from his family for years, and his father thought him dead. But God used Joseph to save his family, even his evil brothers, from starvation."

Hunter stood again. "Interesting story. I suppose next you're going to tell me that God is going to use you to do some great thing now."

"I don't know what God will do, but I know he's in control here, not you."

Dark anger crossed Hunter's features. "You don't know how wrong you are! *I* am in control! *I* broke away from the jail! *I* kidnapped you! *I* killed Uncle Palmer! And *I* will decide what happens next! Do you understand me?" Large veins bulged on his forehead as he shouted at Jade. The wild look in his eyes frightened her, and she wisely remained silent.

Hunter turned back to the entrance and his horse. He removed some packages from a saddlebag and threw them to her.

"Make us something to eat," he ordered. He pointed to a ring of rocks and a stack of wood nearby. "Get a fire going."

Jade looked at the fire ring for the first time. It occurred to her that the cave Hunter had chosen to hide in was not unknown to the others. Hope leaped in her. Tyler would be coming, of that she was sure, and he probably knew about this cave. In fact, he may have been the one to leave the wood, he or one of the men from the settlement. Somehow she had to help them find her.

Jade looked through the packages Hunter had thrown to her. She found some matches and set to work on the fire. Several matches later she still hadn't succeeded. Never before in her life had she lit a campfire. The servants had always taken care of their fireplaces, and her mother had taken care of the cottage.

"What are you doing?" Hunter impatiently swept her aside. He got a fire going with one match and showed her how to feed it. "Guess a city girl like you doesn't know too much about camping out." He laughed at her.

Curiously she looked at him. "You're from a city too, aren't you?"

"Philadelphia. But unlike you, I had to help with the work at my house. My parents, rich as they were, thought they were doing Cecile and me a favor by teaching us how to live without money like poor people." His look darkened again. "We had the money to live like kings, and they made us work like servants. But we got the money—Cecile and me—we got it all."

He pulled a pan from one of the packages and rummaged through the others. "What's in these anyway?" he questioned her.

"Don't you know?"

"Haven't had time to look. I took the horse from a hitching post back in Freesburg after I got off the train."

"You *stole* the horse?"

"Who me?" Hunter asked with mock innocence. "No, I've got a bill of sale right here." He reached into his pocket and drew out a small gun. He flashed it at Jade and grinned. "This is all the bill of sale I need. I can buy anything I want with it."

She looked at him without speaking.

"Here, fry up some bacon and beans, and do you think you can manage some coffee? I'll get water from the stream outside."

She took the things he thrust at her and numbly began to fix the meal. Evening was settling in, but she was not hungry. She silently prayed while she worked and watched Hunter. He paced in the cave or sat by the entrance, staring out at the deepening shadows.

Jade looked slowly around the dim cave searching for something, anything that might help when Tyler came. The cave seemed small, but as she fed the fire more of the wood and it blazed brighter and higher, she was able to see that what she thought was the back wall of the cave was not a wall at all. The cave was deeper, and the blackness that the fire couldn't penetrate was an opening that apparently went farther into the hillside. Jade swallowed nervously. Would she dare run into that blackness to get away from Hunter?

The coffee boiled, and the food bubbled in the pan. Jade poked another stick into the flames and looked up as Hunter approached the fire. He sniffed the aroma emanating from the pan, and an appreciative smile lit his face.

"Food!" He rubbed his stomach. "It's been awhile since I've seen any food. That looks pretty good, Jadyne. Where did a rich city girl like you learn how to cook?"

Jade ignored his sarcasm and added another piece of wood to the already blazing fire. Hunter dug through the packages again and found a cup and plate. He scooped up some beans and bacon onto the plate and handed it to Jade.

"Here, you eat this. I'll eat from the pan. Pour me some coffee. We'll have to share the cup."

Just then the coffee began to boil over, and the hot liquid sizzled as it hit the flames. Hunter looked at it absently while he began devouring the food. Suddenly he jumped up and kicked at the burning wood, sending fire scattering in all directions.

"What do you think you're trying to pull?" he shouted at Jade. "A fire that size will be seen for miles!" He turned back to the entrance then glared at Jade again. The wild look had returned to his eyes. "You better hope they didn't see it, my girl. If I can't use you to get ransom money from Uncle Amos, you're no good to me alive. I'll kill you before I let your friends take you back. Remember that the next time you try to signal for help."

Jade stared at him mutely. The anger seemed to seep away from him again, and he resumed eating. He held up the coffee cup and motioned for her to fill it. She lifted the corner of her skirt and used it to lift the hot pot from the fire. She poured the boiling liquid into his cup, and as she started to set the pot down on a rock near the flames, her eyes caught a movement in the black space beyond the fire.

She started and gave a little scream, causing the coffee to slosh onto her hand so that she jerked away. Hunter jumped up and grabbed his rifle, and at the same instant Jade recognized a man's boot before it was pulled back into the blackness.

"My hand!" Jade moaned quickly. "I think I burned my hand!" She shook her fingers and grimaced in assumed pain. Hunter looked around with the rifle ready; then he set it down against the cave wall again and resumed eating.

"That's the least of your worries, my dear Jadyne. Hurry up and eat. We're moving out of here. The sooner we get away from this area, the better I'll feel. That fire may have drawn someone."

Jade picked up the plate but shook her head as Hunter offered her the coffee. When his head was down, she glanced at the dark area again. She saw nothing. But she knew there was someone there. How did he get there? Was it Tyler? Was there another entrance to the cave? She didn't know what the person or persons there wanted her to do, but she would be ready.

A scrape of boot on stone, and suddenly Tyler *was* there, but he stood in the entrance of the cave, not in the back. His gun was held ready, and he spoke harshly to Hunter as the fugitive grabbed for his rifle.

"Don't touch it, Granville!"

The rifle clattered against the cave floor as it fell. Hunter lifted his arms slowly, but his eyes darted in all directions, looking for a way to escape.

"Are you all right, Jade?" Tyler asked the words without taking his eyes off Hunter.

"I'm fine," was the trembling answer.

"Jade, step back and away from Granville. Keep far away from him. Granville, step over there, and keep your hands up."

Jade moved slowly to the other side of the cave. A figure stepped out of the dark shadows behind her and startled her so that she jumped.

"It's me, Ty." Buck announced his presence.

Hunter saw his chance as soon as Tyler's eyes left him to look at the man. He reached into his pocket and grabbed the small pistol he had shown Jade. Tyler looked back in time to see the gun flash, and he was thrown back by the impact of the bullet as it hit him.

Jade screamed as Tyler fell and red rapidly covered his shirtfront. An arm grabbed her and pulled her roughly into the safety of the dark recess of the cave. Another shot rang out, and she felt its impact throw her against the cold rock wall. More shots, running feet, but all she could see was the blackness, and then she heard nothing.

Chapter 33

The Settlement

Jade opened her eyes slowly and blinked to adjust her vision. It was dark. She blinked again and waited; then she began looking around without turning her head. She listened to the stillness as she struggled into consciousness, and she became aware that she was in a bed, but she was bound again. Her arms were tightly bound to her body, and her head felt tight. She tried to move and couldn't; she tried to speak, but her mouth felt dry, and she couldn't force a sound from her throat.

She tried to remember what happened, why she was here. Brief images swept through her mind, and she pressed her eyes tightly closed and concentrated on them. Her hands were tied, and Hunter was galloping. Palmer and her mother were falling to the ground. She was eating bacon and beans with Hunter, and the rifle was nearby. Tyler was falling, and his shirt was red with blood.

Her eyes flew open, and she tried to sit up. Sharp pain made her groan and fall back. She felt nauseous and knew she was losing consciousness again. A light was suddenly in the room, and someone was bending over her. She shrank back, afraid. Before she slipped into the deep sleep again, she felt a cool hand touch her forehead, and soft words spoken kindly were the last things she heard.

"Is she awake yet?"

Whispered words penetrated into Jade's hearing, and once again she blinked her eyes open. The bright sun was filtered by a soft curtain, and she recognized one of the rooms in Buck's hotel. Relief washed over her. She was safe.

Jade turned her head toward the voice, and immediately her mother was beside the bed.

"Jadyne, honey, how do you feel?" Concern and fatigue lined Hazel's lovely features. Jade started to reach for her mother but found she couldn't move her arm.

"Wha—" A cottony, dry mouth prevented her from saying what she wished. She struggled to swallow and lifted her head for her mother to assist her in taking the much-needed water. She savored the cool refreshment a moment then spoke again.

"Mother, what's happened? Why ... why can't I move?"

Hazel smiled reassuringly at her daughter, but it was Mallory who approached the bed and answered.

"You took a ricochet bullet from Hunter's gun in your shoulder, Jade. We wrapped you up pretty good because we didn't want you to move your arm. You're going to be kind of sore for a while, but you'll be fine. I'm sure glad Buck got you out of there."

"My head?" Jade felt the throb of pain as she moved.

"You hit a rock when you fell. You've got a nasty lump there." Mallory started gently unwrapping bandages, and Jade groaned as she was lifted to a sitting position. When her good arm was free, she felt her bandaged head. It was tender all right.

Suddenly she stopped Mallory's hands with her own. "Tyler! Mallory, is Tyler all right? He was shot."

Mallory avoided looking at Jade. "He'll be fine, Jade. Now you need to rest some more. Here, have another—"

"No! Tell me, Mal! Tell me now! What's wrong with Ty?" Jade saw the uneasiness in her friend's face. She looked at Hazel. "Mother, where's Tyler? What's happened?"

Mallory gently but firmly pushed Jade back. "Just lie down again, Jade."

"No, Mallory, she needs to know, or she'll get no rest." Hazel took Jade's hand. "He's not awake yet, Jadyne. He has a bullet in his chest, and he's lost a lot of blood. We're waiting for the doctor from Sand Creek because the bullet will have to be removed. Sky is taking care of him now."

Jade watched her mother's face closely. "Will he live?"

Tears sprang to Hazel's eyes. "We hope and pray that he will, Jade, but only God knows that."

Determination came over Jade. "I need to see him." She pushed the covers away then looked at Mallory's protesting face. "Are you going to help me or not?"

The two women wrapped Jade in blankets and slowly led her down the hall to the room where Tyler lay. Sky was leaning over the bed when the three walked in.

"Jade! You shouldn't be up!" Sky admonished softly, but she gently hugged the injured woman and led her to Tyler's side without argument. "He hasn't been awake yet, but you can sit beside him for a while."

Jade looked at Tyler's white, still face, and tears streamed down her cheeks. She gently took his hand and without looking at the others said, "I'll be staying in here."

The women looked at each other in concern, but Hazel resignedly went for more bedding to make her daughter comfortable on the floor. She knew Jade would not leave Tyler now.

It was Rooney Nolan who arrived with the doctor and the sheriff two days later. Two long days of waiting and praying. During that time Jade learned that Hunter Granville was the one who shot his gun twice in the cave, and Buck had finally stopped the madman with a single shot to his heart. Palmer Granville was back on his feet and deeply saddened at the actions of his nephew. Dugan was resting in Sand Creek after his race for the doctor, and he would return with the rest of the town's supplies as soon as the horses were ready. Rooney had volunteered to make the ride to the settlement with the doctor.

Jade waited anxiously with the others for the doctor to finish his surgery. Sky was assisting the older man, something she had done many years earlier. Finally they were done.

"He needs lots of rest and care around the clock," the old doctor instructed as he wiped his wire-rimmed spectacles. "He's strong and healthy"—he smiled at Jadyne—"and he has a good reason to want to recover quickly. I don't think there will be any danger. Now let me take a look at that shoulder, young lady. Seems to me you folks have had enough excitement around here for a while. You keep this up, and you're going to need your own doctor."

"Please, wait." Jade stopped the old gentleman. "You can check me later. I want to see Tyler now."

The doc smiled. "I guess I can check on Palmer first, but you're not getting out of an examination, missy. I'll see you later."

Jade looked closely at Tyler's sleeping form. He looked the same to her. Would he get better now that the bullet was out?

Chapter 34

The Settlement

"I'm not staying here a moment longer and neither are you!" Gwyneth's sharp voice carried through the hotel. "Men with guns! People getting shot! What next? Do you have to have a bullet in *you* to see that I'm right? We're leaving, Cora. We're leaving today!"

"But, Winnie!"

"No, Cora, this place is too wild for us, too uncivilized. We were better off in the city, and that's where we belong. I should have known this was a mistake. Just look at these primitive surroundings."

"Winnie, please, lower your voice," pleaded Cora.

"I will not! I thought I could find someone willing to marry you here, but I don't want even you stuck way out here where people shoot each other. No, we'll go back to the city. I'll marry someone and convince him to let you live with us. I'll always take care of you, Cora."

"Winnie, I don't need to be taken care of."

"Why, how could you possibly take care of yourself? You do so need me. Now, get your things together. That nice Mr. Nolan said we could ride to the town with him. Hurry up, he's waiting! I can hardly wait myself to get back to civilization."

Jade looked anxiously at Mallory and Lucy. They were sitting in the hotel lobby together, enjoying a cup of coffee while the doctor again checked on Tyler. The voices from the hallway above them were clear, and Jade felt anger stir in her at Gwyneth's control over her cousin.

"Go get Ray," she said suddenly to Mallory.

"Ray?"

"Yes. If I'm right, he won't let Cora leave so easily."

Mallory nodded in understanding and hurried off while Jade and Lucy waited in silence. Presently Rooney entered the hotel and looked around. When he spotted the two women, he headed toward them then stopped abruptly when he realized that Lucy was one of them. A red flush crept over his face, and he looked everywhere but at her, finally turning to leave.

"Rooney, wait," Lucy called to him softly, not wanting the two women upstairs to hear.

He looked uneasily at her, but he waited for her to speak.

"Rooney, I wanted to thank you for bringing the doctor so quickly for Ty."

"Glad I could help," he mumbled while he avoided her eyes.

Lucy felt badly that she had inadvertently hurt him; she had never meant to. An idea occurred to her. "You're taking Gwyneth to Sand Creek?" she asked.

Rooney nodded.

"It's a shame she's decided not to stay here," Lucy continued. "I guess she'd be happier in a bigger town, though, you know, something like Sand Creek. She's very pretty, isn't she?"

Jade glanced curiously at her future sister-in-law.

"I guess so. I don't know." Rooney shrugged.

"You know, it's a shame she's leaving. Her cousin Cora wants to stay, but Gwyneth won't be parted from her. If only she would decide to stay nearby, you know, somewhere close like Sand Creek."

Jade watched Rooney look oddly at Lucy. She smiled to herself.

Gwyneth's voice again was heard in the lobby.

"Cora, will you please hurry up! Quit stalling. We're leaving as soon as Mr. Nolan calls for us. At least he's a gentleman. You can tell he has a refinement that these 'lumberjacks' don't have. He's handsome too, isn't he?"

Jade suppressed the giggle she felt inside her as she watched Rooney Nolan's ears turn red. Lucy seized the opportunity.

"You see, Rooney, she likes you a lot, and she'll like a big town like Sand Creek. Maybe you could convince her to stay ... for Cora's sake."

Rooney cleared his throat nervously, but the staccato of heels on wooden steps prevented him from speaking.

"Why, Mr. Nolan! I hope you haven't been waiting long. We would have been down a lot sooner if we had known." Gwyneth's tone had changed to a feminine sweetness at the sight of Rooney. Cora set down the bags she was carrying. She glanced at Jade and Lucy then looked down at the floor and bit her lip.

Jade winced when her arm bumped the chair arm as she stood. Somehow she had to stop Gwyneth from making Cora leave.

"I'm not going, Winnie."

Jade stopped where she was, surprised at the determined look on Cora's face.

Gwyneth glared over her shoulder at her cousin then smiled pleasantly again at Rooney. "Nonsense. Mr. Nolan has gone to all the trouble to come and get us. Of course we're going."

"You can go if you want. I'm staying here. I belong here."

Gwyneth spun around, startling Rooney into taking a step back.

"Belong here? Cora, don't be ridiculous. No one belongs *here*."

The determined look remained on Cora's face.

Exasperated, Gwyneth asked, "Where will you live? I haven't seen any of these men falling over themselves to marry you. What will you do? You have no skills, and even if you did, what good would they do you here? Now stop this nonsense and come along."

"If the lady doesn't want to leave, she doesn't have to."

Heads turned to the voice, and Jade heard Cora's sharp intake of air when she saw Ray in the doorway.

"Mr. Tunelle, this is none of your business." Gwyneth's remark was meant to warn him away.

Ray ignored her and strode to Cora's side. He took her hand in his, forcing her to look up at him. "Cora Macardle, will you marry me?" He asked the question softly as if they were the only two people in the room.

Cora was stunned. "Are … are you sure?" she stammered. "I'm … I'm not—"

"I'm very sure, Cora. I was planning to ask you as soon as we got to know each other a little better, but when I heard you might leave, I figured the time to ask was now. Will you? I'll be a good husband to you, Cora."

A beautiful smile lit Cora's face. She nodded quickly.

"Wait a minute! Just wait!" Gwyneth was furious. "Cora, you can't marry him and live here. I promised your parents I would look after you, and I will! You don't have to stay here. Don't you see that?"

Cora clung to Ray's hand as she smiled calmly at her cousin. "You've kept that promise too, Winnie. You've always watched out for me, and I appreciate it. But I'm old enough to make my own decisions now. I'm going to marry Ray and live here in … in … " She searched the others' faces. "What are we going to call this grand place anyway?" She laughed.

"Grand place," mused Jade aloud. "How about Grandville, Grandville, after Palmer Granville?"

"Perfect!" exclaimed Lucy. The others agreed. Just then, Mallory pushed through the doorway, followed by Malcolm Tucker, who was clearly out of breath.

"You…needed…me, Ray?" Malcolm gasped out. "What's wrong?"

"There's nothing wrong, Pastor Tucker. I just wanted you to perform the first wedding ceremony in Grandville." He questioned Cora. "Will you marry me right here, right now, before your cousin leaves?"

Cora nodded again and took Ray's arm to face the out-of-breath preacher. Malcolm was surprised, but he gamely reached into his breast pocket and took out a small Bible to begin the ceremony.

"Grandville?" Mallory whispered to Jade.

"Now hold on!" Gwyneth held up her hands to stop Malcolm.

"Winnie, please! Don't interfere," Cora started.

"If we're going to have a wedding, we're going to do it properly. You!" She pointed to Ray. "Haven't you a suit or something to put on? And you." She turned to Malcolm and inspected his dusty work clothes.

"Yes, ma'am, I've got a suit," he said quickly.

"Winnie," Cora pleaded.

"Cora, you have a beautiful dress that will be perfect. Five minutes is all I'm asking. Just five minutes, and then we'll have a proper wedding."

"Oh, Winnie!" Cora threw her arms around her cousin. "Thank you," she whispered.

There was scurrying in every direction as people rushed to prepare for the first wedding in Grandville. The news spread quickly and so did the name. Palmer beamed when he heard it.

"Grandville. It has a nice ring to it."

Fifteen minutes later Ray waited impatiently in the hotel lobby alongside his brother Ralph. They were both scrubbed and dressed in their best. Malcolm stood before them, and they watched the stairway together.

Jade slipped back into the lobby after a quick check on Tyler, who was still sleeping. She didn't want to miss Cora's wedding! Nearly everyone in the small settlement was there, and couples were smiling at each other, likely wishing today was their wedding day.

Gwyneth came down the stairs first in a slow, reverent walk. She seemed to have made up her mind that if Cora was getting married, she was going to do it right. Cora soon followed in a lovely peach gown complete with a small hat. In her gloved hand she held a bouquet of wild flowers.

"Buck picked her the flowers," Lucy whispered to Jade. Buck smiled at Lucy, and she moved closer to him.

The ceremony was brief, and tears stung Jade's eyes as she watched Ray tenderly kiss and embrace his wife. A cheer broke out over the group, but it was quickly hushed as they remembered the injured man in a nearby room who was in need of rest.

Gwyneth finally left with Rooney and the doctor. "I'll stay in Sand Creek for a while," she told Cora. "If you need me."

"I'll ... we'll be fine, Winnie. We'll be fine."

Things quieted down as the newlyweds left for home. At least they were quiet for a while. That is, until Malcolm Tucker was fairly mobbed by couples who wanted to set up wedding dates with him.

Chapter 35

Grandville

"We do need our own doctor, you know," Jade commented to Tyler as she wrapped a fresh bandage on his healing wound. The process was rather clumsy with her sore arm, but she worked slowly while she talked. Tyler was anxious to be up and about, but the doctor had insisted that his patient stay in bed a full week; then he could sit up in a chair, and then he could try walking a little each day. Jade had a hard time getting Tyler to obey the doctor's orders.

"You're a pretty good doctor, ma'am," Tyler teased. "At least you're a pretty one."

"Ty, I'm serious. Grandville is growing and will need a doctor. It won't be long and babies will be on the way, you know." She blushed at his look. "Just think. Counting the Tuckers, we have five married couples already and three more waiting, including us."

"I wish I could have been to the weddings, but I guess I don't blame anyone for not waiting."

Jade laughed. "Nothing would have made them wait, Ty." She counted off on her fingers. "After Cora and Ray, Bernie and Pearl were married. Then Dugan and Melody and Gabe and Leigh had a double ceremony. I liked your Uncle Evan and Aunt Ella. They're coming back for Michael and Mallory's wedding tomorrow. Then next week is Buck and Lucy's, and as soon as you are fully recovered, we can make plans." She smiled shyly at Tyler.

He slipped an arm around her and pulled her closer to him. "I can hardly wait, Jadyne. There is one problem, though," he added regretfully.

"What?"

"I was so sure I wasn't going to find a wife that I never put up a house, any kind of house."

"That doesn't matter, Ty. We can stay here."

"No, we're not staying at the hotel. You've lived here long enough already. We'll just have to wait until I can work on something. We'll have to start out kind of small, I'm afraid."

"What about your room at the mill?"

Tyler laughed. "That's all it is, Jade, a room. I can't ask you to live like that." He sighed in frustration. "If only I could get started!"

"It's okay, Ty. The Lord will work something out." Then, to get his mind on something else, she said, "Wasn't it wonderful what Mother told us about Amos?"

The worry left his face as he grinned. "He finally accepted the Lord as his Savior! That was great news! It took nearly being killed to get him to see that he wasn't ready to die. I'm sure glad your mother stayed with him that night when he needed someone to talk to. When Palmer was in to see me yesterday, we talked about it too. It sounds like Palmer will be going to the city soon to see Amos."

"I know. He and Mother were talking about traveling together, but Mother doesn't want to leave until after we're married."

Tyler scowled, and Jade regretted bringing the subject up again. Just then, Michael appeared in the open doorway.

"How's the patient today?" he asked cheerfully. "You know, Jade, I think he's just faking that wound so he can get all this female attention."

Tyler ignored his friend's teasing and spoke with earnest what was foremost on his mind. "Mike, have you got extra lumber sawed? I mean, more than you'll need for the Tucker's house? I want to get started on a house for Jade and me as soon as I'm out of this bed. Now, I figure I'll just put up a small cabin to start with so I'll need—"

"Whoa, Ty." Michael laughed. "You're not ready to be handling lumber for a while yet according to the doc. I've got a better idea. Why don't we add on to the room at the mill? We could make it comfortable enough for the two of you until you're ready to handle the house project next year. Then we'll have plenty of office and supply space at the mill when you move out."

Tyler looked questioningly at Jade, and she nodded a quick reply.

"I guess that would work out, Mike. As soon as I'm up, we'll get started."

"No need for you to rush things, Ty. The fellas and I can handle this in an afternoon, but we probably won't get started for a couple of days. I got a wedding to go to tomorrow, you know—mine."

Tyler looked at his friend carefully. "Where has everyone been lately, Mike? I haven't seen much of the guys."

"We stop to see you, Ty, but you're either sleeping or staring at your pretty nurse."

Michael grinned and left. Jade looked at Tyler with sparkling eyes. "Now all you have to worry about is getting better, Mr. Newly."

The smell of freshly cut boards permeated the small church. Wild flowers in two small baskets at the front blended with the aroma, giving pleasure to the assembly waiting for the ceremony to begin. Tyler and Jade sat near the back, and Sky sat on the other side of her son and kept a watchful eye on his pale face. He was going back to the hotel as soon as Mallory and Michael's wedding was over.

Lucy started down the aisle first and smiled as she passed Jade and Tyler and her mother. Michael looked nervous in his broadcloth suit, but Gabe, as his best man, was relaxed, and Jade saw him wink flirtatiously at his own bride of a few days. She knew she and Tyler would have been included in the ceremony if Tyler had been well enough, but she was content to sit beside him and clasp his hand with her own.

Mallory Riley entered the small church on her father's arm. Jade watched for Michael's reaction at the sight of his beautiful bride. She wasn't disappointed, and she had to suppress a giggle when Gabe nudged his stunned brother to take Mallory's hand while Hank waited with a grin on his face. Jade silently thanked the Lord that these wonderful people were her friends and would soon be her family.

The days passed quickly, and it was harder and harder to keep Tyler quiet.

"I'll be glad when Russ gets back from Sand Creek. Maybe he can convince Tyler to wait until he's well enough to be up and around." Sky sighed. "Although I don't know why, Russ can be as bad a patient as his son."

"I'm sorry he had to miss Michael and Mallory's wedding," Jade said.

"He was too, but when you own a ranch, you just can't leave it forever. Our good friends, Clyde and Belle Moore, have been staying there taking care of things, but Russ felt we had been away too long. He has to come back soon, though. Lucy's wedding is only two days away."

Jade went to help her mother in the kitchen. She and Hazel had been helping with the cooking and baking at the hotel while Lucy prepared for her wedding day. Jade hoped she could continue to help with the baking even after she and Tyler were married. It was fun.

The next day as Jade worked, she heard the stagecoach coming. *Dugan must have more passengers,* she thought excitedly. A family had come through on the stage a few days ago on their way to Norris. They had been served a meal at the hotel and had taken rooms for the night. Jade thought the stagecoach business was going to work out fine.

Flour covered her apron front, and her sleeves were rolled up, but Jade hurried out of the kitchen to the front door of the hotel to see who Dugan had brought to their new town this time.

It was Gabe driving instead, and Jade was surprised to see that his usual smiling face wore a scowl. Tyler was seated in a chair on the porch, and he had thrown off the blanket covering him. He started to rise as Jade went to his side, but she gently pushed him down with a reproving look. He sighed in mock exasperation and grinned at her.

"You've got flour on your nose." He laughed.

Jade absently rubbed her spotless nose, leaving a trace of flour where none had been. She was watching the coach eagerly, and, chuckling to himself, Tyler turned his attention to it as well. Gabe was looking at the two of them oddly, so Tyler called to him.

"Have you any passengers for us today, Gabe?"

Gabe's answer was ominous. "Oh, yeah!"

Jade was puzzled, and she questioned Tyler with a look. He shrugged, and she was sorry when she saw him wince from the action. They both turned when they heard a voice.

"It's about time, Gabriel! We've been kept waiting long enough!"

Jade was even more mystified when Tyler sighed deeply beside her.

Gabe rolled his eyes as he opened the door and assisted a woman out. Jade looked at the woman in the frilly dress and then realized she had seen her getting out of a coach somewhere before. Where?

The woman shook out the ruffles of her dress and straightened her hat. She searched the faces on the hotel porch until she spotted Tyler. Then she gracefully ran up the steps and fell to her knees at his side. Jade stared at her openmouthed while Tyler braced himself beside her.

"Hello, Philippa," Tyler began.

"Oh, Tyler! I heard you had been injured, and I came as fast as I could. Oh, my darling, are you all right? I will stay right here and take care of you. I'm so sorry I left you to go to the city. I'll never leave you again, dear Tyler."

"Philippa."

"Yes, dear?" Tears sprinkled daintily from Philippa's eyes.

"Philippa, there's someone I think you should meet."

Philippa raised her head from Tyler's knee.

Tyler cleared his throat and coughed, and Jade could have sworn he was trying not to laugh. She was too shocked to know what to do, but she couldn't see anything funny about Philippa's arrival.

"Philippa, this is my—"

Philippa stood abruptly and reached for Jade's hand. "You must have taken care of Tyler up to now. I don't know how to thank you. I'm so glad he's out of danger. Now that

I'm here, I'll be taking care of him, so you can return to your other duties."

"Now, wait a minute," Jade began.

Tyler coughed again, and Jade cast him a suspicious look. She tried to speak again, but Sky spoke first from behind Philippa.

"Hello, Philippa. How nice of you to come for a visit. Have you met Tyler's fiancée Miss Crandall? They plan to be married in a few days."

Philippa gasped. "Fiancée!" She stared critically at Jade until Jade realized her unkempt appearance was being noted in detail, yet she stood regally, outstaring the rude woman.

"What are you doing here, Philippa?" Tyler asked tiredly.

They all watched Philippa's stunned face as Tyler's tone finally got through to her. No doubt her trip to the city had been a disappointment. Jade wondered what she must have thought when she learned that Wilbert was a just a groom, not a man of means.

"I heard you were wounded, and I wanted to help," she answered lamely.

"How did you hear?" Tyler asked.

"Oh, Mr. Granville told me." She waved at the coach, and the group on the porch saw an elderly man leaning heavily on a cane.

"Mr. Granville!" Jade exclaimed. She rushed past Philippa, down the steps, and embraced the old gentleman. "What on earth are you doing here?"

"Amos!"

Jade stepped back to allow Palmer and Amos the opportunity to look at each other.

Amos opened his arms, and the two brothers embraced. Hazel stepped in next for a hug. Then she firmly took the old man's arm, and Palmer took the other, and they led him to a chair on the porch beside Tyler.

"Mr. Granville, it's great to see you in such good health!"

"Me? Young man, you're the one I've been worried about. Ever since the news was wired about Hunter, I've been praying that you'd pull through, and you"—he pointed at Jade—"and you too." He clasped Palmer's arm and shook his head. "How can one man do so much damage?"

Sky handed a glass of water to the elderly man. He thanked her appreciatively while Tyler introduced his mother and the others on the porch. Philippa was totally forgotten, and when Tyler took Jade's hand and gave her a special look, Jade felt more than saw the defeated slump of the young woman's shoulders and heard her sigh.

"Welcome home, Philippa."

Ralph Tunelle looked bashfully at the pretty woman. Philippa's eyes narrowed thoughtfully; then a small smile stole over her face.

"Why, Ralph! How nice to see you again. I had forgotten that you were one of the men in this settlement. How silly of me!"

"That's okay, Philippa. It's good to see you."

"Thank you, Ralph." Philippa batted her eyes at him, and Jade looked on in amazement at the transformation in

Philippa's face. "This little town is really growing, isn't it? Maybe you'd like to give me a tour?" she coaxed.

"Sure, Philippa," the bedazzled man said eagerly. "Let's start with my store. Well, it's Ray's and mine actually. We call it the Tunelle Brothers General Store."

Jade listened to Ralph's voice fade as the two walked away. She sighed with relief that Philippa had turned her attention on someone else, but poor Ralph!

"Amos, I wish I would have known you were coming. Hazel, uh…Mrs. Crandall and I were going to make a trip to the city soon ourselves."

"I'm glad I came, Palmer." Amos studied the small street of the town and the surrounding hillside and forests. "I'm glad I could see the beauty of this place. What do you call it?"

Palmer chuckled. "It's been named Grandville in honor of us, Amos. How about that?"

Amos smiled. "It is grand!" He turned his attention back on Tyler and Jade. "So that woman has no claim to you, Tyler?"

Tyler was puzzled, then, "You mean Philippa? No, sir, none at all."

"I'm relieved to hear it, son. She had me pretty worried for a while when she insisted you promised to marry her and that she needed the money to get here."

"What? Mr. Granville, I'm truly sorry for the trouble she caused, and I'll gladly repay you whatever she took from you."

Amos held up his hand. "No need. Things worked out just fine. I'm finding out that *our* God can work things out that look pretty hopeless to us."

"That's right, sir. He can. Welcome to the family."

Amos grinned. "Took me a while to get here, Tyler, but even a stubborn old fool like me can get saved. Now, when's this wedding taking place? I've come all this way. The least you can do is get married while I'm here."

"Well, things aren't quite ready," Tyler began to explain.

"They are now," Michael walked up. "The fellas and I are finished with the addition, so it's ready when you are."

Jade's eyes sparkled, but Sky protested. "You have to wait for your father to get here. He wouldn't want to miss your wedding, Ty."

"And we shouldn't interfere with Buck and Lucy's day," Jade admitted slowly.

"How about the day after, then?" Tyler suggested.

Jade nodded happily. She reached for Amos's arm. "Mr. Granville, will you give me away?" she asked.

Amos beamed with pride. "I'd be honored, my dear. And if I'm not mistaken, I'd venture to guess there will be another wedding while I'm here."

Jade was puzzled, but Tyler was grinning at Palmer. "Mother?" Jade asked.

"Yes, Jadyne. You've been so busy taking care of Tyler and cooking at the hotel—"

"Cooking! Oh, no!"

Jade rushed into the hotel, leaving the people on the porch laughing.

"Do you think she minds?" Hazel asked Palmer.

"You know better than I do what she thinks," Palmer replied. He studied the frown on the face of the woman he had come to love in such a short time. "Why don't you go talk to her?"

Jade pulled a beautifully browned apple pie from the oven just as her mother entered the kitchen.

"They aren't burnt!" Jade said with relief and a laugh. Her face was flushed from the heat, and her copper curls were hanging down to her shoulders.

"Mrs. Todd would be very proud of you, dear." Hazel waited, hesitant to continue until Jade had put the last of the pies on the table to cool. "Jadyne, what do you think about Palmer and me getting married?" she asked bluntly.

Jade turned back to the cook stove and brushed some crumbs from its surface. "Do you want to know what I really think?" she asked quietly.

Hazel steeled herself. "Yes, I do."

Jade moved to her mother's side. She had a mischievous glint in her eye. "I think God answers prayers mighty fast!"

Hazel was startled.

Jade reached for her mother and hugged her tightly. "It wasn't long after I met Palmer that I thought he would be a perfect husband for you and a perfect way to get you and Sidney to live closer to me. Isn't God wonderful, Mother?"

"You don't mind?" Hazel insisted. "I mean, your father hasn't been gone that long, and you're getting married too, and everything has happened so fast!"

Jade took her mother's arm and led her to a chair. "I don't mind, and you shouldn't worry about things happening too fast. You can get married the same day, the same time as I do, and I wouldn't mind. I'm just happy for you and for Sidney and for me." She sighed happily. "We're going to start a new life here. What could be better than that?"

Chapter 36

Grandville

Lucy was radiant on her father's arm as he led her down the aisle. Jade thought Buck would burst with pride as Lucy took her place beside him. She sighed, and Tyler squeezed her fingers. She smiled happily at him. Tomorrow would be *their* wedding day.

The day passed quickly, and Buck and Lucy left for a short honeymoon in the hills where Buck had a hunting shack. They would return to the business of running a hotel and restaurant all too soon. Palmer and Hazel would be married a week later just before they returned with Amos to the city for their own short honeymoon, during which Sidney would remain in Grandville with his sister and new brother-in-law, and Jade knew Sidney was happy about that. He had taken an instant liking to the wilderness town even though he took a fair amount of teasing from the women when they reminded him of Jade's impersonation of him as "Sid."

The women of the town now turned their attentions to preparing for Tyler and Jade's wedding. Jade was shooed out of the kitchen by Cora. "You've done enough cooking getting ready for Lucy's wedding. Now it's our turn to get ready for yours, and you are not welcome here. Go on!" Cora laughingly scolded.

Tyler met Jade in the lobby. "Shall we take the wagon over to the mill and check out what the guys have done?" he asked.

Jade nodded eagerly, but then she asked with concern, "Are you feeling up to it, Ty? You still seem pretty weak."

"I feel great! I'm anxious to see what kind of a home we have."

They left soon. Jade watched Tyler anxiously on the short trip to their future home. He looked around him eagerly, and she realized how he had hated being confined to the indoors for so long.

The mill was quiet when they arrived, and Tyler began apologizing again for not having a real house ready for her. Jade stopped him.

"Please, Tyler! You have to believe me when I tell you that it won't matter where we live. I'll be happy here or anywhere as long as I'm with you."

Tyler drew her close for a moment. "I'm sorry. It's just that my dream to build a wonderful house has been with me for so long that I find it harder to swallow starting out like this. Oh, I know." He put up his hand. "I've given up that way of thinking. The Lord has shown me a lot these last couple of months." He leaned against the still closed door. "You know, my folks talked to Lucy and me last night, and they gave us each our inheritances." He chuckled. "If I would have gotten it a few months ago, I would have started right in building. Now, I want us to pray and seek God's will for how we use that money. It's a blessing from him, and I want to use it for him."

"So do I."

They entered the back room of the mill together. The addition broadened the small bedroom into a bedroom plus a kitchen and sitting room. It was small. But it was cozy too. The ladies of the town had been there, and dishes and linens sat ready to use on the shelves. Jade looked around her in delight.

"Oh, Ty! This will be perfect! I know it's small, but won't that be fun!" She walked around the tiny area and nodded her approval. Tyler watched her carefully.

"Are you sure, Jade? Can you really live here for a year?"

"Of course! What do I have to do to convince you? What's the matter? Don't you think you can live with me in such close quarters?" she teased.

"I love you, Jadyne Kathleen Crandall."

"I know."

Tyler reached out and pulled Jade to him. The way he looked at her made Jade breathless, and he was just bending forward to kiss her when the clomping of hooves made them turn to the door. Michael Trent lightly knocked then entered the small room, making it seem smaller with his large frame.

"Everything satisfactory, Ty? Jade?"

Slightly frustrated at the interruption, Jade nevertheless was glad for the opportunity to thank their friend. "It's wonderful, Michael! Thank you for all the work you and the others did to get it ready." Jade stood on tiptoe and gave him a kiss on the cheek.

"We really appreciate it, Mike." Tyler shook his friend's hand. "I think I'll drive Jade up to my—*our* land and show her where our real house will be someday."

"Sorry, Ty, but your mother needs to see you back in town. You're looking kind of pale too. Are you sure you can make it back okay?"

"Ty?" Jade looked at him closely.

"I'm fine. Really, I am. I'm sorry. We'll have to take that drive another day if Mom needs to see me for something now. We'll see you, Mike, and thanks again."

Chapter 37

Grandville

"It's raining." Jade peered out the window at the light drizzle. Her mother straightened the sleeves on the white wedding dress she had brought for her daughter from the city.

"Don't let that spoil your day," she advised.

"Spoil it!" Jade laughed at her mother's expression. "I think a summer rain is perfect. By evening everything will be fresh and clean and brand new again. Mmmmm! Smell that!" She leaned out the window to enjoy the fragrance.

"Jadyne! Get back in here before you ruin your hair! Honestly, Jadyne, sometimes I worry that you won't have enough sense to manage a home of your own," Hazel teased her daughter.

"Are you ready, Jade?" Mallory tapped on the door then poked her head in. "Oh! That dress is fabulous, Mrs. Crandall! Wait 'til Ty sees you, Jade. You look stunning!"

"Thank you, *Mrs.* Trent. You look pretty good yourself for an old married lady." Jade smiled and accepted the light hug Mallory gave her.

"Jade, are you okay?" Mallory stepped back and studied her friend's face.

"Why?"

"You're acting kind of funny. Aren't you nervous? At my wedding, I was a nervous wreck! Michael said my hand was trembling the whole time."

Jade's green eyes squinted with her smile. "I don't feel nervous. I just feel so happy that the day is finally here that I don't have any time for being nervous. Is Tyler ready?"

"Ready and waiting at the church. Palmer will ride over with you, and Amos is already there, ready to take you down the aisle."

"And I'm ready, so let's go."

"Jadyne."

Jade turned at her mother's voice. Hazel took both her daughter's hands in hers and struggled to blink back the tears that threatened to fall. "Oh, Jadyne, you look so beautiful!"

"Mother, don't cry." Jade's voice trembled, and her gaiety melted into seriousness.

Hazel pulled Jade to her and held her close. "God bless both of you," she said in a choked voice.

Jade blinked rapidly to hold back her own tears. *I'm not going to cry*, she thought. *I'm not going to cry.*

Palmer was ready downstairs, and he whisked them into the waiting stagecoach. Dugan held the reins, and he tipped his hat in the drizzle and smiled at Jade and Mallory and Hazel as they climbed in.

Jade pressed her hands tightly together in an effort to control their trembling. She was not going to cry! Mallory was just in time to rescue the flowers Jade held before they were completely crushed.

"Now you're acting more like a bride," Mallory softly teased.

Jade tried to smile, but she found it impossible. She felt cold and clammy and then hot and stuffy. The short ride in the rain seemed endless.

"Jadyne?"

Jade stared at Palmer, who stood patiently with water dripping from his hat waiting to help her out. Her mother and Mallory were already inside! She gathered her gown around her and let Palmer lift her to the church steps and hurry her inside.

Mallory and Hazel fussed with Jade's gown and hair, and Mallory placed the flowers back into Jade's hands. In lieu of any other musical instruments, Bernie used his harmonica to play the familiar wedding march. Hazel and Palmer were seated next to Sidney, and Mallory left Jade's side to begin down the aisle ahead of her.

"Those flowers are too beautiful to be dropped to the floor, my dear." Amos reached for Jade's trembling hands and patted them. "Everything will be fine, Jade. Are you ready?"He pulled her hand through his arm and took a step forward. When she didn't move, he stepped back and chuckled.

"Jade, I think it would be better if you came with me. I don't think Tyler wants to see just me coming down the aisle next. Poor boy! Just look at him, Jadyne. He's more nervous than you are!"

Jade's head snapped up, and she took a step forward. "Where? Where is he?"

Amos chuckled again and kept her moving now that he had gotten her started. "He's waiting right there," he said softly.

Jade looked through the crowded room and met Tyler's eyes, which had been following her every movement. A radiant smile lit her face, and Tyler's tight features relaxed into an answering smile. In no time, Jade was by his side.

"You could have at least waited for me," Amos complained, a step behind her.

"Oh, Mr. Granville! I'm sorry." Jade kissed the old man's cheek. "I'm okay now."

"I see that." Amos smiled at both of them then sat down with the rest of the amused onlookers.

Malcolm spoke reverently about marriage and new beginnings; then he began the ceremony, and in moments Jadyne Crandall became Jadyne Newly. She heard Tyler breathe a sigh of relief beside her and say, "About time!" under his breath. Michael, who was standing beside Tyler, suddenly coughed.

They turned and faced their relatives and friends, and then Tyler kissed her and a cheer broke out. Hazel dabbed at her eyes and rushed to hug her daughter and son-in-law. Sky and Russ were close behind her. Sidney manly shook hands with his new brother-in-law and reluctantly accepted the kiss his sister planted on his cheek. He looked on with the rest of Tyler's brothers and sisters as the newlyweds marched down the aisle together.

For the next couple of hours they were surrounded by well-wishers as they returned for a wedding dinner at the hotel. Jade felt her heart would burst with happiness as she looked around her at all their friends and family. The rain had stopped, and everything sparkled in the setting sun.

"A lot has happened since you dressed like a boy in the city, hasn't it?" Cora stood at Jade's side.

"Cora, who would have known then the changes that would take place? I guess only the Lord." Jade answered her own question. "He has a way of leading us to where he wants us to go, hasn't he?"

Cora nodded. "I never thought I could be so happy!"

"Is Gwyneth staying in Sand Creek?"

"For a while. Rooney has been so nice to her. I don't know if she'll stay for good, though." She nodded to a corner of the room. "Ralph seems to be enjoying Philippa's company."

Jade watched the couple and then shook her head. "Only the Lord knows, Cora." She laughed.

Michael approached. "Ty wants to know if you're ready to go, Jade. I'll be driving you home in the coach."

"But it's not raining anymore, Michael. Doesn't Tyler just want to take our wagon?"

"Well, yes, he does, but I told him since I'm the best man that I get to drive you home and that I wouldn't take no for an answer. So if you're ready, Mrs. Newly, I'll be happy to escort you." He held out an arm.

Jade allowed herself to be led through the crowded room. She said quick thank yous and good-byes as they went, and finally she and Tyler were in the coach and on their way.

Tyler slipped an arm around his wife, and Jade gazed lovingly into her husband's eyes. They talked softly, laughing now and then about the mishaps of the day. The ride seemed endless, yet they were surprised when the coach abruptly stopped.

"Now all we have to do is get rid of Michael," Tyler said in Jade's ear.

She giggled.

"He's been bird-dogging me for the last two days. Every time I turn around, he's there."

There was a quick knock on the coach door, and then Michael opened it and poked his head in. "Welcome home, Mr. and Mrs. Newly!"

Tyler stepped down, and Jade waited for him to help her, but it was Michael who assisted her out while she held her billowing skirts. It took a few moments to gather them as she held them up off the wet ground. Finally she turned to Tyler, but he was standing still, staring ahead of him with such an unusual expression on his face that she looked to see what was wrong.

"Oh, my!" Jade dropped her skirts and reached for Tyler. They stood together in silence until Tyler finally found his voice.

"When did you do it, Mike?"

"We've been working on it pretty steady since your injury." He hesitated. "I know it's not exactly what you wanted, but—"

"It's perfect," Tyler interrupted.

"It's so beautiful." Jade wiped a tear off her cheek.

They stood together on a hill. In the fading light stood a magnificent house. It was made of logs, giving it a rustic look but also was perfectly harmonious with its setting. A large porch encircled the front, and from the big windows shone lights to welcome the new owners. The roof was peaked quite high, and Michael, following Tyler's inspection, explained.

"There's an upstairs with two rooms and a loft, but why not go inside and check it out yourselves?"

The stunned couple moved forward and up the steps into their new home. The door opened before them, and Mallory smiled a welcome to them.

"How did you get here?" Tyler asked in surprise.

"Your wagon is out back. I left early to finish getting things ready for you." It was obvious she was enjoying their surprise.

"Where did all these things come from?" Jade exclaimed.

The house was completely furnished with what appeared to her to be items of excellent quality. Michael calmly sat down in a handsome rocking chair and explained while Tyler and Jade stood openmouthed and stared at him.

"As soon as Palmer was able, he wired the news about Hunter to Amos, and he also told Amos about you two getting married. Amos had all these things shipped here for a wedding present as soon as he heard, with instructions that they were for your new house." Mike grinned. "Gabe and Dugan have been so busy hauling your belongings they've hardly had time to run a coach line. Anyway, the guys all agreed to build your house as quickly as we could and surprise you. Surprise!"

Tyler's voice was choked with emotion as he answered. "I don't know what to say. You didn't need to do all this!"

"Ty, for goodness' sake! You helped all of us and sawed lumber for everyone. You were the only one left without a house. We wanted to do it! Besides, you had the toughest job of all of us—bringing us our brides."

Michael grinned happily at the couple until Mallory nudged him on the shoulder. "Uh, Michael, I think it's time we were going."

"Huh? Oh, right! Time to go!" He clapped Tyler on the back and quickly hugged Jade. Mallory kissed Tyler's cheek then Jade's, and they were gone.

For long moments, Tyler and Jade stood looking at their new home, and then Jade slipped over to Tyler's side and laid her head against him. He brushed back her hair.

"Who would have thought that after all our careful planning and decision making about no longer wanting or needing all this, we have it given to us? The Lord certainly has blessed us."

Jade smiled up at him. "I think the Lord has blessed us in more ways than we will ever fully realize, Tyler. We have been blessed with wonderful friends and family who care enough about us to do this for us, and we have the opportunity now to use our beautiful home to serve the Lord. We have a new home, a new town, new friends, and a wonderful new life together. There's no place on earth I'd rather be but right here where the Lord has led us."

For more information about
A Newly Weds Series or
author Margo Hansen, visit her at
www.margohansen.com.

Margo would enjoy hearing
from her readers. Send your
comments or questions to
margo@margohansen.com.

Other books by Margo Hansen
Sky's Bridal Train